Praise for *Stop at Nothing*

"A fast-paced thriller by an author who has mastered his craft, with lots of action, knowing detail, plenty of twists and turns and characters to cheer or hiss."

—*Forbes*

"This book [is] worthy of going to the top of your must-read list, thanks to Ledwidge's peerless setup and execution of each and every scene."

—*Bookreporter*

"Ledwidge knows how to tell a fast-paced story, and he has created an appealing maverick hero.... Give this one to those who remember and still love John D. MacDonald's Travis McGee."

—*Booklist*

"Fans of...page-turners will be entertained."

—*Publishers Weekly*

"Michael Ledwidge has the gift—he knows how to involve us in the story from page one. The writing is sharp and the action doesn't let up. *Stop at Nothing* is FLAWLESS."

—James Patterson

"I literally could not put down this book. I loved it. *Stop at Nothing* is a timely, perfectly paced, character-driven thriller with fun twists and intense action. Michael Gannon is the next great hero in popular fiction."

—Allison Brennan, author of *The Third to Die*

"*Stop at Nothing* is my kind of book. Shades of John D. MacDonald's Travis McGee. Great characters, lots of action, and a razor-sharp plot. Good stuff. Really good."

—Marc Cameron, author of *Tom Clancy Oath of Office*

"I'm not sure how he did it—it seems to defy science—but Michael Ledwidge figured out a way to write a book using pure, distilled adrenaline. Michael Gannon is a fantastic protagonist, destined for the pantheon of characters we love to follow through countless adventures. Here's hoping for many more."

—Rob Hart, author of *The Warehouse*

"In *Stop at Nothing*, Michael Ledwidge gives us sharply drawn characters in a tense, fast-paced adventure that keeps the reader entertained from the intriguing start to the wild finish."

—Thomas Perry, author of *The Burglar*

"*Stop at Nothing* is a smart, brawny thriller that moves fast and surprises often. The action is tense, the characters are surely drawn, and a wonderful sense of authenticity drives the story. Best of all, the writing is assured and stylish. *Stop at Nothing* is a high speed roller coaster that will carry you away."

—T. Jefferson Parker, author of *The Last Good Guy*

RUN FOR COVER

RUN FOR COVER

A NOVEL

MICHAEL LEDWIDGE

HANOVER
SQUARE
PRESS

**HANOVER
SQUARE
PRESS™**

Recycling programs
for this product may
not exist in your area.

ISBN-13: 978-1-335-50997-0

Run for Cover

First published in 2021. This edition published in 2021.
Copyright © 2021 by Michael Ledwidge

This edition published by arrangement with Harlequin Books S.A.

Hanover Square Press
22 Adelaide St. West, 41st Floor
Toronto, Ontario M5H 4E3, Canada
HanoverSqPress.com
BookClubbish.com

Printed in U.S.A.

For the Lawtons and the Luceys

PROLOGUE

MOUNTAIN RETREAT

1

When they turned the vehicle in off the blacktop at the trailhead, all the land still lay in shadow, and the coming sun was just a faint ribbon of paleness in the dark of the open sky.

With its big all-terrain tires, the Tahoe made steady progress at first. But as the grade of the slope increased, even at a crawl, it began to buck and spin and bottom out off the deep pits in the trail-like dirt road.

Two thousand feet up the mountain wall, National Park Service ranger Owen Barber stood beside his jacked-up pickup, watching the headlights of the Tahoe as it climbed up slowly through the dry prairie grass and lodgepole pine. After another minute, he lowered his binoculars, laid them on the hood of the truck with a clunk and turned.

On the other side of the ridge saddle he was parked

upon was a descending hollow of exposed rock that looked almost lunar in nature. Beyond the hollow in the northwestern distance stood a line of immense mountains, high and jagged against the paling sky like the graph of some volatile company stock.

Barber rapped on the side of the pickup with a knuckle as he gazed out at the sublime landscape.

He'd been to Iraq and Afghanistan with the 101st Airborne, but west Wyoming was beyond anything he'd ever seen.

It was coming on fifteen minutes later when the Tahoe finally arrived. The first one out of it was small and bald. Teton County sheriff Jim Kirkwood.

"Morning, Owen," Kirkwood said, handing Barber the warm steel thermos he held in his hand.

"Morning, Jim. Thanks," Barber said, turning and looking over at the FBI agents Kirkwood had just chauffeured up the off-road slope.

There were two of them, a man and woman, sitting in the sheriff's vehicle talking to each other. Through the windshield, Barber could see they were wearing navy blue windbreakers just like on TV.

Barber was pouring out his second coffee when they finally emerged.

The man was a burly individual in his early forties with some muscle on him. The female agent was younger, Barber saw, about thirty-five. She was a little on the short side but quite pretty. Even with her brown hair pulled back tight.

They were both wearing fleece under their raid jackets as well as hiking boots.

So maybe they weren't completely stupid, Barber thought as he tipped the camp cup to his lips.

"Hi, I'm Dennis," the male agent said. "Dennis Braddock."

"Owen Barber," the ranger said, raising the cup lid at him.

"Thanks for standing post until we could get here, Owen. It really means a lot," Braddock said, looking him square in the eye.

Barber nodded again then sipped some more coffee.

Former military, he decided. Man had some grit. Or at least a passable appearance thereof.

"Which one is Grand Teton?" Braddock said, looking to the northwest above the hollow at the slightly off-kilter peaks.

"It's that one there," the FBI woman said, suddenly standing beside them, pointing.

"Right?" she said, turning to Ranger Barber with a radiant smile.

Barber looked down at her in the waft of the wind. At her light brown eyes. The spark there.

"You're right," he finally said with his own smile back. "That is it."

"This is Agent Hagen," Braddock said.

"You can call me Kit," she said to Barber with another smile.

A man could get used to those, Barber thought.

"How far down are we looking?" Braddock said, gazing over the ridge saddle down into the blue-shadowed hollow.

"A little less than a mile, but it's slow going. Trail's pretty steep," Barber said.

"You were the one to find the body?" Sheriff Kirkwood said.

Barber nodded as he finished the coffee and screwed the cap back on tight.

"Yesterday at sunset," he said as he handed back the thermos to the sheriff. "We had a call from a camper about a light they saw from a trail off on that hill on the left there, so we were looking around. They had a screw-loose arsonist two summers ago over in Idaho who burned down a hundred square miles so they're always quick to send us out for violators."

"Violators?" Agent Braddock said, squinting down into the shadowed landscape below them.

Barber nodded.

"Yep," Braddock finally said. "They send us out on those calls, too."

2

Down the hollow's steep and tricky zigzagging trail, Kit Hagen was sweating in less than three minutes.

She had never seen so much rock. Rock in ridges and in slopes and slides and in crevices. All of it as gray as ashes. Born and raised outside of LA, she took in the bowl-like indentation and was reminded weirdly of Dodger Stadium of all things. It was as if God had chiseled an immense baseball stadium of rock into the side of a mountain, and they were now heading down from the nosebleeds for the field.

A sudden crunching sound of falling rocks just below on the trail made Kit stop in her tracks. As she watched, Braddock lunged forward and caught Sheriff Kirkwood by his jacket's back collar just before he could fall.

"Thanks," the sheriff said as he stepped to his right and peeked over the trail edge.

Kit Hagen looked down with the both of them to where the land fell off sharply. Four or five stories below thcre was a stream, green and bubbling as it wound its way down the mountain through a serrated ravine.

"Pretty steep indeed," Agent Braddock said, looking back at her with a wide-eyed nod.

They continued their descent. Six feet even and broad-shouldered with close-cropped hair, Section Chief Dennis Braddock looked more like an ironworker foreman or a professional rugby player than an FBI agent. For his homicide course at the FBI Academy, his wife, Anna, had valiantly attempted to soften the former marine's bulk and blunt-edged features with professorial khakis, tweed blazers and dad ties. But it didn't work.

"Watch your step," Ranger Barber called back from farther down the trail.

Hagen smiled as she watched the lanky ranger duck under the trunk of a huge dead branchless pine sticking out over the trail at a rudely phallic angle.

She was still smiling to herself at the weenie tree when the trail finally leveled off another fifty feet below it. As she stood in the base of the hollow, its high rock walls didn't remind her of Dodger Stadium anymore.

Then her smile evaporated as she looked over a tumble of rocks a few car lengths away, and finally found what they had come here to see.

3

Sticking straight up in the gap between two exercise-ball-sized rocks, thirty feet to the right of the trail, was a foot.

The pale bare foot of what seemed to be a young woman.

Obscured by the rock, the rest of the body wasn't visible.

Thank God for small mercies, Kit Hagen thought.

She and Braddock glanced at each other grimly in the hollow's half-light.

"What time yesterday evening did you arrive here?" Braddock said to the ranger as he unslung his pack.

"It was a little after eight," Barber said. "Eight oh seven, I think. It's in my report up in the truck."

"And no one else has been here? No supervisors or coworkers? No one?" Braddock said.

"No one," Barber said. "Not unless they snuck in under my truck last night. A hundred feet down the trail is covered with a rockslide. That trail we came down is the only way in or out."

"Give us a break already," Sheriff Kirkwood said to the agent. "We weren't down here taking selfies if that's what you're worried about. I wanted to bring in county homicide from the second the call came in, but Park Service said you guys said to hold off. I know this isn't DC, but even hick hayseeds like us like to think we're at least a little professional."

"So you've been here all night?" Kit Hagen said to Barber.

Barber nodded.

"It's okay. I got no problem with overtime."

"And I take it you're wearing the same boots," Braddock said as he sat on a rock and pulled a pair of blue surgical booties over his own.

"Yep," the lanky ranger said, looking down at his Red Wings. "These ones aren't even hardly broken in."

"Okay, gentlemen. You can wait right here," Braddock said, tossing Hagen a pair of latex gloves. "This won't take long. We're just going to go over and look and take some pictures, and we'll head back up. The other members of our team will be by later for the full scene processing."

"Actually, do either of you have a phone?" Kit Hagen said. "I left mine back in the Tahoe."

"No, sorry," Barber said, patting his pockets. "Mine's in my truck, too."

"I have one, but good luck getting service," Sheriff Kirkwood said, taking a smartphone out of his jacket pocket.

"He's right," Barber said. "Nearest cell site is thirty miles away. If you need to call someone, only the radio back in my truck is powerful enough to reach the station."

"No, it's not that," Hagen said as she started unzipping her camera bag. "We need video. Could you tape us working from over here? We usually forget where we step or what have you so it's helpful to have everything documented when we look back later."

"Okay, sure," Sheriff Kirkwood said as he stood up from the rock he'd been sitting on.

He took out a pair of reading glasses and began tapping and flicking at the phone screen with a forefinger.

"Say cheese," Kirkwood said and had just begun to lift the phone upward when the first crack of a rifle sounded out from somewhere above them, and the killing began.

4

Three hundred yards to the northwest up the curving wall of the hollow, Westergaard watched the head-shot sheriff teeter and fall away off the scope's reticle as he jacked the glass-smooth bolt back and forth.

Then he pivoted the rifle very, very slightly left to the male FBI agent, huge in the precision German optics, and took him through the back of his neck just below his brain stem with another .338 Lapua Magnum round.

The long crashes of the rifle were still whining and reverberating off the bare rock as he jacked the bolt again. He pivoted back where the other two were, but they were wisely sucking ground now behind the clearing's low trail rocks.

Westergaard watched patiently. He had put a tiny pebble in his mouth as he had tracked them all down the rock trail, and now he rolled the smooth little bit of basalt back and forth behind his teeth with his tongue as he calmly assessed.

The ranger and the woman were pinned behind half a dozen close-together squarish boulders. The rocks were actually quite small, each about the size of a mini-fridge.

No matter, he decided as he blinked through the Schmidt & Bender scope.

He flexed his jaw against the soft chamois that padded the Accuracy International AW sniper rifle's cheekpiece.

He just needed to wait but a second or two.

It actually didn't take that long. Just between two of the squarish rocks, there was movement, and then the heel of Ranger Rick's boot was on the pin of the reticle.

Westergaard lay breathing calmly, looking at it. The boot had a high serrated heel and nice reddish-brown leather and looked expensive.

The ranger probably oiled them every night before bedtime with some special hiking boot leather maintenance oil he learned about in the Eagle Scouts, the killer thought.

He wondered about the FBI woman down there with him. She was quite the little number. He wondered if she had the hots for the ranger there in the close confines. He was older but a flat-bellied rugged stud. For some, it was all about older, wasn't it? He knew all about that.

Oh, well. Back to work, he thought as he pulled the silk-smooth trigger and blew the ranger's beautiful boot to smithereens.

5

When the sledgehammer impact of the rifle round struck, Owen Barber had thought his whole right foot had surely been obliterated. But as he looked down at his annihilated boot and counted all five of his wriggling toes, he saw that by some holy miracle, the bullet had only cut a perfect stripe-like groove across the sole of his heel.

Barber untied what was left of the boot and lay there breathing with a deliberate slowness, trying to calm the mad frantic pumping of his heart. He glanced down at Kit Hagan where she lay with her face pressed into his chest, shivering. He could see that she was still in the black zone, mentally undone with shock.

Then he glanced over at Sheriff Kirkwood and Agent Braddock where they lay blown to pieces against the rocks.

No blame there, he thought.

Barber's hands squeezed involuntarily, longing for the M4 he had slept with for over a year in the Kush Mountains. What he wouldn't do for its undermounted M203 grenade launcher right now. Damn had he loved the forty-millimeter grenades, the coppery smell of them, the hollow thunk of loading them, the nothing click of the trigger followed by the distant thunder boom when they landed three hundred meters out.

If wishes were fragmentary ordnance, he thought, as the woman clutched at him even harder behind their extremely inadequate rock cover.

Okay, Barber thought, looking up at the still-dark morning sky. *You've done this before. You're back on the firebase, and there's a sniper. What's the plan?*

First thing was finding where the shots were coming from. Get a grid. Second was getting to his radio. As in Afghanistan, the radio was life.

That was it. Get a grid. Get to the radio. That was the plan.

Sit still, you dirty murdering son of a bitch, Barber thought as he wiggled very slowly on his back through the dust toward the sheriff's body. *I'm going to call in an air strike on you.*

"Wait!" Hagen said.

"It's okay. Everything's going to be fine," Barber said, surprised at the calm in his voice as he reached back as far as he could. He just managed to grab the fallen sheriff's cell phone with his fingertips.

He turned it over as he brought it up in front of his face. The video screen was still queued up and the time stamp was still rolling. It had already started recording.

Good, Barber thought as he tilted just the camera part of it up above the rock and panned it back and forth.

6

The shot, when it came a fraction of a second later, shattered a sizeable portion out of the rim of rock just above Barber's face. It showered the both of them in jagged shards the size of playing cards and covered them in a plume of gray rock dust so fine it was like talc.

What was this boy shooting? Barber thought coughing. *A Howitzer?*

He wiped dust from the screen of the miraculously unharmed phone with a licked thumb and played back the footage.

"Ah, there you are. Say cheese, jackweed," he said as he saw the muzzle flash on the screen.

Barber watched the video again and paused it and zoomed the still. The shooter was behind some rocks up the rim of the hollow to the left of the clearing. He was well back in some good cover with only the barrel showing. It looked like he'd built a little blind or something with the rocks.

A crazy thought—*Barney Rubble goes postal*—came into Barber's head as he unzoomed the still. He gauged the distance. Five hundred yards at least. Plus, you'd have to compensate for the difference in elevation a bit.

Barney had some skill, Barber thought. *Just great. Okay, got my grid. Now for the hard part.*

"Okay, Kit. Do you have your service weapon?" Barber said calmly to the agent shivering slightly less now but still attached to him like a tick.

She immediately handed him something. It was a small backup gun, a Glock 27.

"How many rounds? Ten?" Barber said.

"No, eleven. There's one in the pipe," the agent said from where her head was pressed against his stomach.

His Glock 20 had sixteen, and he had another magazine, so they had what? Forty-three?

Forty-three, he thought biting his lip. That wasn't a lot.

What was also not, not, not in their favor was the distance. Five hundred yards plus uphill with a handgun was laughable. Hitting this son of a bitch would be like getting a hole in one with a blindfold on.

But then again, he just needed to get a few in close to get his jackass head down. Like the agent here was finding out, shooting a gun was one thing. Getting shot at was quite another.

Besides, what else could they do?

There was literally no other cover. If he flanked

them up along the bowl-like rim of the ridge he was up on, they were toast anyway.

"Okay, Kit. Take a look at this," Barber said, showing her the video. "See where this joker is? On our left here? Here's what we're doing, Kit. I'm going to shoot at him while you run up the trail back to my truck and call for help. I'm going to shoot four times, spaced out a little. At the fourth shot—or even the third—you run and get to new cover, okay?

"I'll wait twenty seconds for you to catch your breath, then shoot four times again. Every time, you have four shots to run. Then you have to put yourself between a rock and this loser on the hill, okay? It sucks, but it's what we have to do. I'd run myself, but it looks like I'm currently down a boot, and I actually shoot a bit better than I run anyway."

"Okay," Agent Hagen said, forcing a brave smile on her terror-stricken face. She took a deep breath as she moved off him slowly and got up on her knees a little.

Barber even shocked himself when he reached out and touched her tear-streaked cheek.

"You got this, Kit," he said.

She nodded.

"Remember, look for cover while you're running. I've got an emergency six-pack in my truck, and in about ten minutes, we're going to be pouring it over each other's heads as we mount this son of a bitch to the grille, okay?"

"Okay," she said.

"On three then," Barber said, slipping his gun out of its holster. "Ready? One…two…"

7

Westergaard was still aimed at where the phone had popped up when the gun started going off five feet farther to the right. He ducked down as a bullet strike whined off the rock somewhere not too far below him. When he got back onto the scope again two shots later, he saw the woman twenty feet up the trail, diving behind another rock.

"Oh, so you guys want to play after all?" the killer said with a smile as he blasted away the top edge of the rock the woman had dived behind.

He ditched out the first magazine and had just snapped in another when the return pistol fire started again. One of them hit only ten feet down now. There was a blast of four again. The ranger was walking the rounds up the hill. With a handgun no less!

"Very clever, Ranger Rick," Westergaard said.

He waited and when the pistol fire started up the

third time, he ignored it and looked up the trail as the female agent ran out from behind cover again. He slid a bead on the woman's running back and gently squeezed the sleek springy euro trigger.

The butt of the gun kicked into his shoulder as the round drilled a neat hole through the top part of the yellow F on her FBI raid jacket. She ran on for three more strides and then went down sprawling, arms out and headfirst, like a base runner trying to steal second.

"You're out!" the killer said as he shot out the casing.

When he sighted back on the ranger's position, he had stopped firing. When the Glock appeared again at the same spot above the rock twenty seconds later, it was right in the center of the reticle.

He squeezed the trigger. The handgun along with a spray of blood went airborne.

There was a long pause before he heard the ranger's unholy scream.

"Finally," Westergaard said, rolling the kinks out of his neck as he stood with the rifle.

He clambered over some rocks to his right for a hundred yards and lay down and got the attached bipod set and sighted down again.

He could see the ranger there now completely exposed, clutching at his blown-apart hand.

He couldn't get a good head shot because of a pesky jutting rock, but he was able to quickly shoot him once and then twice high in the chest.

"Game, set, match," Westergaard mumbled as he watched the ranger's arms drop.

As the ranger bled out on the stone, the killer stood

and gave him the two-finger-over-the-right-eye Boy Scout salute.

"Least you tried, brother," he said.

Who does that anymore these days?

It took the killer less than five minutes to scoop his brass and pack his kit and another twenty to clamber down the stones to where the three dead men lay splattered across the clearing.

He fished the truck keys from the ranger's bloody khaki pants and found the cell phone and bagged it. He thought about things and took the man's wallet and badge. Then he went to the others and took their wallets and credentials, as well.

If this doesn't blow a lot of minds, he thought to himself with a giddy giggle as he tucked everything away into his knapsack.

"What in the hell?" he said, halting immediately as he came up level on the part of the trail where the female agent had gone down.

She wasn't there.

He ran over to where there was a huge red ink blot splat on the rocks and quickly tracked the bloody drag trail through the dust to where the trail fell off above the stream.

No, he thought, looking down at the trees and water far below. The crazy agent had jumped!

"Damn, damn, damn," he said as he searched the evergreens and white water with the rifle's scope.

He couldn't see her. He passed a hand through his hair as he lowered the rifle. Now he would have to go down there.

He checked his watch.

He didn't have time for this.

No, no, he thought after a minute. Calm down. Think, moron. It had to be what? A five-story drop? He had probably heart shot her anyway. Nicked the aorta. Hell, with 250 grain .338 Lapua Magnum boat tail that traveled about a thousand yards a second, nicking a toenail usually did the trick.

He looked down at the roiling water, then up at the hovering peaks, then down at the water again.

Get real. She was dead. They were all dead.

"Get moving," Westergaard said, finally shouldering the strap of the rifle as he turned.

PART ONE

HOME ON THE RANGE

8

At seven thirty in the morning, the sun had not yet risen over Carbon County in Eastern Utah. In the distance out the glassless window beside where Gannon sat was a line of the high desert cliffs that were huge and ominous in the predawn dark.

The fantastic mesa-like vista looked like an advertisement for something, Gannon thought. And then he remembered it.

It looked like one of the cowboy ads for Marlboro cigarettes they used to have in magazines when he was a kid.

Welcome to Gannon Country, he thought with a grin.

He stood and turned from the windowsill and glanced around the second-story room of the abandoned house. The old wood beams above were coated thickly in dust, as were the exposed brick walls.

The formidable structure had once been the headquarters of a surrounding coal mining operation that had gone bust in the 1950s, he knew. Now its occupants consisted mostly of desert rats and birds.

And various other strays, he thought as he went over to the cheap leather office chair in the room's center and sat.

The old battered green metal office desk in front of it looked army surplus circa WWII. Upon it was a Toshiba laptop that was wired into the old building's interior and exterior security camera array.

Gannon clicked at the mouse and brought up the three-by-three rows of screens.

It was 7:32 a.m. on the button when Gannon detected movement on the uppermost left-hand camera. He put eyes on it just in time to see the tall figure with the rifle emerge from the mountain junipers a hundred fifty yards northwest of the house.

He made the screen larger. The figure came slowly as he skirted the shadow of the abandoned coal mine's tall, looming wash plant. But then as he came past the long line of rotting wooden barracks dead west of the house, he sped it up into an almost jog.

There was a ragged creak in the cheap chair as Gannon leaned forward.

Beside the computer on the desk was a brown paper bag from which he removed a single banana. He examined it in the computer screen's bluish glow. Still a tad green but acceptable.

He broke the stem and peeled some of it back.

Better early than late when it came to bananas, Gannon thought as he took a bite.

By the time he had tossed the empty peel into the room's corner trash can, the figure was less than twenty feet from the house's north side. He was moving slowly again now, silently heel-to-toe, with his carbine's buttstock up on his shoulder.

"Come to papa," Gannon said with a smile as he drew his sidearm from its thigh holster. Then he lifted a flash-bang grenade out of the milk crate beside the desk and stood.

Down the stairs, he stood for a moment looking out the old house's doorless front entry into the cool morning dimness of the outside, listening.

He couldn't hear anything, and he had just pulled the grenade's pin with his teeth and had turned to his right to chuck it into the front room when he heard the footstep behind him.

That's when he dropped the flash-bang. It bounced off the hardwood floor and then exploded at his feet at the same exact moment he was shot in the side of his head.

He staggered around the narrow hall for a second, blinded, his ears ringing despite his earplugs.

"Dad, Dad, you okay?" Gannon's son, Declan, said, lowering the rifle as he climbed up the porch.

Gannon lifted his goggles up onto the skateboard helmet, shaking away the cobwebs. The goggles were critical because the state-of-the art paintball guns they used for the drills were filled with a powerful pellet called Simunition that could take out your eye.

"No, I'm not all right. Somebody just shot me in the head," Gannon said, holstering his paintball pistol.

His son's face broke into a huge grin.

"I actually did it!" he said, raising a pumped fist. "I finally did it. I actually got you for once!"

"Very clever of you running all the way around

from the back," Gannon said. "I thought you were coming in the side window like last time. Nice head fake."

"This is unbelievable. Woo-hoo! I just dropped a navy SEAL! I'm invincible!"

Gannon frowned.

"Well, sort of," he said.

"Sort of?" Declan said, throwing up a frustrated hand. "What? No sort of. I got you for the first time ever. What did I do wrong now? C'mon, this is bull, Dad. I got the drop on you fair and square. You said it yourself. I put one in your head! You're dead!"

"But how many times do I have to tell you? It's twice," Gannon said.

"Twice? You can only die once!" Declan cried.

Gannon walked past him out the door. He took off the helmet and stood in the morning breeze, looking out at the horizon from the old rickety porch. The sky was lighting up now over the still dark endless-seeming desert, and in the far distance the top of the Utah-side Book Cliffs were now glowing with a pale gold light.

"To the head, son," Gannon finally said. "To the head."

"To the head?"

Gannon turned back as he pointed a finger gun at his temple and double tapped.

"When you shoot a man, remember, it's double or nothing. Never pull the trigger once, son. Always twice."

9

When Kit Hagen woke with an electric-like charge of shock, she found herself cold and soaked and tangled up in brush with turbulent water rushing and roaring in her ears.

She was just about to start roaring herself when the gargantuan tree branch that she was using as a flotation device finally popped free from the rocks it had gotten caught on.

Then she was free flowing again, spinning sideways back out into the fast-running greenish-brown mountain river.

Every time she was about to completely fade out of consciousness, the cold metallic smell of the fresh river water in her nostrils would jog her awake again. As she breathed it in and out, a happy childhood memory began to form. They were on vacation somewhere, and she was on an inner tube beside her older brother and sister and daddy when they all suddenly started singing. It was the theme song from that hilariously stupid Saturday morning TV show, *Land of the Lost*, and they all sang it together with gusto as they went merrily down the stream.

"Marshall, Will, and Holly," Kit mumbled facedown as she floated along, "on a routine expedition…"

Her voice trailed off as her eyes fell closed again. She listened to the soft gurgling sound of the water. So soothing, so tranquilizing, so serene.

Maybe she should stop fighting it, she thought. Daddy was here. She could sleep. It was okay. Daddy would take care of her. She could go to sleep, go down where it was safe and cool and Daddy and—

"No!" she suddenly yelled as her eyes shot back open.

Sharp pain pierced her entire left side as she tried to adjust herself a little on the huge floating branch she'd found after hitting the water. She looked to her left. The high bank she was passing was edged in rough gray rock. Beyond it were more rocks and brush sliding past on a tan-colored endless wilderness shoreline.

Where am I? she thought. *What is this?*

Then she remembered.

The sniper round had blown open a half-dollar-sized bloody exit wound hole just above her collarbone. She would have died from blood loss right there and then if her Quantico training hadn't kicked in.

The very first thing she did as she lay there in shock with her adrenaline still pumping was take off her fleece and fold it and pack it down into the hole as hard as she could. Then she'd cinched it painfully tight to her torso with the raid jacket and her belt.

She looked down at the makeshift dressing now, scanning it carefully. It was almost completely soaked through with water, but she couldn't see any blood blotting through it. At least not yet.

She looked up. It had still been somewhat dark when she'd slid down the almost sheer rock slope into the water, but now the Wyoming sky was a bright cloudless blue.

How long had she been in the water? Five minutes? An hour?

She had no clue.

The current took her out into the center of the stream as she came around a bend. When she looked left at the shore again, she could see the Wyoming mountains in the distance above her now, bright in the morning sun.

A sense of bone-deep sadness hit her as she suddenly thought of her partner, Dennis, up there somewhere facedown in the rocks, shot dead, all alone.

No! Stop it, she thought as she began to cry. *Stop it. Stop thinking about death. Not now. Just hold on. Just—*

She jerked her head up at a sudden louder sound in the river ahead. It was a low scary freight-training rumble, and she gripped the slimy branch harder as she felt herself moving faster.

The branch went sideways on her as she tracked out into the center of the stream again. When she looked to her left, she saw where the riverbank had suddenly become high slabs of gray stone. They were terracing down like descending stairs, and when she looked forward again, there was white water ahead shooting up in geyser-like spurts.

Shit, she thought as she dipped down and rose up and then plunged down even lower. Her stomach dropped as she lurched down in a rush through the center chute of it. When she rose up again, she was in the white-water geysers and then she was turning. She went under with the spinning log branch and then popped back up, coughing water.

She saw the fisherman as she drifted into an eddy beside the bottom of the rapids. He was on one of the lower rock slabs to her right, an old man in dark green rubber waders and a dark cowboy hat. The way he hovered above her, backlit against the sky, she thought she was hallucinating him. She didn't think he was real.

Was it God?

"Ma'am, are you okay?" the old cowboy fisherman said calmly as she floated in a slow spin. "Do you need help, ma'am?"

"Yes!" Kit Hagen screamed.

10

On Tuesdays, they did Mexican, so as Declan took the first shower, Gannon put on the eggs and set out the tortillas and salsa and hot sauce on the table. After he clacked down the plates, he made a fresh pot of coffee and poured himself a cup and took it with him into the living room.

Of their bus.

It actually wasn't as bad as it sounded. It was a slick shiny black rock-star-style bus with tinted windows and an interior like a Manhattan penthouse. It had all the amenities: stainless-steel appliances, a washer and dryer, a steam shower. It even had a new Chevy Colorado pickup truck hitched to the back of it that they used to do their monthly grocery run.

"All the comforts of home," Gannon mumbled as he pulled up the window blinds and looked out at his little slice of the middle of nowhere.

The elevated promontory their rock-star bus was perched upon afforded a clear view of a long curving dried arroyo that was used as a drive up into the desert canyon mine site. The high hills on both sides of the canyon were colored in muted tans with patches of green where the slopes were lightly bearded with shrubs and firs and spruce.

Gannon came forward to the window and tilted his head up at the highest eastern ridgeline. In the month and a half they'd been there, he'd seen several animals. Desert rabbits, bobcats, mule deer, even a bighorn sheep once.

There was a hunting hawk up there in the bright blue morning summer sky now. He watched it turning and turning and turning over the textured hills.

"Yeah, what else is new?" Gannon said as he finally sat on the couch beneath the bunk bed with his coffee to ponder his crazy situation for the millionth time.

Though the off-the-grid Utah desert lifestyle had its high points, his recent entry into it with his son wasn't solely for recreational purposes.

Not long ago, he had run afoul of some people.

It had started out innocently enough. He'd been fishing down in the Caribbean and found a bag of money and diamonds in a crashed corporate jet. Thinking it was dope money, by the age-old law of finders keepers, he'd decided to keep it.

As it turned out, he probably should have thought again. Because wouldn't you know it, instead of dopers, the money belonged to a bunch of corrupt-to-the-bone top-secret-clearance FBI counterintelligence people in the midst of committing a multitude of high crimes and treason.

Due to this unfortunate turn of events, there had been some problems. Problems involving the kind of automatic gunfire, violence and death Gannon had thought he'd put behind him when he'd left the navy SEALs and the NYPD.

Everything he had done was solely in self-defense, and he would have gladly tried to explain it to an honest judge and jury in an open court of law.

But that was actually sort of the problem.

Since the incident had involved a cabal of corruption at the tippity-top of the federal government food chain, it seemed like the whole bloody body-strewn incident had somehow been kept out of the papers and swept very deeply under the rug.

He'd had his old NYPD partner, Stick, discreetly look into it for him to see what was up. But there was nothing. Nothing in the computers. There was no open FBI investigation on him, no FBI warrant out for his arrest.

Or at least no formal official legal warrant, Gannon thought.

Call him crazy, but since he'd banged heads with the psycho killer lunatic wing of the shadow government, his thinking was they could still be out gunning for payback unofficially.

The fact that he was still in possession of the very large bag of corrupt loot that he'd salvaged from their crashed FBI Gulfstream 550 only seemed to add to this depressing theory.

Or maybe not, he thought for the thousandth time. Maybe no one was looking for him. Maybe it had all blown over and all the corrupt bozos involved who'd come out of it alive were happy to let bygones be bygones.

Then Gannon suddenly remembered the look on the face of the assistant deputy FBI director that he'd impaled with a scaffolding fence pole out in front of the Chilean embassy in London, England.

Or then again, he thought.

Gannon sighed as he heard his son start to sing in the shower.

It was true that the bus confines were tight for two people, he thought as he finally savored a sip of French roast.

But compared with a pine box or a prison cell, he decided with a nod, it wasn't too bad after all.

11

Gannon was in the bus galley plating scrambled eggs a few minutes later when he heard the engine.

At the living room window, he saw a large vehicle coming up the dry streambed. It was an old wide-tire desert-beige Hummer truck, and Gannon's face broke into a smile as he went back into the galley to turn off the burner.

He was outside with his coffee cup when the massive rumbling vehicle came to a halt in the gravelly desert dirt beside the bus. Gannon watched as its door shrieked open and a pretty college-aged blond girl in a Cabela's hoodie and shorts climbed out from behind the wheel.

The lovely young lady's name was Stephanie Barber, and she was the oldest child of Gannon's old war buddy, John Barber, who owned the remote Utah property where they were currently hiding out.

Gannon's friend John and his wife, Lynn, and two other kids lived down in the valley below the mine, where they raised some sheep and ran a weekend-warrior-style shooting resort camp for deep-pocketed corporate executive types.

The outfit was called Hotel Juliet Bravo, and the old house he and Declan had just been goofing around in was its main attraction. Barber had spared no expense to convert the old brick house into a state-of-the art tactical firearm training shoothouse really no different than the one he used to train in with his SEAL team outside of San Diego.

"Morning, Mr. Gannon," Stephanie said.

"Good morning, Stef," Gannon said. "What brings you up here so early?"

They both turned as Declan emerged from the bus with his hair still wet, buttoning up his plaid shirt.

As if I didn't know, Gannon thought as he saw Stephanie staring dumbstruck at his lean, nice-looking twenty-year-old son.

Gannon stifled a smile as Declan stepped over and gave the pretty college girl a hug and a little hand squeeze. They'd both hit it off pretty well in the almost two months they'd been staying there.

Gannon and Declan had actually gone on a rafting trip on the nearby Green River with the whole Barber clan the week before. Come to think of it, he couldn't help but notice the two of them cutely holding hands as they all sat around the campfire. Since then, Stephanie was visiting more and more.

Go figure, Gannon thought.

"You're lucky you caught us, Stef," Gannon said. "Me and Dec and the rest of the dwarves usually like to get heigh-hoeing down in the old mine there real early, but wouldn't you know it? Dopey broke the pickax again. That Dopey. Second time this week."

"That's real comical, Dad," Declan said, rolling his eyes. "Desert mining humor isn't easy. Most say impossible. But you manage to pull it off every single time."

Stephanie smiled.

"Hey, I actually have a surprise for you guys," she said as she turned and opened the Hummer's back door.

On the floor of the back seat was a cardboard box. It had a blanket in it, and from the blanket came a high yip.

"What in the world?" Gannon said as he came in closer and saw a cluster of extremely cute tiny black furry creatures climbing all over each other.

"One of Dad's dogs had puppies," Stephanie said proudly.

"No way. Look at them," Gannon said shaking his head. "What are they? German shepherds?"

"No. Malinois," Stephanie said, petting one.

"Of course," Gannon said, laughing. "What else would they be?"

John Barber, like Gannon, had been in the Special Forces, and Belgian Malinois were one of the breeds of dog SEALs and other Special Forces units used sometimes for bomb sniffing and raids.

"How many are there?" Declan said. "It's hard to tell."

"There's eight of them. Dad's busy out at the range with a new group that came in last night, but he said to come up this morning first thing and see if you guys want one."

"Get out," Gannon said, smiling down at the squirming bunch of them. "The pick of the litter, huh? You guys are too nice. What do you think, Dec? We could use a dog up here."

"Hell, yes!" Declan said.

Gannon picked one up and was peering at it when there was a weird ringing. It was coming across the sandy clearing from the direction of the shoothouse.

"I got it," Gannon said, handing Declan the puppy and jogging down to the old house.

He came in through the shoothouse's doorless threshold and continued straight past the stairs into the ground floor kitchen. On the counter there next to an ancient soapstone sink was a dusty green box with an old telephone handset on it.

The box was actually a US Army Vietnam-War-era field telephone. In addition to his shooting ranch down the canyon, his buddy John Barber had a kind of war museum with hundreds of weapons and war paraphernalia. He had all kinds of stuff. Artillery pieces, WWII samurai swords. The Hummer out in the yard was actually a real one he had bought from army surplus.

Since they were SOL up here with no cell service, John Barber had run a mile and a half of some old copper military phone line up the canyon so they could still reach out and touch each other off-the-grid style.

Gannon smiled as the beat-up green field box that had probably called in more than its share of napalm strikes began to jingle again.

Like Gannon himself, his buddy, John Barber, was paranoid and nuts in the most beautiful way possible.

Only the paranoid survive, Gannon thought, lifting the ringing handset.

"Gannon residence," he said.

"Hi, Mike. Is Stephanie there?" John's wife, Lynn, said.

Gannon's grin disappeared as he heard the no-nonsense tone in her voice.

"Yes. She's out talking to Dec. What's up? Is everything okay?"

"Could you just put her on, please? It's important."

"Sure."

Gannon put down the phone and jogged over and stuck his head out the shoothouse front door.

"Stef, it's your mom."

"What's up?" Declan said on the porch as Stephanie went inside.

"I don't know," Gannon said.

They didn't have to wait long to find out. When Stephanie came back out a minute later, there were tears in her eyes.

"What is it, Stef?" Gannon said.

"My uncle Owen," she said sobbing. "He's a park ranger up in Wyoming, and his boss just called the house and said somebody shot him dead."

12

Declan went down to the house with Stephanie in the Hummer while Gannon followed in the unhitched Chevy pickup.

As Gannon drove down the desert dirt road, he found himself thinking about his friend, John Barber, and the time they had spent together during the war.

Their former unit had been called a bunch of stuff over the years but when he and John were in it, it was called Task Force Orange. It was a special mission reconnaissance unit specializing in electronic surveillance and covert border transit. High-risk, sneak-and-peek missions where they wanted to softly penetrate into places where US forces weren't officially supposed to be. Sometimes roping in off a Night Stalker chopper in the dead of a moonless night. Sometimes doing a High Altitude High Opening jump out the back of a C-130.

After they hit some jackpots, one of the brass pulled some strings and had them sent back to the States to go through the CIA espionage course in Virginia called the Farm. There they'd been taught the fun James Bond stuff. How to steal cars and pick locks and bluff their way through border checks. Then when they got back to the war, they started going into places on commercial flights in civilian clothes with passport cover. Those trips were especially great since they actually got to land inside the aircraft and use a set of stairs for a switch.

They'd send them in first before they did anything big. To listen and to find out things. Get coordinates. Count things like troop numbers or guards in prison towers.

Gannon remembered how on walk-in sneak-and-peeks they'd move nights, sleep days. They'd sleep in the brush undercover, taking turns to stand the two-hour watches.

John, who was five years older and who had started hunting with his own father at the age of seven out here in the Utah wilderness, had taught Gannon so much.

How to read a trail like a novel. How to cover your tracks. How to be completely silent. How to listen.

They'd become like brothers on those long nights listening. Deep listening, hours and hours of it. Listening so intense you started to hear the footfalls of insects. Think you were melting into the landscape, actually becoming the grass, the wind, the stone.

If there were anyone better at recon on the planet, at tracking someone down, and moving in and out of places at whim and without a trace like a ghost, Gannon couldn't imagine who it could be.

He shook his head as John's lake house came into view down in the valley below.

Whoever had murdered John's brother better start praying that the cops caught him very quickly, Gannon thought.

And had a quality bulletproof vest for him to wear to the arraignment.

13

Getting out of the truck in the yard, Gannon found his old friend alone sitting at a picnic table in the side yard of his log-cabin-style house beside his small lake.

John Barber was a lean, wiry man of five-foot-ten. When Gannon had first met him in Afghanistan, his hair was longish and almost blue-black, but it was cut in a flattop now and streaked with bits of gray, as was his mustache. As Gannon sat across from his friend, he could see that he was still in his polo shirt that he wore on the firing range, and there was a book in one of his big muscular hands.

Gannon winced as he looked at the old family Bible. The cover soft, the old onion skin pages yellow and worn with handling.

"John, I'm so sorry about your brother," Gannon said. "What in the hell happened?"

"We don't know," Barber said. "His boss and buddy, Don, called. He could only talk for a second. He just said Owen was working up in Grand Teton Park, and that there was a shooting sometime this morning, and that Owen was dead. It's not even on the news yet. I checked twice."

"That's unbelievable," Gannon said.

"That's the word," John Barber said, placing the Bible down on the weathered wood as he looked out on the lake and cliffs.

"Was he one of your younger brothers?" Gannon said.

"No, Owen was the oldest," Barber said, wincing.

"Married? Kids?" Gannon said.

"No, thank goodness. He was a lifelong bachelor. There was a woman he loved when he was young, but she died and that was that."

"Your mom know?" Gannon said.

Barber nodded.

"Just got—"

Barber turned and looked off over the dark blue-green lake. Gannon looked with him out at the wind drawing silent lines and curves there on the water. Then John Barber took a breath and looked back.

"Just got back from telling her," he finished as he turned and looked over at the front porch.

"I remember how he was laughing going down those steps two months ago. He always came down for Steph's birthday. Looked great as usual. Happy. We'd made plans to go up to Alaska in the fall for fly-fishing. I guess I'll need to cancel that."

"Stef said you're going to fly up to Jackson?" Gannon said.

Barber, in addition to so many other things military, was an avid pilot. He was a partial owner of a Beechcraft King Air 200 at the airport in Moab that he used for his more action-oriented corporate clients for skydiving.

Barber looked at Gannon with his placid brown eyes and nodded.

"I need to go and get Owen and bring him back for my mom. She wants the funeral down here so they can bury him next to my daddy."

Gannon bit his lip. Barber's wife, Lynn, was completely hysterical about the flying issue. She'd told Stef that she didn't want John driving feeling crazed and heartbroken the way he was, let alone flying.

And it wasn't just that, Gannon knew. After his military service, like so many other great soldiers, John had some trouble transitioning back into civilian life. Not that long ago, he'd gone on a tear of drinking, then sunk into a deep spiraling depression. He and Lynn had really struggled for over a year to finally pull him out of it.

Gannon peered at his old buddy.

"When are you going to leave for Wyoming?" Gannon said.

"In a minute. I already called the guys at the airport to reconfigure the plane so we can fit in the casket. I know what Lynn's saying, but I'm fine."

"I know you are. I'd like to come with you," Gannon found himself saying.

Barber smiled.

"No, that's not necessary, old friend. I appreciate the gesture, but you have your own scenario. This is family stuff. I got this."

"Just let me tag along for the flight."

"No," Barber said.

"John, how many times have you saved my ass? How about letting me pay you and your wife back a little, huh? You need help, so I'm going with you, you hardheaded son of a bitch, and that's that."

John looked at him again.

"There'll be law enforcement. Federal. Owen worked for the US Park Service."

Gannon had told him all about his recent run-in with the FBI.

"I'll just come along for company. I'll stay at the hotel until you get stuff settled and then we'll head back."

Barber shook his head.

"Do it for your wife, man," Gannon said. "She wants someone to watch your back. You think she wants you up in a plane alone? She's freaking terrified."

Barber thought on that, then finally nodded.

"Suit yourself. You ready? Some bad weather's coming. We need to leave now to beat it."

Ready? Gannon thought. *Shit no!*

"Of course," Gannon said standing. "Let's go."

14

Twenty minutes later, Gannon got out of his pickup back up at the bus.

Inside he found a knapsack and began tossing in items. A couple of pairs of jeans, some underwear, some T-shirts. He found an anorak and threw that in along with some socks.

When he was done, from under the bed, he took out a shiny black strap bag the size of a small briefcase. It was a fireproof document case, and he flipped up the Velcro lid and spun the combination lock.

Inside the bug-out bag, there were a bunch of separators, and he flipped past the pistols toward the back and reached in and took out a stack of twenties and fifties. He counted out five hundred and folded it and clipped it with one of the stainless-steel money clips there beside the money.

He was slipping the case back under the bed when Declan came in with the puppy.

"Hey, Dec. You name him yet?" Gannon said as he stood.

"No, not yet. Um, Dad?"

"Yes?"

"What's going on? Where are you going?"

"I'm going to take a little trip with John up to Wyoming to get his brother's body."

"But how?"

"He's going to fly us up there in his plane."

"Okay. But, I mean like how, as in I thought we were supposed to lay low here. At least for the summer, you said," Declan said.

"I know but this is…a special occasion," Gannon said.

"I don't know, Dad. I don't think you should."

"It's not a matter of should, son. It's a matter of have to. John needs help. His wife needs help. They need me to watch their back. Least I could do after all they've done for us."

"Yeah, sure, but it was a shooting, right? So there's going to be cops and stuff?"

"It's fine, son. I got this. You know the combo to the bug-out bag here, right? And where everything is? The ATM card? The info for the bank back in the Dominican?"

"See, Dad? I knew it," his son said, giving him a doubtful look. "Why would you even say that? This isn't a good idea."

Gannon knew he was right.

But he shouldered his duffel anyway.

The tiny puppy in Declan's hand made the cutest

whining sound there ever was as Gannon scratched him under his chin.

"Dec, listen. Trust your old man, okay? I'll be back tomorrow. We're all good here. I promise," he said.

15

When they got to the airport in Moab, it was just before noon, and within twenty minutes, John Barber was taking them up to fifteen thousand feet in his roaring twin prop.

They began their bumpy descent into Jackson only a little over an hour later.

Gannon, who had never been to Wyoming, looked out the window in awe. At the flat glass lakes, the flat grass plains, the mountains and cliffs sharp-edged as cutlery.

If the hugeness of the Utah landscape made you feel like an ant, he thought, shaking his head, Wyoming made you feel microscopic. How could the mountains actually still have patches of snow on them here in August?

As they touched down, the tower directed them over to the private plane aviation company hangar tucked at the airport's southwest corner. Surprisingly, the plane parking area was actually quite full. Gannon counted three large corporate jets before John taxied them in beside a small Lear.

Barber powered down the plane and flipped the door. They crossed the tarmac into the lounge of a sleek polished glass-and-mahogany pagoda-style building that looked brand-new. Barber was sitting by its front exit doors holding a couple of bottles of water two minutes later as Gannon came back out of the head.

"Rental company is sending over a car," Barber said, handing him a bottle. "Owen's buddy, Don, isn't picking up his phone. Where do you think we should head first? Sheriff's office?"

"Do we know where the crime scene is?" Gannon said.

"No."

"Then we should go to the medical examiner's office," Gannon said.

"The medical examiner?"

Gannon nodded.

"They'll know as much as the sheriff's office and being doctors, they'll be far more likely than the cops to actually tell a family member what's up. Especially if you're staring at them face-to-face."

"You don't think we should call them first?"

"No way. Let's just show up," Gannon said. "Did you call your wife? Tell her we made it?"

Barber nodded.

"Funny, you're starting to sound just like her," he said as they saw a white Nissan Pathfinder pull up outside the glass doors.

As Barber drove them up the airport road, Gannon wasn't done gaping at the landscape. In the northern distance, out the windshield, there were massive mountain ranges and unfenced grasslands of a vastness he'd never experienced before.

There wasn't a house. Not a tree. In every direction for miles and miles and miles, there was nothing. Nothing but grass and wildflowers until your eyes gave up.

"What's up, city slicker?" Barber said, noticing the awe in Gannon's face.

"How much land do you think that is out there?" Gannon said.

"That little field there?" Barber said squinting as they came to the turnoff for US 191. "Oh, I'd say that's in around about the size of Connecticut."

It took them twenty minutes to get into Jackson. There was a welcome arch made of antlers set up in a park by the main road. Gannon looked out as they passed it. There was an A-frame log cabin diner. A bright shiny gas station. A two-story motel with batwing saloon doors.

It looked like a life-size Western town from a model train layout, Gannon thought.

The medical examiner's was in the Teton County Health Department building on Pearl Street deep in the east part of town past all the tourist stuff.

Gannon had thought there might be some media news vans but as they approached, he saw that there were just some regular cars and pickups in the lot.

Barber parked and killed the engine and took a deep breath.

"Okay, wait in the car," he said as he opened his door.

"No," Gannon said, getting out with him. "I'll tag along if you don't mind. I need to stretch my legs."

16

The reception area inside the medical examiner's office was low-ceilinged and painted a dreary beige with a scuffed linoleum floor. The man on the other side of the reception desk was heavyset and about fifty, wearing glasses. They watched as he stacked some papers on top of a whirring laser printer.

"Help you?" he said, staring at them, puzzled.

"I'm John Barber, the brother of Owen Barber, the park ranger who was shot up on Grand Teton. Is his body here?"

"I'm so sorry, Mr. Barber," the heavy man said. "I'm the medical examiner, Dr. Walter Thompson. This must be so hard on your family. This is a real tough, tough day."

"You're right about that. Is Owen here?" Barber said.

"No, your brother isn't here. No one is here yet. All

of the, um, decedents are still up at the crime scene. They're still processing it."

Barber and Gannon looked at each other.

"Wait a second. Decedents?" Barber said. "As in plural? You're saying more than just my brother was shot?"

Dr. Thompson looked at them with a sudden uneasy look on his face. The room went starkly silent as the printer shut off.

"Did you talk to the sheriff's office?" he said.

"No, I heard from one of Owen's coworkers that he was shot dead, so we just flew up here from Utah. Decedents? What do you mean, decedents?"

"I'm not supposed to be talking about this," the man said as he grabbed a clipboard. "You really need to call the sheriff's office."

"Give me a break. I'm not calling anyone when I'm right here standing in front of you. What the hell happened to my brother?"

Dr. Thompson passed a hand over his mouth.

"Can I see some ID?" he finally said.

Barber showed him his license.

"You're not a reporter, right?"

"I look like a damn reporter to you?" Barber said with a cold squint.

"There were four law enforcement shot," the doctor said. "Your brother and the Teton County sheriff and two FBI agents. They actually got one of the FBI agents out of the Snake River. She's in surgery over in St. John's. That's what I heard."

"Four shot! FBI agents! What in the world? Four?" Barber said.

"It's even worse than that," the doctor said nodding. "They were up there investigating a homicide at the time. So there are actually five victims on the mountain. We have MEs coming in here from three counties."

"So you're saying my brother was killed at a crime scene?"

The doctor nodded again.

"He was guiding in the sheriff and federal agents to a body that was found yesterday. After two hours of not hearing from anyone, the park station tried to establish radio contact. Then they sent up some more Park Service personnel. All of them were shot dead except the one FBI woman. She might be dead, too. I heard they had to medevac her to the hospital."

"They went in to look at a body and somebody shot them down?" Barber said.

"It's looking like it, but like I said, they're investigating it. It's still an extremely kinetic situation, Mr. Barber. If you have any more questions, talk to the sheriff's office or to the FBI, please. All right? If you'll excuse me."

"But wait, wait. Why was the FBI there?" Barber said.

"You'll have to ask them," the doctor said, turning back toward his printer. "They're over at St. John's, waiting for the agent to get out of surgery."

17

Kit Hagen sighed as the softly moving hospital bed came to a gentle stop. The air was cool here, smelled of lemons and antiseptic. She listened to the light clicks of things being plugged in around her, the muffled rattle of a curtain being drawn.

"You're here in your room now, okay?" said a woman's voice.

"Okay," Kit said, smiling as she allowed herself to sink even deeper into the delightfully soft, warm, clean and dry sheets.

She listened to the soft footsteps trail off. When she peeked down at herself under the white towel-like blankets, she thought about when she was little again. Saying prayers with her mother after her bath and then giggling with her father as he tucked her in tighter and tighter until she was wrapped like a mummy.

Wow, was she wasted, she thought. She peered up at the ceiling. She must be on a massive amount of painkillers. The good stuff, too. The top-drawer stuff they kept under lock and key.

Sometime later, she lifted her cotton-filled head as the sound of something close cut through her drowsiness.

"Hi, Kit. Do you know who I am?" said a new voice.

She turned her gaze to her right and blinked up at the woman there at her bedside. It was a blond woman with a pinched-looking tight face.

It definitely wasn't her mom.

How many guesses do I get? she thought and laughed.

"Kit? Are you awake? Can you talk?" the blond woman asked.

"Are you my doctor?" she said.

"No. I'm from Justice, Kit. I cover environmental stuff with the Parks. I was actually at a conference nearby and came as soon as I heard."

Kit squinted at her.

Justice?

Then she frowned.

Work? Ugh!

"I'm Dawn Warner," the woman said.

Who gives a shit? Kit thought.

Then her eyes shot wide as she remembered it all in cut flash images. The sheriff dropping with half of his head gone. Then Dennis. The horror of them facedown on the raw bloody rock. She remembered the ranger. The calm in his voice reaching through her terror. The pops of his cover fire as she ran for her life.

Something stung in her arm as she tried to sit up. As she opened her eyes wider, she noticed there were two men there beside the blond woman. They were agents, she saw. A tall younger one and a squat veteran dad-like one. The tall one was holding a cell phone and the other had a notebook out.

Locals, she thought. From the Denver office probably. Dennis and she had been coordinating with Denver. They had crime scene people ready to go waiting on the word from Dennis the second that he confirmed the victim was the NATPARK killer's latest.

"You got him, right? Tell me you got the son of a bitch," Kit said, looking at the agents pleadingly.

"We'll get to that," Dawn Warner said. "This is Agent Fitzgerald and Agent Harris from my team, Kit. Tell us what happened."

"The sheriff met us at the airport, and we drove straight to the mountain. We had to off-road up the slope and then the ranger—" she paused and took a deep breath "—the ranger who had found the body led us down into a rock ravine. We saw the foot of a body among the rocks, and we were about to get closer when there was a rifle shot.

"The sheriff was killed first. Shot in the head. Then Dennis was shot in the head a second later. The ranger and I got down in some cover, and he shot back so I could run. But then I was shot, too. Then I jumped into the water to get away."

"Did you see who the shooter was?" asked the shorter agent. "Did you see his face?"

"No. He was hidden in the rock at a distance up above us somewhere. He must have used a rifle with a scope. Was the ranger killed, too? Did he make it? Just before I jumped into the water, I heard him scream."

Dawn Warner shook her head.

"No," she said. "I'm sorry, Kit. The park ranger is dead, too. You're the only one who made it out alive."

Kit started to cry.

"He was a good man. A good, good man. The ranger. He…he saved my life. There was no way I would have gotten out without him."

"Is there anything else you can tell us?" Warner said after a bit.

She looked down at the bottom of her bed as she shook her head.

"Wait. There is something," Kit said. "The ranger filmed the shooter or at least where the shots came from. It's on the sheriff's phone. He used the sheriff's phone. You need to look at the sheriff's phone. Do you have it?"

"We'll look, Kit," Warner said. "That's good info. Good enough for now. You need to get your rest now, okay?"

"No, wait. You didn't tell me. Did you get the shooter? Did you catch him?"

"No, Kit," Warner said. "No, we didn't. But we will, okay? I promise. Now get your rest. We'll talk later."

18

There was a loud racket as the excavator's blade dropped with a heavy clatter and began to tear open the run-down sunny suburban Los Angeles street like a thumbnail through the peel of an orange.

Crouched in the shadow of the 405 San Diego Freeway overpass, Westergaard sweated as he watched.

He was in Los Angeles now, four or five miles north of LAX. Flying got him wound up so he always liked to get out of airports as fast as he could on foot. He'd get some exercise in and a few hours of walking actually made him feel mentally better.

He'd been walking for a while rather aimlessly before he saw the construction here in Sunkist Park. Already feeling hot and tired, on a whim he had decided to throw his carry-on over his shoulder and climb up the weedy embankment to stop and to watch.

The hard-hatted men seemed to be in the midst

of replacing a water main, he thought as he took a warm water bottle out of his roller bag. He watched them, watched the excavator. There was something stabilizing in the normalcy of it. Something soothing in the simple act of men working together. People set to a purpose. The knowable symphony of cause and effect.

Westergaard took a sip of his Dasani, then closed his eyes, listening to the rushing ocean sound of the traffic over the sound wall behind him. When he opened them, a pudgy white kid was jogging by the construction workers. When he looked above him in the sky, a yellow DHL cargo plane was soaring in toward the airport, the air screaming off its steel skin with a high-pitched whistle.

Westergaard squatted there absorbing the nowness of everything, letting things be. He never planned these things, just went with them. He knew it seemed weird, but he'd just have to live with that.

Everybody had his own way of decompressing, he thought.

It was ten minutes later when the horn honked. Westergaard turned down the embankment. Parked at the curb, there was a white sporty Jaguar with its top down. An attractive young blond woman sat behind the wheel. She had big Gucci sunglasses on, and she tilted them down as she looked up at him with her sky blue eyes.

Even with her massive baby bump in her stretched-to-the-limit tank top, his wife was smoking, just smoking, Westergaard thought as he stood. Just turned twenty-six, she was half an inch under six feet and had been a genuine Friday night lights Texas cheerleader before she'd headed out west here for the bright lights.

The construction workers were noticing her as well, Westergaard saw as he dusted off his pants and scrambled down the embankment. His wife had stopped all work.

"Back to work, boys," Westergaard said in his clipped South African accent as he arrived beside the car. "Get your own Texas piece of prime ass, eh."

"Get in here," Elena said, scooting over to let him drive. "What the hell were you doing up there? Taking a leak?"

"No, I was watching the construction."

"Watching the construction? Why?"

"I don't know," he said truthfully. "I got tired of walking, and I guess it seemed interesting, eh."

"You should have said yes, eh, I was taking a leak, eh," she said, making fun of his accent. Then she kissed him. "You're always so weird after your trips. You're lucky you're so cute."

"I know," he said kissing her again. "Screw that Lou Gehrig. I, Clarence Westergaard, am the luckiest man on the face of the earth."

"Speaking of screwing. Screw any hookers at the convention, Clarence Westergaard?" she said as he gunned it past the whistling hardhats. "Be honest. I'll be scrubbing it with boiling water and a wire brush anyway before it comes anywhere near me."

"Not this trip. Too busy," he said, winking at her.

"Well, you better stay busy," she said, "you want to keep it attached."

"Okay, okay. Enough banter. Lay the update on me."

She lifted her phone and tapped it, bringing up an

app she had that showed different everyday objects that matched the size of the growing baby inside of her. She showed him the screen.

"A baseball mitt!" he cried. "Two seconds ago our progeny was the size of a peppercorn."

"Yeah, well, time flies when you're giving Momma stretch marks."

"I can't wait to see those stretch marks, Momma," he said, tickling her as they pulled up to the red light.

"Right here? Really? That's weird, but okay," she said, grabbing the bottom of her tank.

"Come on," he said as she paused. "What are you waiting for? Do it, you tease. I double dare you."

"Fine. I'm really going to do it," she said as she began sliding her tank top slowly up her belly. "Oh, are these folks at this light in for a treat."

She laughed and then stopped as he finally slapped her arm down.

"Stop!" he cried.

"Ha-ha. I win. Don't you mess with momma," she said.

"You're crazy, eh," he said, laughing. "You're a genuine nut."

"Takes one to know one," she said as she snuggled up against him.

Westergaard didn't say anything to that as the light changed, and he hammered it up the ramp for the highway.

19

St. John's Hospital was only a block north from the medical examiner's office on East Broadway Avenue.

John Barber pulled the Pathfinder into the parking lot of the Baptist church across from it, and he and Gannon sat looking through the windshield.

It wasn't a big facility. To Gannon, it looked more like one of those urgent care medical offices than an actual hospital. Like most other buildings in Jackson, it was trimmed with wood beams for a rustic look.

Gannon looked at the ER entrance sliding doors. He shook his head as he thought about the amount of FBI personnel that were probably in there right now. And more on the way, no doubt.

How do you like that? Gannon thought. He and the good old FBI. What was that Buck Owens cowboy song? *Together Again*?

He glanced over at John. He wasn't looking too

hot. Ever since he heard about what happened, he was looking like he wanted to kill a few people himself.

"You ever hear of anything like this when you were in the NYPD?" Barber said, squinting. "Cops getting shot on their way to see a body?"

"Cops getting shot, sure," Gannon said. "But actually at a crime scene? Never."

Barber nodded.

"Those cars there near the ER entrance look like government to me," he said.

Me, too, Gannon thought, swallowing.

"How likely you think it is they tell us anything?"

Uh-oh. Here we go, Gannon thought, taking in the thousand-yard stare in Barber's eyes.

There were people who followed normal channels. Barber wasn't even close to being one of them.

"If they're state cops, not likely," Gannon finally said. "If they're Feds, no chance at all. What are you thinking?"

"About taking a walk," Barber said opening his door.

20

Gannon had to hurry to catch up with his friend as they crossed the street for the hospital. He wasn't surprised in the slightest when instead of heading for the ER entrance like normal people, Barber veered off left into the lot.

Around the corner at the rear of the facility was an enormous dumpster with a loading dock on the other side of it. Gannon groaned silently as he noticed the propped-open door atop the concrete.

"Are you sure about this?" Gannon said as Barber immediately mounted the steps beside the dumpster.

The narrow corridor inside was dim and empty of people. As Gannon entered it, Barber was already a half dozen steps ahead, pulling open a door on the left.

It led into a cement stairwell, and as Gannon caught up on the second story, Barber opened another door into a bright hallway.

They walked down between what looked like patient recovery rooms. A man with a broken wrist was inside the third one they passed. An old smiling woman in a wheelchair was in the next.

On the other side of the push door at the end of the hall was a nurses' station with a black-haired very young-looking nurse behind it. She looked up at them in surprise.

"Sheriff's office," Barber said without the slightest hesitation. "I think we got turned around somehow. We're here to talk with the wounded FBI agent?"

"Of course. Miss Hagen. Room 207. First room on the left through the hall door there," she said pointing. "She just woke up."

Room 207 was a large suite with a huge window behind the bed that showed a stunning view north of the snowcapped mountains. Lying in the bed beneath its window was a woman asleep. She was pale and pretty with reddish-brown hair. As they stepped over, Gannon looked at the massive wrapping of gauze at her left shoulder. Her entire left arm was strapped into an elaborate sling.

The woman's eyes suddenly opened. They were pale brown and glazed from the painkillers. They fixed immediately on Barber's face.

"You...you made it," she said.

Barber smiled down at her.

"No, Agent Hagen. I'm not who you think I am. I'm Owen's younger brother John. Owen died. He was shot dead. You were there, right? Did you see it? That's why I'm here. I'm trying to find out what happened to him."

"What in the hell is going on here?" said a woman's voice from behind them.

Gannon turned to where three people—two men and a blond woman—had just come in through the hospital suite doorway.

"Shit," he mumbled as he noticed the blue windbreakers the men were wearing over their business clothes.

Why didn't I wait in the car, again? Gannon thought as half of the FBI west of the Mississippi suddenly appeared in front of them.

"Are you deaf? Who are you? And who the hell let you in here?" said the woman.

Barber and Gannon looked at her. At her short blond hair that looked expensively colored. At her slightly masculine strong-jawed face that looked surgically tightened. Her clothes were too nice for an agent.

Some kind of lawyer, Gannon thought. Some jackass Fed administrator or Fed PR spin doctor or something.

"My brother, Owen Barber, was killed this morning is who I am," Barber said glaring right back at her. "Who the hell are you?"

"Owen what?" the snippy blond woman said, baffled.

"The Park Service employee who was killed, ma'am," said the taller of the two FBI agents with her.

The woman's taut cheeks puffed and her eyes flashed as she wheeled around at the guy.

"You have got to be shitting me!" she cried. "What in the hell is this, Patrick? A joke? This is secured? You call this security?"

"I'm sorry," the tall agent said stepping forward. "Mr. Barber, is it? I'm Agent Fitzgerald. I'm so sorry for your loss, but you can't be in here. No one can talk to the agent. She just came out of surgery. You have to leave immediately. Please."

"And you are?" the other shorter agent said, suddenly standing there right next to Gannon.

Gannon blinked at him. He was in his early forties, broad-shouldered and thick-featured with receding blond hair. Beneath his intelligent blue eyes, his slightly homely plain face exuded an almost convincing harmlessness.

"I'm...nobody. I'm Mike," Gannon said nodding calmly. "I'm John's friend. I'm just a family friend of the Barbers."

"What happened to my brother up on that mountain?" Barber said, still glaring as he stood his ground beside the hospital bed. He looked past tall Agent Fitzgerald, who was practically breathing on him, at the pushy woman.

"What happened up on that mountain?" he said again.

"I'm done with you," the woman said. "You're not authorized to be in this room. You have exactly one second to leave or you will be cuffed."

"Cuffed?" Barber said, tilting his head back with a genuine laugh. "Cuffed? Is that right? My brother is dead and now you're going to cuff me? That's interesting. Really? I gotta see this."

"Please, sir. Everyone, let's be reasonable," Agent Fitzgerald said.

Barber stared at the blond lady for a long beat, then slowly turned down toward Agent Hagen in the bed.

"You get your rest, okay?" Barber said, smiling with a wink. "We'll talk later."

"Oh, no, you won't," said the woman in the suit.

Barber ignored her. He was too busy staring at Agent Fitzgerald until the agent finally stepped out of his way.

"Alrighty then," Gannon said as they came out of the room. They headed quickly past the nurses' station and down the hall toward the back stairs.

"I told you this was family stuff," Barber said. "I told you to wait in the car. Hell, I told you to stay back in Utah, but you insisted."

"Don't remind me," Gannon said. "Now what?"

"How about we find a hotel? Cool our heels for a bit?" Barber said.

"I like that idea," Gannon said as they reached the back stairs. "A lot."

21

When Gannon woke in the hotel room, it was pitch-black, and he clicked on the bedside light and sat up. It was 3:00 a.m. on his phone. He thought there might be a message from John, who had left the hotel that afternoon around two, but there was nothing.

The tiles of the dark kitchenette were cold on the soles of his bare feet as he came out of the suite's bedroom. He took a bottle of water out of the mini-fridge and took it to the window. It gave a view of the hotel's rear parking lot. He stood and drank some cold water, watching in the silence. The fluorescent light on a dozen lonely cars. The darkness beyond. Everything still.

He'd just finished the water bottle when he heard the rattle at the door. He turned and watched it open.

"You hungry?" John Barber said.

The all-night diner they found twenty minutes later

was near the entrance of town by the antler arch. Barber took out his reading glasses as they slid into a booth. He took a little notebook from his pocket and began to mumble to himself as he went over his notes.

When the tired-looking waitress came over, they both ordered the same thing, eggs and bacon with french fries instead of home fries. Gannon yawned as a tractor trailer pulled out on the other side of the window beside them. The grumble and scratch of its upshifting made the plate glass wobble. After it left, the only sound was the country music that was playing low from the kitchen.

"The FBI agent who was killed was named Braddock," Barber said.

"And you found this out how again?" Gannon said, squinting.

"My brother's coworker and friend, Don Hicks. I spoke to him and several of his Park Service buddies. One of the buddies is dating the local DA who is working a task force on this case with the Feds. Turns out there's a lot going on with this thing. A hell of a whole lot."

"I'm getting that impression," Gannon said. "So this Braddock was Agent Hagen's partner?"

"Yep. They were both from the Bureau's Behavioral Science Unit."

"Behavioral Science? Wait. The serial killer squad?" Gannon said holding up a finger.

Barber nodded.

"They'd just flown straight in from DC when it happened. They came looking for a serial killer they've been after. The NATPARK killer, they're calling him."

"The what?"

"The NATPARK killer," Barber said, tapping at his notebook with a finger. "Over the past three years, three women—all young, all attractive—have been abducted, raped, and tortured in three separate national parks while on camping vacations. Two were taken off hiking trails during the day and one out of her tent in the middle of the night. Each victim was strangled to death after extensive torture, and in each case, there's been a very distinctive..."

Barber licked a thumb and went through his notes.

"Postmortem posing," he finally said.

Gannon took a sip of the water the waitress had poured, then shook his head.

"What's highly unusual even for a serial murderer is the massive distances between the crimes," Barber continued. "The first victim had been taken at the Great Smoky Mountains in North Carolina, the next at the Grand Canyon, and the most recent was at Rocky Mountain Park in Colorado last year. Without any witnesses, the FBI worked out a profile and have been doing a lot of investigating in the RV community for people with histories of sexual violence."

"You'd think this case would be front page stuff," Gannon said. "Let me take a wild guess. The Feds are keeping a tight lid on it?"

"Yep," Barber said, turning a page in his notebook. "National parks have millions of visitors each year so the rumor is the Bureau of Land Management especially have their undies in a bind about making sure it doesn't leak. They wanted it investigated discreetly. Didn't want it to cause some kind of panic."

"Guess those Fed pencil pushers take their family

vacays at the beach these days, huh," Gannon said. "So Braddock and Hagen came here to look at victim number four?"

"Yes. Owen found a dead young woman up in the foothills of Grand Teton the evening before around eight. Hagen and Braddock were actually waiting on the next killing to see the fresh crime scene so when Owen called it in, they immediately jumped on a plane. They actually told Owen to stay put at the crime scene until they got there. Then yesterday morning as they were heading into the site, they were all shot as they stood right beside the body. With a rifle. Apparently from some distance. All the bullets match. Lapua Magnum .338 boat tails."

"Lapuas," Gannon said with a whistle. "That's a long-range cartridge. Sniper rounds?"

Barber nodded again.

"That's completely bananas. Was it an ambush?" Gannon said.

"Maybe. But it's a remote area with only one way in or out, so maybe they're thinking the killer got boxed in just after he dumped the body."

"Couldn't get out so he up and started blasting away at two FBI agents, a park ranger, and the county sheriff with a safari big game sniper rifle," Gannon said.

"Worst thing of all, it worked," Barber said, snapping his book closed and tucking it into his pocket. "Since the son of a bitch got clean away."

"Well, at least the rocket scientists down at the BLM are in for some bad news," Gannon said. "Law enforcement killed by serial killer is the kind of juicy headline even the government won't be able to cover up. Good luck keeping the lid on this now."

"Exactly," Barber said. "Especially since I already anonymously emailed every news outlet in the state about it."

"What now?" Gannon said.

Barber took out his phone and looked at it and took a deep breath.

"We're to get Owen later this morning. His autopsy is done. After we eat and get a few hours' sleep, we need to head over to the funeral parlor to pick out a coffin and arrange transport to the plane."

Gannon shook his head. Then he reached out and put an arm on his buddy's shoulder.

"I'm so sorry, John. About all of this. Your poor brother. This isn't right. They have to catch this son of a bitch."

"Well, if they don't, I'm going to," Barber said coldly as the waitress approached with their plates. "If it's the last thing I do in this world."

22

A little after breakfast, Kit Hagen was on her feet coming out of her recovery suite's restroom. She was trying to tie her skimpy hospital gown closed behind her with her free hand when she turned to see her Behavioral Science coworker, Francis Sinclair, standing there in the suite's doorway.

How do you like that? she thought. *Her butt was literally in the breeze, wasn't it?*

"Oh, hey, Kit," he said, immediately turning around. "I'm sorry. Hey."

"That timing, Sinclair. Impeccable," she said as she finally got things secured. "I don't know about you, but they never showed this kind of tight-knit team-building in the FBI recruitment video they played me at Pepperdine Law."

"You need the nurse?" Sinclair said, still turned around as he stood by the door.

Kit managed to carefully back toward the bed and drop into it without knocking over the rolling IV stand.

"No, it's okay. You can come in now," she said.

"First off, about Dennis. I'm so, so sorry," Sinclair said as he stepped over to her bedside. "Everybody is. I keep getting texts. There's literally hundreds of them. Mostly students."

She thought about Braddock. How he was the most beloved teacher at Quantico. How he hadn't even wanted to go into the field.

She thought about his wife, Anna. How nice she was. How they were college sweethearts. She thought about Anna's garden, the way she kept their house. You could eat off the floor.

This would shatter her, Kit thought. Just full obliteration.

The only consolation was that he'd been killed instantly.

Then she thought, no, the only real consolation was that she had been shot, too, so she didn't have to tell Anna herself.

"Everyone is asking about you, too, of course, Kit. They're overjoyed that…that you made it. I am, too," he said.

She looked up at Sinclair. Tall and skinny with slightly spiky black hair, she always thought that the boyish thirtysomething looked like an aging skateboarder. No one would ever guess that he was an FBI profiler. Or had been with the marines thick in the shit at Fallujah.

"How's the arm?" he said.

"The bullet just missed my collarbone. As my

funny doctor put it, I dodged a bullet there. Get it? Anyway, I heard you've been up to the crime scene."

Sinclair nodded.

"Just got back."

"Do you have photos?"

He gave her a hesitant look.

"Isn't this too soon, Kit? I just actually came up to visit. They said that…"

"What did they say?"

"They said to take it easy on you. Not to stress you out. That you might have suffered a concussion in the fall."

"A concussion? Really?" Kit said. "Interesting. That's news to me. Give me a break, Francis. My eyeballs work. I'm awake and over eighteen. Let me see the photos."

"But—

"But what?"

"Some of them are pictures of Dennis."

"I don't want to see those obviously or of the ranger or the sheriff. Just show me the ones of the original victim. I need to know."

"Know what?" Sinclair said.

"If it's him," she said.

Sinclair took his Nikon out of his kit bag and queued it up and handed it over.

Braddock, who had been a profiler for twenty years, had taught her not to jump to conclusions, but at the very first photo, she started nodding.

It was him, she thought. It was actually him. Shit! All the signs were there. The way the victim was positioned. The braided bungee cord ligatures at the wrists. The folded clothing left beside the body in a neat pile with the underwear on top.

She looked over the victim's body. The height was right. Five-seven or eight. He liked them tall. She was slender yet shapely at the bust and hips, especially the bust. That was a little off. He seemed to like them a tad thinner up top.

As she did with the others, Kit took a deep breath before she finally looked at the face. Like the others, the hair was tied up with a black scrunchie, and the ears were removed and the face was cut up beyond all recognition.

She looked through it all again before she handed back the camera.

"So," Sinclair said.

She took a breath thinking about it.

"It's him, and he was waiting for us," she finally said.

Sinclair looked at her.

"He had built a kind of perch up above the body. He lurked there waiting for us like a cat leaving out a chunk of cheese for a mouse."

"You don't think the ranger interrupted him dropping the body?"

"No," Kit said, shaking her head slowly. "Why wouldn't he kill just the ranger if he wanted to get out? Sneak up and shoot him while he sat in his truck. He had a scope on the rifle and Ranger Barber had to have catnapped a little. He was there all night."

"Good point."

"No," Kit said. "I don't think we just came upon him. If this perpetrator is anything, he's meticulous. I think it was an ambush. He waited for us. And by us, I mean me and Braddock. He shot us on purpose."

"Why?"

"I'm not sure. I've been wondering about it myself. Because we're covering it up? He's pissed that we're leaving the murders out of the papers?"

"You think he's upping the ante so we can't keep a lid on it anymore? He's looking for fame now?" Sinclair said.

"Maybe. I mean, why go to all this trouble if no one knows how fiendishly clever he is? Do we know who the victim is yet?"

"No, not yet. Like the others, he took the ID."

"Is it just you on this?" Kit said.

"Yes. For now, it's just me and the forensics team out of the Denver office. It's all still such a scramble. With Dennis passed, they haven't even appointed a new section chief yet."

"How's the press on this?" Kit said. "On me at least. Are the jackals down there waiting? I'm getting out of here later this afternoon. Last thing I want is an O. J. Simpson white bronco ride out to the plane."

"The nationals aren't here at the hospital yet, but I saw some vans setting up back at the mountain as I was coming down. Though I think I saw some local press hanging with the town cops in the waiting room off the lobby."

"Can you help sneak me out the back? I should be getting out around three, they said. My flight back to DC leaves at five. I just booked it."

"Of course, Kit," Sinclair said as he put his camera away. "Of course. Least I could do. Kit, I'm so sorry again."

Kit looked at him, then turned and looked out the window at the distant mountains.

"Me, too," she finally said.

23

Kit was in no way ready for Dennis's funeral back in Boston a week later.

In no way shape or form, she thought as she sat in the crowded pew.

It was the saddest thing she'd ever been a part of in her life. The church in Dorchester Heights in Southie was small, and it was filled to capacity like it was a Fenway Park World Series game. Everywhere large men were crying. The amount of people Dennis knew from his time as a Boston cop and then as one of the country's most renowned experts in homicide investigation was astounding.

And they all apparently loved him like a brother or a father, she thought as she stood in the second row behind Anna and the kids and the grandkids.

She lost count of how many cards she was handed by state troopers and FBI agents and DEA guys who told her if she needed anything—and they meant anything, any help whatsoever in nailing the son of a bitch who killed Dennis—she was to give them a call.

"There goes the greatest cop who ever lived," said a well-dressed broad-shouldered hulk of man in front of the church as four full-dress marines put Dennis into the back of a Cadillac hearse.

Kit turned to him.

"Hi, you're Kit, right? I'm Bill Ferguson," the big man, said gently shaking her hand. "I'm so sorry."

"Thank you. Wait. Bill Ferguson?" Kit said peering at him. "Head of the New York Office Deputy Director Bill Ferguson?"

"Since last year, guilty as charged," he said as another football-player-sized fiftysomething offered his hand. "This is my brother, Judge Joe."

"I remember now," Kit said, shaking his hand. "The Ferguson brothers. You grew up with Dennis, didn't you? Dennis told me stories about you two."

"He lied. I wasn't there. Bill did it," Judge Joe said, smiling.

Kit smiled as she remembered that he was actually a federal judge. Not just any federal judge either, but the chief judge of the US District Court of Maryland.

"You guys went to grammar school together?" Kit said.

"Yep. Went to St. Margaret's together, then the police academy," Bill said. "I was the one who got him his application. He didn't even want to go, but I convinced him. This was before he met Anna. See, before Anna, Dennis was different. Before Anna, Dennis was…"

"Completely stone-cold crazy," Judge Joe said.

"In the best way possible, of course," Deputy Director Ferguson said. "I mean, he was a legend. He ever tell you about his first arrest?"

"No," Kit said. "Never. I have to hear this."

"He's nineteen, okay?" Director Ferguson said. "Just got out of the academy. Day one, he's sent out on a foot post by himself. Two minutes out the door, two blocks from the station house, he comes across these two huge rough punks beating the living crap out of each other in the street. Dennis immediately goes for his belt. For his radio, right? Call it in?

"Hell, no. This is Dennis the menace. Out comes his piece. 'Freeze, you blankety blanks! Up against the mother-blankin' wall!' Like he's the star in a *Starsky and Hutch* episode. The two guys immediately do as this insanely fired-up kid tells them, and then what does he do? Call for backup?

"Hell, no. He handcuffs them together, and he marches them back into the station house through the neighborhood at gunpoint. 'Hey, Sarge, two for assault,' he yells, like he's been there for twenty years. Imagine. This is five minutes in on day one at nineteen."

"Wow," Kit said, smiling. "He never told me that."

"Yeah," Bill said shaking his head. "What a crazy, good, fun-loving, life-loving, caring cat he was."

Kit looked over at the hearse. They were closing the door now.

"Listen," Deputy Director Ferguson said as he passed her something.

Kit looked down at his card.

"My personal is on the back. You need anything on his investigation, you call me, okay? I mean it," he said.

24

The funeral for John Barber's brother, Owen, was on the same day as Dennis Braddock's back in Utah in a place of worship called the Harmony Church of Our Lord.

Off Route 191 several miles south of Barber's ranch, it was the only structure visible in a vast desolate stretch of high desert.

Gannon, running a little late at the wheel of his pickup, saw it from miles away. You couldn't not see it if you wanted to, he thought. Against the immensity of rock and pale dusty land, its high glowing white spire drew the eye like a magnet.

The lot was so full he had to park on the shoulder of the desert road. He sat for a second looking at the summer sun glinting off all the police vehicles among the pickups. There were ones from Arizona, Colorado.

Gannon tightened his just-bought stiff black tie as he looked out at them.

More cops. Super. He had seriously debated whether to come at all.

His son, Declan, in his own new dress shirt and black tie, sat in the passenger seat, looking at the police vehicles along with him. Looking with concern.

"For people who are supposed to be living under the radar, I have to say, we sure have a real funny way of doing it, Dad," he said.

"C'mon, this is a funeral. You think they'll be looking for fugitives?"

"Yeah, you're right," Declan said as they got out. "What kind of fugitives would be dumb enough to attend a cop funeral?"

There was a US Army color guard in the vestibule just inside the church's door. The church itself held about four or five hundred people, and it was all but standing room only. Up on the altar, a cello was playing music so sad and beautiful, it was torturous. Gannon did a double take when he saw that the female soloist was actually Stephanie Barber.

Down in the front, Lynn was a puddle, but John Barber looked to be fine as he stood in the front row beside his eighty-five-year-old mother, who was in a wheelchair.

Gannon watched him squeeze his mother's hand. Truth be told, he was pretty concerned about his friend. Ever since they'd flown back with his brother in the rear of the plane, the man had been quiet.

Too quiet.

Once Stephanie was seated, the preacher, sitting beside the altar, stood. He was a very thin and tall handsome young man still in his twenties. Gannon didn't know why him being so young made things even sadder but it did somehow.

"Blessed are the peacemakers," the young preacher said, "for they shall be called the children of God. Let us bow our heads and pray for God's blessing."

Gannon looked out at the crowd as five hundred heads lowered.

He had been to his share of funerals. Sometimes they made him sad, and sometimes they made him angry.

This one made him feel very weary, Gannon thought, as he bowed his own head and looked down at the hard, white marble of the floor.

25

Kit Hagen's morning drive to work down 619 from her condo in Bristow was always one of the best times in her day. It was an almost perfectly straight shot on a country lane lined with white horse fences and gorgeous rolling fields and American flags on poles by dirt drives.

Exactly two weeks from the morning she got shot, she was at the wheel of her Crown Vic zipping east and heading back into work at Quantico bright and early. Waking up, she'd been somewhat worried about what kind of face she would show to her coworkers after the shooting. But now as she found herself back in the rhythm of her commute on such a beautiful morning, she thought, who gives a shit.

The funeral was over, she thought as she looked at the sun breaking over the rolling hills. The tears had been cried. Now it was time to do one thing.

Tear up the country from one end to the other to find the monster who had killed her partner, Dennis.

A quarter mile before where 619 made the turnoff to the south, her phone rang. She glanced at it there in the drink holder. It was a 575 area code.

575?

The phone had stopped ringing by the time she put on her left clicker and pulled into a gas station.

She looked up the area code on Google. 575 was for New Mexico.

"New Mexico," she said, her eyes going wide as she thumbed the Call Back button.

"There you are," said a man's voice. "This is Detective Lampard. Dan Lampard, San Juan County sheriff's office. How are you doing today, Agent Hagen? This is Agent Hagen, right?"

"That's me," Kit said.

Kit remembered San Juan County because it was where they had picked up their best and pretty much only lead in the NATPARK case.

After the Rocky Mountain Park murder, the female victim's pickup truck had been stolen, and they had found it in the parking lot of a motel over the state line in New Mexico. In the truck was a bottle of Gatorade with some backwash in it that contained male DNA. It wasn't the victim's fiancé's or brother's or father's, so they had sent it into the Bureau's NDIS, National DNA Index System. But there had been no match.

"I do remember you, Detective. How are you?"

"I'm doing fine. Sorry for calling so early. I read about your situation there in Wyoming in the paper. We're real sorry about Agent Braddock. He was a real nice fella. And we're pulling for you. I've actually been trying to contact your office, but they said you weren't back to work yet. I take it you haven't received the report I sent you from that online DNA place? Genodex Labs?"

"No. I'm heading back into the office for the first time this morning. DNA lab? What's going on, Detective?"

"Well, it's one of those things," he said. "I don't know if you remember my boss, Sheriff Harlan? Well, he retired, and we were going through some of the cold case stuff, and I came across a package. It was the results from Genodex Labs. I hate to say that it's been sitting there for six months, but it has. There's no excuse. Just stone-cold incompetence."

Kit quickly remembered the details. Due to a pending lawsuit, the FBI wasn't allowed to solicit the DNA companies to cross-reference crime scene samples, but for some technical legal reason, some of the states still could. Which was why they had made arrangements with Sheriff Harlan at the San Juan County sheriff's office to send the evidence in to Genodex for them.

"You're kidding me," Kit said. "I thought we'd arranged everything. Sheriff Harlan assured me he'd stay on top of it."

"Yeah, that's Sheriff Harlan, all right. Lots of assurances, not too much follow-up action. Especially after he turned seventy-five. Would you be shocked to hear some people around here aren't all that sad that he's finally gone fishing for good? Anyway, I hope you're sitting down because we got a match on your DNA."

26

Kit's windowless work space in the corner of the Behavioral Science basement office was way in the back by the mechanicals. Since the whole office was always so dim and depressing, they'd finally gotten the powers that be to rehab the entire floor two months before. There were nice espresso-brown wooden cubicle walls now and overhead pin lighting and a row of shiny new reference books in the open-walled cabinet above her two monitors.

She was standing up and slipping out the latest copy of *Federal Rules of Evidence with Objections* from the new cabinet when Francis Sinclair walked in.

"There you are," Kit said. "Sit down, Francis. Boy oh boy, do I have news for you."

"I have news for you, too, Kit," Sinclair said.

"What?" Kit said looking at him. "No, scratch that. Me first. Sit down."

She rolled her spare chair over to him.

"Believe me," she said. "You have to hear this."

"What is it?" Sinclair said as he sat.

"The shooter on the mountain. That wasn't our guy. I don't know who it was, but it wasn't the NATPARK killer."

"What?"

"It was a copycat or something, Francis. This whole thing is so crazy."

"What are you talking about, Kit?"

"I'm coming in this morning, and I get a call from the detective in New Mexico we worked with when we got the DNA in victim three's truck over a year ago."

"The Rocky Mountain Park murder?" Sinclair said squinting. "The Gatorade bottle?"

"Uh-huh. Well, long story short," Kit said, lifting up the Genodex Labs report she'd been mailed, "we have a hit on the DNA with a sibling match."

"A sibling match?"

"Two months ago, a woman named Johanna Halstead had a minor health scare and wanted to check her ancestry roots, God bless her. She's the sister of the unknown subject who left the DNA in our victim's truck. The beyond awesome news is that it turns out Johanna only has one sibling, a man named Cameron Ketchum.

"Here's where it gets good," Kit said, putting down the DNA report and lifting up a spreadsheet. "I've been scouring the database all morning about Cameron Ketchum. He's a long-haul trucker from Indiana, and I called his company, and his routes line up with the national park locations, Francis. They are a perfect match.

"He was in North Carolina when victim one was killed and in Grand Canyon for victim two. And not only was he near the Rocky Mountain Park for victim three, he was staying in a trucker's hotel on the same road within walking distance of where the pickup was found! That very night! Not only that, he's got some burglary charges from when he was in his twenties and a rape arrest.

"It's him. Ketchum is the NATPARK killer."

27

"Wow, that is some incredible news," Sinclair said. "This Ketchum guy does look good, but I don't get it. The other part you said. Why isn't Ketchum the Wyoming shooter? Why isn't he the one who shot you up in Grand Teton?"

"Because," Kit said as she handed Sinclair another printout. "He's been in custody at the Lansing Correctional Facility in Kansas *for the last nine months*! Last year, he was blind drunk and got pulled over and decided to run. They tried to throw down one of those stop sticks, and as he tried to avoid it, he ran right over a Kansas state trooper and broke the poor young rookie's leg. He's been in custody ever since on attempted murder of a police officer."

"I see. So you're saying the good news is Ketchum looks like the NATPARK killer," Sinclair said.

"At least in the first three killings," Kit said.

"But the bad news is the killer in Grand Teton looks like somebody else?" Sinclair said.

"Exactly! Grand Teton can't be Ketchum. Which is crazy when you consider the posing of the victim's body completely matches the other three. Maybe it's some kind of copycat or something? Or Ketchum had a partner kill a girl and then shoot us to get the heat off himself? Who knows what the hell it is. It's just incredible."

Kit tapped at the report.

"Bottom line, we have to nail Ketchum down and pronto. We need to interview him yesterday, Francis. There's a Delta flight at five thirty. We can be in Lansing in the morning at nine when they let in visitors. I already called the warden's office to schedule an interview. I'm so pumped I can hardly stand it. I can't wait to sink my teeth into this sick son of a bitch."

"This is good, Kit. Real good," Sinclair said quietly. "But—"

"Good? No, this is epic, Francis. We've been on this four years. This is last-second-Super-Bowl-touchdown, go-to-Disney-World stuff. What's the but? But what?"

Sinclair looked at her grimly. That's when she suddenly noticed something odd. Boyish Sinclair didn't look so boyish. He was dressed in a suit and tie and his spiky hair was cut and neatly pasted to one side.

"What is it?" she said uneasily as she remembered she'd never seen him wear a tie before.

"I don't know how to put this, Kit, so I'll just blurt it out. You're off the case."

"What?" Kit said almost falling out of the chair as she reared back.

"I just got back from a meeting at Justice and they are up this case with a flashlight and a magnifying glass. I stood up for you. I really did. But they don't care. They want you off the case."

"But why?"

He clasped his hands together and looked at her over them.

"Did you leak any info to the press?"

"Me? To those hyenas? Are you feeling all right? The only thing I'm leaking is blood out of the hole still in my shoulder."

"I didn't think so. But somebody did and Justice is pissed, and they think it's you."

"But I didn't do it! Check my call records. Go through my texts. They can't take me off this, Francis. Not now. Not after this monster breakthrough. I have to talk to Ketchum. I've been on this case four freaking years!"

"Don't you see?" she said, shoving the report at him. "Maybe he had a partner or something who made it look like it was him on Grand Teton to throw us off or something. We have to find him! We have to figure this out, Francis, and I'm the only one who knows the whole thing. Are you not hearing me? Think about it. Ketchum might know who killed Dennis!"

"It doesn't matter. It's not going to happen, Kit. I'm sorry. You're off. They put their foot down."

"Did this foot have a high heel on it? It's that Dawn Warner, isn't it? Because every time I turn around, I see that our Assistant Attorney General in charge of the Justice Department's Environment and Natural

Resources Division is all over the news. Did anyone check if she's the freaking leak?"

"Kit, c'mon."

"Don't c'mon me. You know what I heard Warner say on CNN? She said that she flew out from Washington immediately after she heard about the shooting. But that's complete bullshit. She was already there!

"She was hobnobbing at some tech conference in Jackson with all these Silicon Valley billionaire people consulting on a new Burning Man event. Then I guess she smelled the potential media coverage on this and was on it like greased lightning.

"I'm fighting this, Francis. Especially with the new boss. Who is the new boss, by the way?"

"Well," Sinclair said standing, showing her his tie.

"What? You? The new section chief?"

He nodded sheepishly.

"What! I mean, no offense, Francis, but you've been here what? Three years? I've been here over seven. Why you?"

"Maybe because I came over from the administrative side? Your guess is as good as mine. You think I asked for it, Kit? I didn't. To tell you the truth, I don't even want it."

"Well, who will you assign the case to then? Grissom? Clay? They've been here for five minutes. Gonzales is good and knows a little, but he's still testifying in Boston, right?"

Sinclair winced, staring at her.

"I haven't even decided yet. But when I do, I'll let you know."

Kit looked at Sinclair for a long moment, then down at the floor.

I'm getting hamstrung, she thought. *But why?*

She stared at Sinclair, wanting to explode. But it wasn't the time.

Kit took a deep breath and put the pin back in.

She suddenly smiled and stood and gave Sinclair a hug.

"I'm sorry, Francis," she said. "Don't listen to me."

"Kit, I'm sick about telling you all this."

"I know. It's fine. Congratulations on the promo. I'm happy for you. Honestly. Are you kidding me? It's actually great. You'll be terrific at this. Besides, you need a promotion to start saving up for braces for those three kids of yours. Congratulations, Francis, really. To you and Naomi, too."

"Thanks, Kit. That actually really means a lot," he said, his face still crestfallen. "You're always so nice. This isn't right. And I know how eager you are to get to the bottom of this. It's completely understandable. They just want you to take a month off, okay? That's all. A lousy month and then I'll get you back on the case or I swear I'll resign. I'll let you know who I give the case to and what happens with the new lead, okay? Just a month. Sound good?"

"Of course. Sounds great," Kit lied as she stood and grabbed her bag.

28

At a quarter after two in the afternoon, Assistant Attorney General Dawn Warner was giving a speech at the Spotsylvania County Regional Criminal Justice Academy in Fredericksburg, Virginia.

Poised, confident, wearing a chic new tailored saw-grass-colored skirt with matching jacket, she stood behind the lectern speaking about her time as a rookie criminal prosecutor in Florida's Southern District. She told a few jokes about the Bush versus Gore debacle and then drilled down into an intensive explanation of how it is the likeliness of conviction rather than the probable cause to arrest that leads DAs to decide to prosecute.

The classroom, the state police academy's largest, was one of those amphitheater-style ones where the lecturer stands at the bottom with the students sitting above in ascending rows like spectators at a basketball game.

Atop the amphitheater just to the right of one of the entrances, Kit Hagen stood looking down over the police academy students' flattops and tightly bunned hair.

She looked at Warner's somewhat pinched face as she spoke. She thought she was Botoxing for sure and had some work done around her eyes. Kit wondered what she had looked like before.

"Great speech," Kit said as she arrived down through the flow of students five minutes later. "I think the crowd really liked it."

"Thanks," Warner said with a shrug of her elegantly tailored shoulders. "Not exactly Virginia Law School out here in the hinterlands, but I like to give back. I believe in sharing your life. Teaching what you learned. Especially to women. Sisterhood is good for the spirit."

Kit had to squint to keep her eyes from rolling as Warner put some papers into a briefcase. Hagen noted the famous Italian designer name subtly embossed beneath the clasp.

"I actually saw you come in," Dawn Warner said, smiling. "How's the arm, kiddo?"

"It's my shoulder, actually. It'll take twelve weeks to heal completely. Luckily, I'm right-handed, so—"

"Thank God for small miracles?" Warner finished for her with a tiny smile.

"Exactly," Kit said as they started up the stairs for the exit.

"What brings you out here?" Warner said.

"Well," Kit said following beside her stride for

stride. "I went into work this morning for the first time after my sick leave, and I wanted to talk to you."

"About?"

"About why was I taken off my case."

Warner stopped at the top beside the exit door.

"What do you mean?" Warner said, not batting a single eyelash. "Why are you asking me about it? Shouldn't you ask your boss?"

"I did," Hagen said. "Now I'm asking you."

"Hagen, I mean, Kit, right? Kit, I know what you must be feeling, but we discussed this fiasco at Justice and decided we need to take a step back. The Bureau agreed. Have you read the papers? We all really took a good hard smack on the nose over this. First of all, you need to heal, of course. But besides that, the optics couldn't be worse. We need the press to move on a little here."

"A smack on the nose?" Kit said staring at her. "My partner had his head blown off."

"See, you're too close, Kit," Dawn said with a nod. "You need to give this some time and distance. The guideline for in-the-line-of-duty shooting incidents says three months, but I relented and agreed to one. You should be thanking me."

"Thanking you?" Kit said, wide-eyed.

"Have you ever thought about therapy? Of the non-physical kind I mean?"

"No, but I have thought about how I'm the only person on the planet who knows anything about this case, and yet I'm being told to stand down. I've tried to piece together how it makes any reasonable rational sense, but I keep coming up empty."

Dawn Warner took out her cell phone and looked at it.

"I'm really sorry, Kit. I have to take this," she

said as she thumbed at the screen. "Honestly, I know you're upset, but therapy, Kit. I wouldn't steer you wrong. My daughter had a bulimia thing last year and her therapist was so incredible."

She took out a business card from her perfectly elegant Italian briefcase and handed it over.

"If you call my assistant, Roberta, she can give you his name and all the details, Kit. Talking things out with a professional. That's the way to do it. You'll see."

29

"Hey, sleepyhead, want to go for a run?" Gannon called over to the lump on the bus's back bedroom bed.

"No."

"Want to go to the shoothouse?"

"No."

"Want to play with Dempsey?"

"No."

"What's the story, Dec? Hey, wait. I know. How late you get in?" Gannon said as he pulled at one of the sheets.

Declan groaned.

He'd started going out with Stephanie and some of her friends to the nearby town of East Carbon after the funeral. Now it was becoming a routine apparently.

"Oh, I don't know. One?" Declan said, pulling the sheet over his head.

"Or, who knows? Two?" Gannon said looking at

him. "Three? I see. Now you're the one gallivanting around."

"At least I don't go near the cops, Dad," he called out from beneath the blanket.

"That's true. You have a point there, son," Gannon said, leaving the room. "But we should probably call a meeting or something. We're really losing mission discipline around here."

Gannon had just clacked a mug of old coffee into the microwave when he heard the phone ring in the shoothouse. Hastily putting on some flip-flops, he jogged over and picked it up at the end of its third ring.

"Hi, Mike," John Barber said. "I was wondering if you could come on down to the house. I'd like to show you something."

"What's up?"

"I just got something in the mail. I want you to see it."

John's wife, Lynn Barber, was alone waiting in the threshold of the house wearing workout clothes when Gannon stepped out of his pickup in the driveway five minutes later.

She was a dark and petite pretty brown-haired woman. Half Cuban and half Irish, John had met her in the 1990s in a bar in Tampa, Florida, outside the MacDill Air Force base, where he'd been first stationed with Delta Force.

As he came up the stairs of the porch, Gannon smiled at her cautiously. He noticed that her dark brown eyes were even more intense than usual. In lying low out here, he knew he was imposing on her the most. Even though he spent most of his time out of sight up in the canyon, whenever he saw her, he always felt like a rude houseguest who had unwisely overstayed his visit.

Probably because he was and had, he thought.

"Hey, Mike," Lynn said quietly as he arrived. "Um, just wanted you to know John's mom had a medical thing last night. We just got back from the hospital."

"No! He didn't even tell me. Is she okay?" Gannon said.

"They don't really know. She's awake and talking, but she's not doing so hot. Her face is numb, and she's having trouble with her left arm. Might be a stroke, they said."

"I'm so sorry, Lynn," Gannon said. "This just sucks so bad. Things just keep getting worse for you guys."

"You're telling me," she said as she held the door open for him. "Just wanted you to know. John's in his office.

"And, Mike," she said as he passed her.

Gannon stopped in the hall.

"Thanks for flying up to Wyoming with him," she said. "I forgot to tell you. It really meant a lot to me and the kids. John needs a friend right now. Thanks for watching his back."

"No thanks necessary," Gannon said as he went inside.

30

John's wood-paneled study was on the ground floor. As Gannon stopped before the glass of its French door, he saw inside that all the wooden blinds were down and there was only a single lamp on at the desk where Barber sat hunched at his computer.

"John?" Gannon said, tapping at the glass as he came in.

"Hey, Mike. Thanks for coming," Barber said, standing up from the swivel chair.

"Sorry about your mom," Gannon said, patting him on the shoulder. "Lynn filled me in."

"Thanks, buddy," Barber said as they shook. "She's been sick for a while, but I guess losing Owen is just overwhelming."

Barber brought them to the office's left-hand corner where there were a couple of leather chairs. When

Gannon was seated in one of them, Barber went over and closed the French door and came back and sat.

Between the chairs was a leather ottoman and from the top of it, Barber lifted a slim black iPhone.

"This is what I just got in the mail," he said, holding up the phone. "My brother's buddy, Don, just shipped it down from Wyoming along with some other effects Owen had at work. Because Owen was out of contact so much, he had a work knapsack he kept in his truck with first aid and survival stuff along with a pair of spare boots. This phone was stuffed down inside of one of the boots."

"Is that right?"

"Let me show you something I came across after I recharged it," Barber said, thumbing at it.

"You know Owen's password?" Gannon said.

"No, but I guessed it pretty quick."

Gannon smiled.

"Let me guess. His old girlfriend's birthday?"

Barber smiled back.

"No. Close. Momma's."

He thumbed some more buttons and handed the phone over to Gannon.

"Now check this out," Barber said.

It was outdoor footage. Raw gray rocks and mountains in the distance.

"Grand Teton?" Gannon said.

"Yep, watch."

The camera was descending a steep trail and then the view showed a flat sort of clearing. The camera blurred as it zeroed in on something. Then there was a shot of a foot between some rocks. Pale and delicate. It looked like it belonged to a young woman.

"This is from the crime scene?" Gannon said. "This the body Owen found? The serial killer's victim?"

Barber nodded.

"Owen had a work phone that they took into evidence, but it looks like when he found the body by himself, he actually recorded his first walk-through with his private phone and must have stuffed it into his boot. Brace yourself for this next part."

The camera came in closer. The footage showed a naked woman. She was small, about thirty. Her head was turned to the side. There were blood splotches and splatter marks on the rocks all around her. As the camera focused in closer, it looked like there were bite marks in her neck and back.

The camera zoomed in on the half-turned blood-splattered face. Gannon looked at her wide open shocked eyes. She was an Asian woman.

"Man, this is sick," Gannon said. "Look at the wounds. This crazy NATPARK son of a bitch must have bitten her to death or something. Then just threw her away like a bag of garbage."

"I know," Barber said. "That's what I thought, too. It looks like she was attacked by zombies."

Gannon was still staring at the real-life horror movie footage when there was a knock on the glass of the French door.

"Hey, hon. What's up?" Barber said as his wife stuck her head in.

"We're not expecting that group from Phoenix until next week, right?" Lynn said.

"Right. Why?"

"The driveway perimeter alarm by the road just went off," Lynn said.

31

John turned and went over to his computer and pressed some buttons, and a grid of security camera boxes appeared on the screen.

Being in the high-end, ever vigilant security biz, Barber had a string of state-of-the-art motion detector cameras set up all over his remote compound.

He clicked on the keyboard. They watched as a car came up his mile-long driveway. It was a small new shiny blue Nissan.

"Looks like a rental," Gannon said from over Barber's shoulder. "Is that a woman driving it?"

Barber clicked another button and stilled the image and zoomed in.

"Hey, look," he said, shocked, as he tapped at the screen. "It's the FBI agent from the hospital."

"The agent?" Lynn said.

"The lady FBI agent who was shot along with

Owen," Gannon explained. "Agent Hagen. We saw her in Jackson at the hospital."

"What does she want?" Lynn said.

"I don't know, but I guess we're about to find out," Barber said as he clicked off the screen and stepped out his office door.

The car had pulled to a stop in the circular drive by the time they all came out onto the porch.

They watched Agent Hagen get out wearing jeans and a white T-shirt. She seemed solid enough on her feet though her color was a little pale.

She certainly didn't look like she was on official business, Gannon thought.

"Hi, you're John Barber, right?" she said as she walked over, extending her free hand. "Do you remember me? I'm Kit Hagen. You visited me at the hospital in Jackson."

"Of course," Barber said, shaking her hand. "Nice to see you again, Agent Hagen. Especially up on your feet."

"Me, too," she said, smiling. "Believe me. And there's no agent. I'm just Kit. Please just call me Kit."

"Okay, Kit. This is my wife, Lynn, and this is my buddy, Mike."

Kit peered at Gannon as she shook his hand.

"You were there at the hospital, too, right? I think I remember you."

Gannon smiled.

"I'm surprised that you remember anything," he said. "You were pretty groggy."

"Groggy," Kit said rolling her eyes. "I'll say. I was high as a kite. I actually just chucked the last of the stuff they gave me for the pain. It was making me cross-eyed. I think I'll stick to Advil from here on out."

"Please come in, Kit," Lynn Barber said. "Get out of this heat. I'll put on some lunch."

"No, Lynn, please. I don't want to bother you guys. I didn't even call. I just came by for a second."

"Sorry, Kit. This is off-the-grid Eastern Utah," Lynn said, waving her toward the front door. "No one is allowed to come by for just a minute. It's a county ordinance."

"How did you get here? Salt Lake City Airport?" Barber said as they went in and sat in the family room.

"Yes," Kit said. "I just went to visit Owen's grave, and before I left I wanted to come by and say hi. I'm truly sorry I missed your brother's funeral but they were burying my partner, Dennis, the same day."

"No worries, please, Kit," Barber said. "We've all been through so much with this. We're all doing the best we can."

"I actually needed to come by," Kit said as Lynn Barber came in with a tray of iced tea and glasses. "I wanted to tell you about what your brother did for me."

"Kit, honestly. You don't have to get into all that if you don't want to," John Barber said. "I know it's all still so raw for you."

"No, thank you for that, John. But I'd like to," Kit said. "You guys should know how Owen saved me. When the shooting began, I saw my partner get killed, and I went into shock. I was completely useless. But Owen wasn't. He immediately hid us both behind cover and then he came up with a plan. He figured out where the shots were coming from by using the sheriff's cell phone. Then he fired at the suspect to give me a chance to run.

"Your brother was a…a hero. Truly, a hero. If it weren't for him, I wouldn't be here right now. I just wanted to tell you. I wanted you—I needed you—to know how terrific he was. He died trying to save me five minutes after we met."

They sat in the room for a long silent beat. John Barber stared at the unlit fireplace.

"Owen was…" he finally said as he shucked away a tear with his thumb. "He wouldn't let down a friend no matter what. Wasn't in him. He must have considered you a friend, Kit."

Kit suddenly stood, wiping at her own eyes.

"Anyway, I've taken up enough of your time. It was nice to meet everyone. Thanks for seeing me."

"Not so fast," Lynn said, standing up as she offered Kit an iced tea.

"But," Kit said.

"But nothing," Lynn said. "Tea."

Kit finally took it. She smiled and sat down.

"Good," Lynn said, smiling. "Much better."

"As you can see, my wife here likes everyone to be comfortable," John Barber said, laughing. "She insists on it."

"I can attest to that," Gannon said. "I recommend you just go along with it, Kit. Resistance is futile."

"Exactly," Lynn said, smiling. "I already started lunch. We actually run a resort here, you know."

"Oh, yes," Kit said. "I saw your website. Hotel Juliet Bravo. Survival training, right? You've got great ratings on Yelp."

"That's right," Lynn said. "Yelp doesn't lie. At least about us. So it's no trouble at all to put you up in one of the bungalows. Coming all this way, you'll have to stay at least for the night."

"Well," Kit said as she took out her phone and looked at it. "I do have a flight tomorrow. I was going to stay at the airport hotel."

"Plans just changed," Lynn said, heading back for the kitchen. "I'll go get my kids to help me fix up the presidential bungalow. We're not the Plaza, but if we can't beat an airport hotel, we need to put out the for-sale sign."

32

When Lynn Barber left, they sat in silence for another long moment.

"So the papers say you were there in Wyoming investigating a serial killer. This NATPARK killer?" Gannon said.

"Yes," Kit said, nodding. "Our unit was operating on the assumption that he was going to kill again, so we had arranged air transport to be on standby to see the fresh crime scene of any new female victim found in a national park. We got the call around midnight and took off a little before two from DC on a Lear business jet we borrowed from the DEA. Owen was there still guarding the victim's body when we arrived early the next morning."

"What do you think happened?" Gannon said. "Is it like the papers say? Do you think you caught this

NATPARK killer as he was dropping the victim's body? Hemmed him in and he shot his way out?"

Kit Hagen was lifting her iced tea as he said this. Then she stopped and put it back down.

"No. I actually…can I talk confidentially?"

"Of course," Barber said.

"I don't think we caught him," she said. "I think he was waiting for us."

"So it was an ambush?" Barber said.

"Yes. I think it was."

"Why would he shoot you? He wanted what? More publicity?" Gannon said.

Kit Hagen opened her mouth as if she were about to say something. Then she closed it.

"Perhaps," she said with a shrug. "It's hard to say."

"So, are you still on the case?" Barber said. "What's the story? Has there been any progress?"

"Well, I can't really say. I'm on leave at the moment because of my injury, but I'm going to get back on it soon as I can."

"Who is on the case, then?" Barber said.

Kit looked at him.

"To tell you the truth, I don't know," she said.

"Don't know?" Barber said, sitting up. "But I saw on the news that Dawn Warner woman said the Bureau is all over it. Top priority."

Kit shook her head.

"Don't believe everything you see on TV," she said. "My boss assured me that he would tell me who he assigned it to. I keep emailing him, but he hasn't gotten back. There seems to be some kind of stall."

"They're not even looking into who killed your

partner?" Gannon said. "The FBI isn't trying to find someone who killed one of their own?"

"I've been trying to figure it out, believe me," Kit said, lifting her iced tea again and looking at it. "I've seen some ridiculous moves before by my bosses over the years, but sitting on this takes the cake."

She finally sipped her iced tea.

"But like I said, I'm getting back on it as soon as I get back to work."

"When will that be?" Barber said.

"In three and a half weeks," she said.

"You have to be kidding," Barber said angrily, suddenly standing, his fists clenched.

"John," Kit said, watching him begin to pace. "I know you're upset, but can I be straight with you? Again, this is completely confidential, but I'm not out West here just for a social visit."

"No?" Gannon said.

Kit shook her head.

"Even saying this could get me into a heap of trouble, but here's the story. They told me to take a breather on the case, but I'm not. I'm the only person who's been on this case from the beginning. I don't care what kind of political shenanigans they want to pull, I'm not letting the trail go cold. Not now. No way am I sitting still for my partner getting murdered. Or your brother or Sheriff Kirkwood. That isn't going to happen.

"I'm on Owen's case, John. Just not officially, okay? The Bureau doesn't know. No one does. Except you now. So please don't tell anyone."

Barber stopped his pacing and suddenly looked

over at Gannon. Gannon looked back. Then Gannon nodded.

"Kit," Barber said, "now I think I know why my brother liked you. Can I show you something?"

"Show me something?"

"Yes," Barber said, walking toward his office. "If you could come back here for a second, I want to show you something that belonged to my brother that I just got in the mail."

33

"What is it?" Kit said as they stepped into Barber's wood-paneled office.

"You'll see," Barber said as he sat her down in one of the corner chairs.

Barber queued the video on the phone again and handed it to her.

"Wait," she said as she sat looking. "This...this is the clearing on Grand Teton. This is where it happened. I don't understand."

"This is my brother's personal phone. I just received it with some other effects from his boss in the mail. It looks like he used his personal phone to film the crime scene when he first came into contact with the victim."

"It wasn't turned in to evidence?"

"No."

Gannon and Barber silently looked on as Kit

watched the video. In the dim room, the screen lit her fine features with a bluish cast.

"Prepare yourself," Gannon said. "There's something stomach-churning coming up."

"No, no, no!" she said after another thirty seconds. "What the hell is this?"

She thumbed at the Pause button. She sat wide-eyed, staring at a still of the victim's face. After a moment, Gannon noticed her hand was trembling slightly.

"What is it, Kit?" Gannon said. "What's wrong?"

Kit said nothing. She just sat there and stared.

"What is it?" Barber said. "Are you okay?"

Kit suddenly put down the phone on the leather ottoman.

Then she stood and went straight for the door.

"Where are you going?"

"My car. I'll be right back," she called over her shoulder.

"What in the hell was that about?" Barber said.

It was a minute later when Kit came back with a laptop. She brought it over to the ottoman, laid it down, opened it beside Owen Barber's phone and turned it on.

Thirty seconds later, she clicked open a folder with a spreadsheet of photos and selected one that filled the screen.

It was a crime scene photo of another naked woman laid out dead in a rocky wilderness. She was a tall, voluptuous white woman with her hands tied up with some sort of braided cord.

Gannon blinked and then looked away as he glanced at her face. It was sliced to bloody ribbons.

"Is that one of the other NATPARK victims?" Barber said.

"No, don't you see? It's Grand Teton. This is the victim we went in to see," Kit said.

"But it can't be," Barber said. "That's a white woman. The deceased on Owen's video is obviously Asian."

"So there were two women killed?" Gannon said. "They found two bodies?"

"No!" Kit said, wide-eyed as she pointed at the screen. "They found one body. This white woman here on my computer. She's the only one they took down off the mountain. The only one in the official file. This Asian woman on Owen's phone here is brand-new."

"So who is she?" Gannon said.

Kit shook her head.

"Got me. This is the first time I've laid eyes on her in my life."

"So this means…?" Barber said.

"The bodies were switched?" Kit said, throwing up her hands. "Somebody took away this murdered Asian woman your brother saw here. And then switched it with this new murdered white woman here."

"How does that make any sense?" Gannon said.

"That's the thing," Kit said, slowly shaking her head. "It doesn't. It doesn't make any sense at all."

34

An hour and a half later, they were sitting outside at Barber's picnic table beside his compound's small lake. They'd just finished lunch and were looking out over the water where Gannon's son, Declan, and the Barbers' children, Stephanie and her two high school–aged brothers, Ryan and Nate, were playing water basketball against a backboard hammered into the side of the old gray wood dock.

On the deck itself, Barber's wife, Lynn, sat in an Adirondack chair reading a book. They all waved as she looked over at them. Gannon noticed how she didn't wave back.

"So, Kit, have you been doing any thinking?" Gannon said, looking across the table at the FBI agent.

"You could say that, Mike," Kit said, lifting her iced tea.

"I'm still trying to get this all straight, Kit," John Barber said.

"You and me both," Kit said.

"From what you told us before, you think the initial killer you've been looking for, the real NATPARK killer, is this Ketchum guy," Barber said. "This guy they have in custody in Kansas. And he's not the shooter on the mountain."

"Correct," she said. "With the evidence we already have, the sibling link DNA evidence from the stolen truck and Ketchum's previous history of sexual violence and his whereabouts matching up with the other three murders, there isn't a prosecutor anywhere in this country who wouldn't sign an arrest warrant on him."

"But only for the first three murders," Gannon said.

"Exactly," Kit said. "Ketchum's been in custody in a Kansas penitentiary for nearly the last year. His being the shooter up on Grand Teton is literally impossible."

"But the crime scene on Grand Teton, the way the victim was posed, the details match Ketchum's other crime scenes?" Gannon said.

"Yes. To a T."

"So the Grand Teton murder is a copycat or something?" Barber said.

"Or maybe Ketchum has a partner," Kit said with a tilt of her head. "As he sat in jail, it's possible he might have thought that we would eventually catch up with him, so he had a partner kill another victim in the same exact way while he was in custody to throw the suspicion off himself."

"But how do the *two* bodies come into play?" Gannon said.

Kit looked out at all the young people in the water. The two Barber brothers were trying fruitlessly to block the much taller Declan, who dodged in the water and leaped up and hooked a shot over them.

"LeBron at the buzzer!" Declan screamed as the ball clunked heavily off the backboard and then made a cartoon boinging sound off the rim as it ricocheted away and splashed in the water.

"You got me on that one," Kit finally said, shaking her head. "That's new to me. I can't even begin to come up with a reason why. I was actually going to head out to Kansas to interview Ketchum after I left here. But now with the switcheroo bombshell we just saw on your brother's phone—that there were actually two dead women and one of them is still missing—I have to say I'm pretty much at a complete loss what to do."

35

"What would you do if you were still lead on the case and found this out?" Gannon said. "That Grand Teton doesn't look related to the other three murders and that the bodies had been switched?"

Agent Hagen put down her glass and looked steadily at him.

"Can I ask you a question, Mike?" she said.

"Sure. Go ahead."

"You seem pretty familiar with investigative work. I saw on the resort website that John was in the Special Forces. Are you military as well or law enforcement or…?"

Gannon took a sip of iced tea.

"Both actually," he said. "Or at least I used to be. I was in the service with this joker, John, here, in the Middle East, but when I cycled out, I worked as a cop in the NYPD. I'm actually recently retired now. My son and I are RVing for the summer, and John was nice enough to let us park our tenement on wheels up in his hills here."

"In the service. Listen to him," Barber said. "So modest. That's an actual genuine navy SEAL commando sitting over there, Kit. C'mon, Mike. Show her your frogman tattoo."

"A navy SEAL? Wow," Kit said.

"Like I said, *was*," Gannon said, holding up a finger. "A long time ago. And despite what my good friend here says, there's no tattoo."

"Were you a SEAL, too?" Kit said, turning to Barber.

"No," Gannon said with a laugh. "Bite your tongue. John wishes but he was just in the army, poor guy. But you didn't answer my question, Kit. What would you do if you were still on the case?"

"Well," Kit said, nodding, "I'd separate out Ketchum for the time being and treat what happened in Wyoming as a brand-new case, then. A new case with two victims. Since one victim is known and the other one unknown, I'd start with the known victim, obviously."

"The white woman?" Barber said.

"Yes," Kit said. "I didn't get a chance to see the autopsy report before they took me off the case so I think I would start there. I'd put Ketchum on the back burner for now and go straight back to Jackson to look at the crime scene again and try to get the results of the autopsy."

"Do you have the paperwork on the shooting itself, the ballistics report?" Gannon said.

"No," Kit said. "I wish. They didn't show me anything before they forced me to go on leave."

"In that case I can do one for you," Gannon said. "I did over a dozen ballistic reports with the NYPD. Even testified in court a few times. Once the brass heard I'd been an instructor in the SEAL sniper school, I started to get assigned over to the CSU to help out whenever it got busy. I also worked some homicides as a detective in Brooklyn, in East New York. Over thirty of them, and cleared most of them, too. So I know a bit about how murder investigations work."

Kit peered at him.

"I really could use a ballistics report. But I don't know if getting someone else involved is such a good thing. I mean, I'm not even supposed to be here talking to you. Like I said, I'm supposed to be off the case. I wouldn't want to get you into trouble."

Gannon smiled.

"Trouble? For what? Going for a hike with a tape measure?"

"Mike's right," Barber said. "You two need to partner up on this and pronto. To get a handle on all this damn craziness, you're going to need all the help you can get. Hell, after hearing about the way your bosses are sitting on this, I'd go with you myself except my mother is still in the hospital."

Kit sat looking out at the lake for a bit. Then she went quickly into her bag and fished out something.

"Okay, let's try this, Mike," she said, offering him a business card. "Here's my number. Despite your wife's generous offer, John, I'm going to head back to my hotel at the airport to get a few things done. But if you want, Mike, how about I meet you tomorrow at the airport. There's a Delta flight at noon back to Jackson. This is a free country, right? I can't stop you from being on the same flight as me, can I? How does that sound? Make sense?"

Gannon took the card and looked at it.

Be careful what you wish for, he thought as he played his thumb over the raised embossing of the FBI seal.

As he began to slip it into his pocket, out in the water all the kids started laughing and howling again as the ball bonged hard off the rim.

"Sounds like a plan," he finally said.

36

Back up at the bus late that afternoon after Kit Hagen had left, Declan came in to catch Gannon already clean-shaven and in the back bedroom, packing again.

"Dad's leaving again. No, it can't be. Oh, well. Whatever. I'm not even going to ask," Declan said as he left the room.

Gannon put down the pair of folded jeans he was holding. When he went out and sat on the couch, Declan was putting some popcorn into the galley microwave.

"Son," he called, "why don't you go into the fridge there and get us a couple of beers and bring them in here. I'd like to tell you a story."

Declan went and got two Coors Lights, handed Gannon one and sat down in the seat across.

"A story?" he said, opening his can.

Gannon cracked his own.

"Yes. This one's a true story, and after you hear it, I think you'll understand a few things better. Why I chose to come out here. Why John and I are so close. The title of it is called, 'The Day I Met John Barber.'"

"Whoa," Declan said, sipping at his beer. "A war story? You never tell those."

"I know. Not normally, but this is important," Gannon said, licking at the foam atop his can.

"When 9/11 happened, I was in San Diego training with the SEAL team I was attached to and within a week, we were on an aircraft carrier in the Persian Gulf doing VBSS operations on any vessel that even remotely looked like it might have terrorist ties."

"VBSS. That's what again? Visit, board, something, something?" Declan said.

"Visit, Board, Search, and Seizure," Gannon said as the Orville Redenbacher's in the microwave started to detonate.

"Got it," Declan said.

"But then after a few weeks, we got a call to send one of us over to some covert special ops task force they were putting together, and I got the short straw. First, I was flown into Oman of all places to some air force base and six hours later, very early in the morning, I was flying nap-of-the-earth on a blacked-out Black Hawk chopper with a team of folks crossing over the border into Afghanistan to fight the Taliban."

"No shit," Declan said.

"No shit," Gannon said, looking out the window at the darkening land.

37

"Was John with you?" Declan said.

"No," Gannon said. "The guys with me were special tactics forward observer air force guys that they needed on the ground to call in air strikes. They were going in to bolster a bunch of their buddies who were already there in the theater of combat and my job, whether I chose to accept it or not, was to provide security for them as we were inserted at some LZ just north of Bagram Airport."

Gannon paused and took another sip of beer as the microwave shut off.

"Now, son, there's this thing called the fog of war. Once things start going hot, there's a lot of moving parts in a very tight area, and friendlies sometimes forget to tell other friendlies what they're doing. Unbeknownst to us as our boots hit the ground, we had all just been dropped smack-dab in the middle of an ongoing fiasco of megalithic proportions.

"The Taliban, who had already been pushed away from the airport a month before, were that very morning about to mount a counterattack. We had no idea, but within a mile west of our LZ was a group of over a thousand heavily armed Taliban jihadis chomping at the bit to chop off some juicy infidel heads."

"Get out," Declan said.

"Gets worse," Gannon said. "The enemy had been spotted by the forward observers already at the airport, and they had already called in an air strike basically right on top of where we were standing."

"No effing way."

"Yes effing way," Gannon said, staring at the bus floor between his sneakers. "And it wasn't just any old kind of air strike either. As we stood there, a B-52 bomber loaded with fifty five-hundred-pound bombs was on its final approach to the drop zone. And as our terrific luck would have it, they weren't even those famous precision munition smart bombs the networks gush about but what they call dumb bombs. The kind that the air force bomb monkeys just kick out the open bomb bay doors and cross their fingers as gravity takes over."

Gannon watched his son shake his head.

"I remember hearing it coming," he said. "B-52s are big-ass planes and this one was flying low, and the rumble of it was like thunder coming down from a mountain. As we were standing there, oblivious to the fact that we were about to meet our maker, over the hill we were walking up appeared a beat-up pickup truck traveling at a very high rate of speed. I imme-

RUN FOR COVER**   **143**

diately got a bead on it with my rifle and was just about to pop the turban-headed driver when I saw an American uniform sitting next to him waving like a nut out the passenger window."

"It was John," Declan said.

Gannon smiled with a nod.

"It was John. His Delta Force guys were attached to the controllers at the airport and by some miracle, he had been on the horn with someone at the base we had just left. He had pieced it together that we were in harm's way so he had grabbed some stone-cold crazy Northern Alliance Afghani he knew with a pickup truck, and they had raced into the zone of imminent destruction to come and get us."

Declan shook his head in wide-eyed awe.

"We only found this out after. As the truck screeched to a stop before us, John leaped out and yelled, 'No questions get in the mother bleeping truck now.' So we did. As the thunder above got louder, into the truck we piled and the Northern Alliance guy dropped the hammer back up the hill. As we reached the crest, I looked up between the three air force guys who were piled on top of me and we all saw the plane. It was coming over us like a gargantuan gray vulture, and there was already a slanted column of large gray objects dropping out of it."

There was silence as Gannon took another sip of his beer in the dimness of the living room.

"We watched the bombs drop down toward us. I remember one of the guys saying a Hail Mary as we began to hear the metallic teakettle whistling of them. Then we looked behind us and watched stunned as the line of the carpet bombs just cleared the top of the hill we had just come over."

Gannon took a breath.

"And then there was a sound like you wouldn't believe. The truck actually started to bunny hop like a BMX bike from the ground swells as five-hundred after five-hundred after five-hundred sank in their teeth and bit a mile-sized chunk out of the stone ass of Afghanistan. It was like we were driving over a fault line during an earthquake. I thought at any moment a hole was going to appear in the earth's crust and we would all be swallowed.

"They had counted over a thousand Taliban at the outset and when the smoke cleared into the early-morning air, they and all their shit—their trucks and their tents and prayer rugs, all of it—was gone. Just gone. One moment they were there and the next, the entire army of them had vanished bippity boppity boo like Merlin had waved his magic wand."

Declan stared at his father as Gannon took a long pull from the can.

"You get it now. Why me and John are tight?" he said with a wink. "Why the man commands a prominent portion of my respect and gratitude. Why I need to help him find out what in the world actually happened to his brother. I mean, the man drove toward that, okay? Toward it. Think about it. Who would do that?"

Gannon took another pull of his beer as his son took a few moments to absorb all that.

"So," Declan finally said in the silence. "How long will you be gone?"

PART TWO

ON THE ROAD

38

Gannon needed to get a haircut and to do some last-minute shopping so he was a little late getting to the Salt Lake City Airport just before noon.

When he finally arrived at the Delta gate, he saw Kit straight off standing at the airport lounge window where a big white 747 airliner was being refueled.

Instead of sitting down near her, he sat away near the flight desk, watching her. He noticed she was wearing business attire now, a nice blouse and skirt with heels. She scrubbed up pretty nice.

He wasn't the only one with that opinion, Gannon realized with a smile as he noticed all the converging sight-line angles of nearly every male in the lounge.

When he looked back, she had spotted him. He watched as she walked out into the concourse and bought something at a kiosk. Then she picked up her bag by the window. All the heads of the men swiveled as she brought it over to where he was sitting.

"You like Twix?" she said as she tore open the wrapper of the candy.

"Of course. You kidding? Who doesn't like Twix," he said, taking one and biting into it.

"I almost didn't recognize you in your business duds without the scruff," she said, biting into the other one.

"I was coming down the highway and saw a Macy's," Gannon said as he smoothed down his new gray linen summer suit jacket. "I thought since we'll probably be talking to other human beings, it might be a good move to go for something slightly less caveman-ish."

They sat chewing. He smiled as he saw all the men now looking at him. Every single one of them was frowning. It took everything he had not to give them a wave with his Twix as they finally started to look back down at their phones.

"I'm sorry for not coming over straight off," Gannon said, slapping crumbs off his slacks when he was done. "I wasn't sure if I should sit down next to you or not. You said back at John's to keep it under the radar. I didn't know exactly how incognito you wanted to take this."

"I think we're good now," she said, nodding. "This flight looks empty. We can even sit together on the plane if you want."

"We leave in what? Forty-five?" Gannon said.

"More like thirty. You cut it pretty close."

"I know. Utah Macy's clerks are real nice but need to

work a tad on the tempo. Moving forward as your ballistic forensics consultant, I'll try to be more punctual."

She smiled.

"I wasn't sure if you were coming at all, actually," she said, looking at him. "You know you can still back out if you want."

"Back out? Are you joking? Can't now," Gannon said, pointing at his cheek. "See? I shaved. All gone. And I got a haircut, too."

"I see," she said, nodding. "You're already fully committed."

"Exactly," he said. "Once the razor comes out, I'm in it for the long haul, Kit."

39

They landed in Jackson at a little after one in the afternoon and changed into hiking clothes. It was about an hour and a half after that when they brought the Nissan Armada they'd rented at the airport to a stop at the rim of the hollow on Grand Teton.

"How you feeling?" Gannon said, looking over at Kit as he ratcheted back the emergency brake.

Kit stared out the window without speaking. She looked tense. She'd been silent on the ride up the base of the mountain. Silent pretty much since they'd landed.

"I guess the bears must have eaten all the crime scene tape," she finally said.

"I can pretty much tackle this part alone from what you've already told me," Gannon said. "Wait here. I'll be back in a bit."

Kit let out a breath.

"Appreciate you saying that, Mike," she said, staring down at the glove compartment. "I'd be lying if I said there is where I want to be right now."

She suddenly threw open her door.

"But that son of a bitch stopped me from seeing that crime scene once," she said. "I'll be damned if I let it happen again."

It was bright and cool outside as they got their bags from the back. Gannon sat for a moment on the tailgate, staring up at the magnificent upthrusts of pale rock.

When he finally stood and turned toward the fall-off, he saw they were almost eye level with a cloud bank. He looked down where its shadow, big as a city, slowly moved across the land far below.

A minute later, he was following Kit slowly down the steep switchbacks into the hollow. He was sweating by the time they halted in a flat clearing.

"What do you need to know?" Kit said as she slung off her pack.

She showed him where they were all standing when the first shot killed the sheriff and where her partner, Dennis, had lost his life. Gannon pinned each location with a handheld GPS tracker he'd brought as Kit knelt down and then lay beside a low rock.

"The shots came from there," she said, pointing.

Gannon squatted down beside her and followed her finger up a slope to their left. There were two rock ridges along the top of it, one in front of the other. She was pointing to where there was a kind of saddle in between them with a small stand of trees on the farther of the two ridges.

"Was he in those trees?"

"No. He was somewhere down in the rock in front of them."

Gannon stood.

"Okay, you're going to take a look at the victim scene over there, right?"

"Yes."

"While you're doing that, if you could leave your bag on the rock where the sheriff was shot, I'll go up to take a look."

Gannon walked across the stony ground. The slope was farther away than it had seemed from the clearing, the terrain dipping down into a dry creek bed before he made it to its base.

It had been like that in Afghanistan, he thought as he scrambled upward. The massive size of the mountains threw off your distance perception, made things look closer than they really were.

It was a good twenty minutes of an uphill slog over the rock until he arrived where Kit had been pointing. He looked around. There was a different angle of the mountain summit from this new perch, and as he looked up, he could see what looked like ice was wedged in between the narrow chambers of rock.

It was a minute later of searching around before he came upon the flattop of a half-buried boulder.

He stepped up on top of it and looked down the unobstructed sightline into the clearing below where Kit was standing, taking a picture.

"Bingo," he said as he took off his backpack.

He whistled as he pinned the GPS tracker and saw that the distance from where he was to the shooting scene was 1,110 yards.

"Eleven football fields and a first down," he mumbled as he took out the Leupold Mark 4 spotting scope he'd brought. He telescoped out its tripod and took a knee behind it as he had a look down the steeply pitched terrain.

Even after he zeroed in the focus, Kit's image danced and wavered behind the reticle. It was because of the distance. The phenomenon, known as mirage, happened because temperature variations along long distances to the target made the light refract like a straw in a water glass. The only thing good about that was, if you were experienced, you could get a decent read on your windage from it.

Kit was really moving around, not just left to right but also up and down, Gannon saw, which meant the erratic wind was pretty much playing havoc between their two points.

Gannon checked the barometric pressure reading off the tracker and took down some notes in a Moleskine notebook, getting his dope. After he was done, he collapsed the scope to rifle level and then took a good hard look around the boulder perch for snakes.

He had a history with mountain snakes. Once while in Afghanistan up in the mountains, one had slithered over the back of his left ankle as he lay half-asleep on the floor of a firebase. The wait before it was gone was among the longest in his life. Being a city boy and no Eagle Scout, he wasn't sure if he should move immediately or stay still or shoot at it or what.

"Gannon mountain sniping rule numero uno," he said as he finally lay prone down behind the scope. "Make sure environment is thoroughly snake-free."

He dialed in on Kit again and mimicked holding

a rifle, right finger along the trigger, left one in and under, firmly gripping an imaginary sandbag rest. He closed his eyes and listened. The sound of the wind, the soft warbling of a bird. The faint smell of the pines.

As he lay there with the cold of the stone underneath him, he could almost feel his cheek brushing the cheekpiece.

He thought about the eye that had been on the glass weeks before. The patience required.

"One," he said, finally opening his eye before the spotting scope and mimicking the trigger pull.

He imagined the crash and buck of the gun as he touched it off, then slid the pretend bolt back and forth and shifted slightly to where the FBI agent was killed, then pretended a second pull.

"Two," he said.

40

"So, what's the story?" Kit said as he got back.

She seemed to have wrapped up what she'd been looking for, Gannon thought as he watched her packing a camera back into her bag. He thought about how hard it had to be, her coming back here. Then he put it aside.

"This guy was damn good, Kit," Gannon said as he sat on a rock and wiped sweat from his forehead with the sleeve of his light fleece. "Even with a one-half minute of angle precision rifle, it was some pretty incredible marksmanship."

"One-half minute of what?" she said.

"Minute of angle," Gannon said. "Think of a slice of pizza with the distance between the side edges as one degree of angle. At the tip of the pizza, the distance is tiny, right? But as you head up toward the crust, it starts to spread wider and wider. The better the rifle, the more you can tighten that spread. Even at long distances, a precision rifle chocked into a bench stand will put rounds on target consistently within a fraction of an inch of each other. You see?"

"Not really. You're saying there's a lot of variables that only an expert would know?"

"Yes. A thousand-yard shot from a higher to lower elevation at high elevation in high erratic winds with no test shot to get a better read on the windage is professional shooting. I mean, with this distance and elevation and this crazy wind, if a novice with a good rifle missed within two hundred feet, you'd buy him a beer. Because under long-range conditions, the temperature of the barrel or even the temperature of the ammo being off a degree or two could cause a wide miss. A human head is only seven inches wide. This guy laid into two of them twenty feet apart from way the hell up there in quick succession. It's not long-range black magic wizardry stuff, but it's damn close."

"Not Tiger Woods, but he's on the tour?"

Gannon nodded.

"Well put. You're looking at a highly experienced hunter for sure or an extreme hobbyist. Probably ex-military shooting with a top-shelf rifle."

Gannon stood.

"I could talk for hours about it if you want, but maybe at a diner or something. I'm starting to get hungry. You hungry?"

"I'm starving," Kit said. "When you were talking about pizza a second ago, I started to salivate."

Gannon laughed.

"Let's get going then. That Twix you gave me was my breakfast. I'm about to eat one of these rocks."

41

After a late lunch at the diner in town, Gannon and Kit checked into two rooms at the same hotel he and John Barber had stayed at.

It was getting dark when Gannon got out of the shower and saw the text from Kit suggesting an attempt to contact the medical examiner.

Gannon cursed softly under his breath twenty minutes later as he brought the Armada into the lot of the medical examiner's office back on Pearl Street and saw only one car.

"Damn, looks like we're too late," he said to Kit in the passenger seat beside him. "We'll have to try back again in the morning."

They were still in the lot making a U-turn when they saw the figure emerge from the small building's front door.

"On second thought," Gannon said as he saw that

it was the same heavyset doctor he and Barber had dealt with the first time they'd been there.

What was his name again? Gannon thought.

"Dr. Thompson?" he called as he pulled up alongside him.

"Yes. Can I help you?" Thompson said as he stepped over, still holding his keys.

"I'm Special Agent Hagen, Doctor," Kit said, leaning sideways to show him her credentials. "And this is my partner, Gannon."

Gannon reached over and extended his hand to the doctor.

"You can call me Mike."

"I was wondering if I could speak with you about the shootings up on Grand Teton."

"You keep some inconvenient hours, Agent Hagen," the doctor said, checking his watch. "I was just about to have dinner. Couldn't it wait until tomorrow?"

"We actually just got off a plane and are starving ourselves," Gannon said quickly. "Could we maybe talk over dinner, Doc? Our treat."

A smile played on the doctor's lips as he thought about that.

Gannon was pleased by the lack of recognition in the doctor's face as he looked back at him. He was newly shaven and shorn and wearing a suit. The doctor seemed completely oblivious that they had already met. He must have thought Gannon was just another FBI agent, Gannon realized. He certainly wasn't going to tell him otherwise.

"A dinner meeting. That's an interesting prospect,"

the doctor finally said. "There actually is a nice new place not far from here."

"Lead the way, Doc," Gannon said.

42

The restaurant Dr. Thompson directed them to was five minutes away on the west side of town in an expensive-looking hotel.

The lobby inside had walls that soared up four stories, and down one of them came a loud and powerful cascade of water. Through some architectural acoustical trick, the rumbling sound of it disappeared as one went deeper into the hotel under an arch.

"This is quite a nice hotel, don't you think?" the doctor said as they headed past the waterfall. "It's designed after that new one in Aspen. There's a whole push in the town now to really compete for the deep-pocket jet-set ski people."

"It's usually not this crowded," he said as he guided them to the left of the check-in desk toward a modern-looking restaurant packed with people. "Some

Silicon Valley conference thing has been going on for the last couple of weeks, I think."

A bartender wearing a shiny black shirt came over and smiled at them.

"They have a great premium scotch collection," the doctor said. "Do you like scotch?"

"We love premium scotch," Gannon said. "Don't we, Agent Hagen?"

Kit gave Gannon a look as the doctor smiled.

"I'm partial to Talisker 18 myself. Is that something you might like?" Dr. Thompson said.

"Hell, yes," Gannon said, tossing a hundred-dollar bill on the bar top. "Set us up. Three Taliskers."

Whatever that is, Gannon thought.

"Please," the doctor said, smiling as the bartender lifted a bottle. "Call me Walter."

Ten minutes later, a tall hostess led them down some steps into the sunken dining room. Like the bar, it was very dimly lit and had a campfire feel from a huge glassed-in electric fireplace tucked into one of its dark stone walls.

"Now, here's what I call my kind of work meeting," the doctor said, raising his cut crystal glass to the flickering light.

"Mine, too," said Gannon, raising his own thirty-dollar highball.

They all turned as a waitress brought a huge cake covered with sparklers over to a table of clapping corporate-suited Asian businessmen who were singing "Happy Birthday."

"Now, what did you specifically want, Agent Hagen?" the doctor said after a fastidious sip.

"Please call me Kit. We were wondering if we

could see your office's copy of the autopsy report on the female victim who was brought down off the mountain," Kit said.

"The Jane Doe?" he said.

"Yes."

The portly doctor took another finicky sip and then nodded as he sat up in the booth seat.

"I did the autopsy myself," he said. "State actually tried to take it away from me with all the publicity and everything, but I put my foot down. I'm a twenty-year veteran board-certified forensic pathologist. I started doing this straight out of medical school in San Francisco. Press or no press, I'm more qualified than the hacks in the State Department to do the investigation, and they knew it. So they finally backed off."

He yawned and sipped a little more whiskey.

"These country people, I swear," he said. "Perhaps you might have noticed I'm not exactly the cowpoke type. I moved out here with my wife because of her family. You can't imagine the kind of blockheads I'm often forced to deal with."

"How did the Jane Doe die?" Kit said.

The doctor swirled his scotch in the firelight as he looked at her.

"She was strangled," he said, turning and staring into the fire. "There was a distinct ligature furrow on the neck and a subconjunctival hemorrhage in the left eye. All the other injuries were postmortem. But I must say, I don't quite understand why you're here now. I sent in the report over a week ago to your office to that… Agent Sinclair? Is that his name? I would have thought you would have ID'd her by now."

"No, Doctor," Kit said, perplexed. "If you consider that the face was disfigured and there was no identification found, even on a high-profile case like this there's at least a three-week wait for any DNA match."

"But didn't you see the report? I would have thought you'd be all over the breast implants. They have the manufacturer identification numbers on them as clear as day."

43

Gannon and Kit exchanged a look.

"That's exactly why we're here," Gannon said, sitting up straight. "There seems to be some kind of mix-up with the reports."

"Could you get us another copy?" Kit said quickly.

"Tonight if at all possible?" Gannon said.

"Tonight?" the doctor said with a pained look on his face.

Gannon lifted his scotch.

"This is as high-priority as you can imagine, Walter," Kit said.

They listened to the clack of plates and murmur of people around them as Dr. Thompson peered deeply into his drink.

"Since you've been so cordial," he finally said with a sigh. "After we eat, it'll be the least I could do."

An hour and a half later, Kit had her laptop out and

open in the dark corner of the fancy hotel bar when Gannon returned from the medical examiner's office.

"This just in. Good news," he said as he produced the manila envelope he was hiding behind his back.

"Oh, fantastic, Mike," Kit said as she immediately tore open the autopsy report.

She put on the flashlight from her phone and placed it facedown on top of her empty highball glass to create a makeshift reading lamp.

"Wow, straight to action," Gannon said, watching her square the sheets on the tabletop. "You don't waste time do you, huh?"

"Never," she said, licking her thumb and flicking the first page over. She looked up at him. "Truly, you did great with the doctor, Mike. You have a soft touch. I like it. You must have been a good cop."

"I had my moments," Gannon said.

"Hey, I was going to grab another drink. That Talisker stuff actually is pretty good. Can I get you one?"

"No. One was enough for me. A glass of water would be great though," she said as she tapped at her laptop.

"Score, Mike," Kit said, smiling from behind the computer as Gannon came back.

"No? What? Not an ID? Already?"

"It's not an ID but the next best thing," she said. "I compiled a bunch of medical device manufacturers' databases and the breast implant serial number came up first thing. The implants are registered to a plastic surgery office in Casper, Wyoming. Fletcher Cosmetic Surgery Center. I was just looking at its website. It's only five years old."

"That's awesome," Gannon said. "So the patient's

name should be in the office file, right? Did you check for any missing women in Casper?"

"That's the second thing I did," Kit said. "But no. There's no one."

"Is Casper far from here?"

"It's east of here. Four and a half hours by car."

"Not around the corner but definitely doable," Gannon said, nodding. "We'll head out tomorrow first thing. Talk about hitting the ground running. This a home run."

Ten minutes later, they were sitting in the waterfall lobby, waiting for the valet to bring their Armada around, when Kit suddenly started shaking her head.

"Shit!" she said.

"What is it?" Gannon said.

"What you said about the ID being a home run. This is a home run on a tee. It took me two minutes and a couple of clicks to get a real lead. And my boss, Sinclair, has this? Has had it for a week? And nothing? He said he'd keep me up-to-date, but I haven't heard a word from him. They're just sitting on it? Because of politics or something? The media? Why?"

They both looked over as the doorman came in waving at them.

"Good question, Kit," Gannon said, standing.

44

They were coming across a bridge over a reservoir on Interstate 25 outside of Shoshoni, Wyoming, at around eight thirty the next morning when Kit in the Nissan Armada's passenger seat closed her laptop.

There were a couple of large cardboard coffee cups with bucking broncos on them in the drink holders from a place near their hotel called the Cowboy Coffee Company. Leaving just after six, they wanted to get a jump on things so instead of sitting down for breakfast, they just grabbed some coffee and takeout.

Gannon watched as Kit lifted one of the cups out and took a sip.

"Penny for your thoughts," Gannon said.

"Sorry," Kit said. "I haven't said anything for an hour, have I? I'm just rereading the autopsy report."

"Rereading it?" Gannon said with a squint. "I thought you were memorizing it."

"I know, I know," Kit said, laughing. "Sometimes I start digging in and I look up and it's the next day. Dennis was funny. He would say, 'Earth to rain woman. Come in, rain woman.'"

Gannon looked out the windshield on the left, where a mesa-like landform was slowly rising up out of the flat horizon as if it were coming up out of the ground.

It reminded him of a crude arcade game he had played as a kid where you were a prism-like tank on an endless horizontal battlefield made of straight green lines.

That's what driving in Wyoming is like, he thought, yawning. Flat and straight-edged as vintage Atari.

"I read in the paper your partner was a cop before he became an agent," Gannon said. "Where again? In Boston?"

"Yes. He was in charge of Boston Homicide. How about you? How long were you a cop?" Kit said.

"Thirteen years," Gannon finally said. "Five as a detective."

"And you said you did thirty murders? Wow, that's a lot in five years."

"Five years. Are you kidding? I worked in Brownsville, Brooklyn, in the middle of a gang war. Most of the thirty I did was in only eighteen months. They were shipping us in and out like it was Vietnam."

Kit shook her head.

"That's an incredible volume. That's what? One every two weeks?"

He nodded.

"It was busy all right. A real bloodbath but practically all of them were drug-related. No serial kill-

ers. How about you? How did you become a serial
killer investigator?"

"I was a field agent in LA for about five years,
and I was looking for a change and the slot came up.
I've been doing it for about seven years," she said.

They drove on for another mile.

"You know, I've always wondered why serial killers actually do what they do," Gannon said, glancing
out at the open fields.

"Making light conversation, are we?" Kit said with
a smile.

Gannon laughed.

"Exactly. Weather, sports, torture, murder. Polite
small talk is my specialty."

Kit took a sip of her coffee and looked at him.

"Dennis actually taught me a basic working theory
he had come up with that I've found helpful. Would
you like to hear it?"

"Definitely," Gannon said.

"Let me ask you a question first. Why do you think
they do it?"

"I don't know," Gannon said, glancing at her.
"Some folks are born nuts?"

Kit shook her head.

"No," she said. "Dennis thought most of the com-
plex psychiatric and psychological and even neurolog-
ical theories are just a bunch of TV show flimflam.
It's really not that complicated. Most serial killings,
like most mass shootings, hell, like most crimes in
general, are merely acts of societal revenge."

"Societal revenge?"

Kit placed the laptop back in her bag as she nodded.

"Though no one really talks about it, when we are

children our first entry into society is often quite brutal. Peers that are put together, especially males, away from the eyes of adult authority will immediately create animalistic pecking orders based on strength, natural social acceptability and competence. Handsome, tall, strong, confident children will be at the top of the human ladder of prestige and those who are less so will be relegated to its bottom rungs."

"So you're talking about childhood bullying?" Gannon said.

"Bullying," Kit said and laughed. "Dennis said he loved when people talked about bullying like it's a bad habit that can be curbed. He especially laughed when people talked about stopping it. As if human beings could stop assessing and outdoing each other."

Kit took a sip of her coffee.

"Every face that we look into we measure and judge. All of us do this. Where there are groups of people, there is bullying. Bullying is just a hamhanded strategy of climbing up the human pecking order ladder. Since to be more socially accepted is to have a better chance of surviving and thriving, social positioning isn't just a hobby or something that some mean snot-nosed punk does to make fun of a skinny nerd. It actually lies at the core of everyone's existential human nature."

"Come on. We're not that monkey-like, are we?"

Kit folded her hands in her lap as she gave him a small smile.

"In every game—even a casual game of, say, cards, checkers, Monopoly, you name it—who wants to win?"

"Everyone," Gannon said.

"Exactly. Everyone," she said. "Now, who wants to lose?"

"No one," Gannon said, looking at her.

"Precisely. It's embedded in the depth of our nature to want to win, to be better than others. It's one of the major prime directives built into nearly everything we do. For example, do you ever get tense as you approach the checkout line at the supermarket? Or feel an inordinate amount of joy when a new slot opens and the clerk says you're next? That's your primal human nature aching to score the best spot over everyone else there."

Gannon laughed.

"You're right. I actually have felt that. But how did you know? You profilers can't read minds, too, can you?"

"Not quite," Kit said with a small smile.

45

They both looked out the window as they came past an old trailer. It was down a soft rolling slope in the landscape to their right and there was a blue-tarp-covered boat beside it that was easily the same size of the home. Next to that was a basketball hoop with a once white backboard that was now black with what looked like mold.

The smallness of the rusty run-down single structure against the immensity of the surrounding desolate terrain was off-putting, Gannon thought as they sped past it. It was like seeing an empty rowboat in the middle of the ocean from the deck of a cruise ship.

Speaking of serial killers, Gannon thought.

"Go on," Gannon said. "You were talking about pecking orders."

"See, the problem is that not everyone can win," Kit said. "The person with the most visible social vulnerability or defect will be placed on the lowest rung of the ladder. They just will. And it is here where we find the first origin for the motivation for inhuman sexual violence."

"So it's the bullied who do it?" Gannon said. "But what about someone like Ted Bundy. He was a nice-looking guy, right? He was smart and socially adept."

"On the surface perhaps," Kit said, nodding. "But who knows what happened to him when he was a boy. I'd venture something quite bad. Because, believe me, by and large most of the violators in our files are former scapegoats.

"See, the problem with human society is that the socially dejected and shunned and spurned are still human beings. Everybody wants friends and a chance to be an accepted part of a group. But some people, because of their looks or a stutter or being the odd one out ethnically or racially, get rejected. For all of them, this marginalizing and scapegoating is an unjust affront. It rightly wounds all who experience it. Most get over it eventually. But a very small minority never does."

"So it all starts in the schoolyard?" Gannon said.

"Yes. Or in an extremely abusive home. Usually both. Denied by nature or circumstance to receive acceptance from others freely and naturally when they are young, serial killers, as they grow in size and strength, decide to make their own personal secret and brutal amends.

"The sexual thrill in killing a victim comes from finally having the chance at dominance that was denied to them. All the hate and pain and humiliating submission they had to accept, they now pass on to another. To rape and kill is in essence to un-scape-goat oneself, to put someone else on the bottom rung for a change."

"I see what you're saying, I think," Gannon said. "It's a pecking order reset."

"Yes, well put," Kit said. "In the mind of the killer, each murder is an attempt to rewrite the sad and sorry tragic history of their youth. They wish to be at the top of the ladder for a time. But after they are done with the killing, the old social shame—and now new social shame of being an actual killer—combine to make the primal pain and rage even stronger. Hence you get more and more murders."

"They're like addicts," Gannon said.

"Precisely," Kit said. "And as with any addiction, the perpetrator thinks that it will be the next one that satisfies the yearning once and for all. But of course, like the drug addict, they're always wrong. They're always just digging the hole deeper."

"But so many people are bullied," Gannon said. "Everybody is at one time or another. Why don't we have more killers?"

"Because most people learn over time through friends and family or just on their own to get over their childhood social wounds," Kit said. "Or they eventually learn to win in other ways. Sports, school, work. Or taking care of a pet. Maybe they discover a religious vocation or maybe they move and finally find a girlfriend. Or maybe they don't and just decide to get a grip and suck it up."

"So these killings stem from our nature, from the way people and society are fundamentally set up?" Gannon said.

"Yes, it's an unfortunate side effect of forming into groups. Groups require hierarchies for order. These necessary hierarchies cause resentment and sometimes a keen desire for social revenge."

"Revenge of the nerds on steroids," Gannon said with a shake of his head. "So it's built in, baked into the cake of who we are. We're basically doomed as a species, then?"

"No, not at all," Kit said. "Serial killings are still thankfully very rare.

"Though our lower nature is potentially deadly, most people learn the mature reality that though being socially accepted is a strong desire, one can decide bravely to be his own successful, productive, peaceful person no matter what other people's opinions are."

Gannon tilted his head and looked out the window. A line of cruciform telephone poles was passing by on the road's edge now, high and dark against the beige of the sunburned grassland.

"Your partner, Dennis, must have been a pretty smart guy," he said. "Because what you just laid out there makes a boatload of sense."

46

A few miles west of the outskirts of Casper, they began to pass huge airplane-hangar-like steel industrial buildings on both sides of the road.

Gannon looked out at the dusty fields beside them where large amounts of heavy metal objects were arrayed in rows. Acres of bulldozers zipped past. Hectares of galvanized pipe.

One of the windowless hangars was actually some kind of bar, Gannon realized as they sped past it. A plastic sign strung from its corrugated steel facade said !!!DELICIOUS BURGERS!!! and beside it another one said !!!SMOKE EM IF YOU GOT EM!!! !!!WE STILL ALLOW SMOKING!!

"Live free *and* die. Interesting," Gannon said.

"You don't smoke, Mike, do you?" Kit said, smiling.

"Not normally," Gannon said. "But sometimes

after a juicy six-exclamation-point steel-warehouse burger, who can resist? What time you got?"

"Ten thirty," Kit said, checking her phone.

They had to slow as they started to come upon more vehicles. The traffic had become bumper-to-bumper by the time they crossed the North Platte River into the center of town.

Down the leafy streets they passed there were American flags flying everywhere. There were sidewalk benches out in front of pharmacies. Ice cream shops with hand-painted signs above the plate glass. Everything clean and shiny and perfect-seeming in the clear desert morning light like they'd suddenly driven into an Edward Hopper painting.

"I like this town," Gannon said as they cruised past an old-fashioned barbershop with a red-and-white spinning pole. "Even if it was named after a friendly ghost."

Fletcher Cosmetic Surgery Center was in a new three-story building a little over a mile south from the city center. There was an empty spot right out front of its main door, and Gannon parked and killed the engine and got out.

It was about eighty degrees outside and humid. Gannon stood by the car rolling his neck for a moment and stretching his legs. Across the street one of those huge cannon-like water sprinklers was going off in an athletic field.

"We're on three," Kit said as they pushed into the building's cool air-conditioned foyer. "It's suite three oh three."

They walked past the elevator and found the stairwell. Lights on a motion detector flickered on above them as they came out into the narrow corridor of the third floor. They made a left past marked and unmarked doors. There was a dentist in one of the suites, Gannon saw, and on the door of another was a sign for a pain management doctor.

Fletcher Cosmetic Surgery Center was the very last door on the end. Gannon arrived a step before Kit and grasped the knob. It wouldn't turn no matter which way he spun it so he gave up and started knocking.

"Closed?" Kit said. "That's weird. It's not even lunchtime."

"Exactly," Gannon said, knocking some more. "Closed at eleven o'clock on a Friday? Aren't plastic surgeons like the busiest doctors of all?"

"Maybe there's something on the voice mail?" Kit said, taking out her phone as they heard it.

From behind the office door came a distinct beep and a loud click, and then the chugging sound of a laser jet printer started going off.

47

Kit hammered at the door with the metal case of her phone.

"Hello?" she called. "Hello? Is there somebody in there?"

They listened intently. There was nothing but the rhythmic hum and squeal of the printer. As it began to power down, there was the loud clack of a door opening twenty feet down the corridor behind them. Gannon turned to see a figure bolting from an unmarked doorway on the right and running down the long narrow corridor.

It was a woman, Gannon saw as he immediately took off after her. A short woman in workout clothes and a black-and-white truckers cap.

"Hey," Gannon yelled as she flew into the stairwell.

When he got to the stairwell, he heard her opening the door of the lobby below and by the time he pushed into the lobby, he saw she was already outside in the parking lot. He watched as she ran full-speed across the street and straight through the athletic field's sprinkler.

"Mike, what's up?" Kit called from the stairwell as Gannon sped across the lobby.

"White female," he called as he yanked the door. "Dark leggings and dark pullover and a black-and-white ball cap."

Gannon pounded across the lot and then the street into what he saw now was a soccer field. Stoneline Community College, he read off a banner strung along a low fence.

Gannon's new shoes and socks were soaked through by the time he cleared the field. When he looked up, he saw the woman still running a couple of hundred feet ahead of him. She was flat-out booking now, Gannon saw, really putting on the jets as she tore down a short road, then disappeared behind a brick building.

A sign atop the door of the building Gannon arrived at a few seconds later said it was the college's cafeteria. On the other side of it was a deserted plaza, three brick buildings in a horseshoe around a green lawn with a limp American flag in the middle of it.

Gasping from his run, Gannon scanned around for the running woman. No dice. He didn't see anyone.

He was bent over, dripping sweat onto his new Macy's slacks, trying to catch his breath when a petite young woman wearing an apron stepped out of the cafeteria entrance a moment later.

"Police," Gannon said to her. "Did you see a woman in workout clothes run past here?"

"Yes. She almost knocked me down. I think she went into Doyle."

"Which one is Doyle?" Kit said as she suddenly arrived beside Gannon with her badge out.

The woman pointed out the brick building on the horseshoe's right-hand side.

"What do you think is up?" Kit said as they hurried toward it.

"I don't know, but I'm dying to find out," Gannon said.

Doyle's front door was propped open, and they went slowly into its dead-quiet dim corridor and went to the left. They were about halfway through scanning the hot, empty classrooms when a middle-aged white guy with a gray flattop burst into the building behind them in a jingle of bouncing keys.

"Charlie Phelps, college security. What in the heck's going on here?" he said.

"FBI," Kit said, flicking her creds at him. "Sorry to barge in, Charlie, but we're looking for a person of interest who just ran in here."

The security guy lifted his radio from his belt as he quickly examined her badge.

"Is it some kind of fugitive, Agent?" he said. "You want me to call PD?"

"No, that won't be necessary," Kit said as they came back to the front door and began to look into the rooms on the right-hand side. "She's not wanted or anything. I just need to question her."

They were coming to the end of the hall when

Gannon saw the smear of mud on the polished linoleum before the women's restroom.

He toed the door. The restroom inside was walled with seventies-style avocado-green tiles and there was a small gray pebbled glass window high in the far wall that looked like it had never been opened. All the stall doors were open except the last one on the end.

After a moment, a gasp came from behind it followed by the sound of ragged breathing.

Kit put her hand to her service weapon in its holster as she fully opened the door.

Gannon noted her setup. A Glock in a concealment holster with two more magazines.

He nodded approvingly at the extra ammo.

Always be prepared, he thought.

He looked in over Kit's shoulder.

"Okay, listen up," Kit said. "This is the FBI. Come out now."

The breathing suddenly stopped.

"Out of there now or we're coming down to that stall and dragging you out feetfirst," Gannon yelled loudly.

Gannon smiled sheepishly as Kit turned squinting at him.

"Too much?" he whispered.

They both jumped back as the door of the last stall suddenly blasted open. The short brown-haired woman who slowly emerged was about thirty-five and more attractive than Gannon was expecting. She'd ditched the hat. He saw that she was crying.

"Fine," she said. "You won't believe me anyway."

She offered her wrists to them as she stepped forward past the sinks.

"Arrest me, okay? Whatever," she said. "It doesn't make any difference now."

48

"Okay, Megan. I understand you're upset," Kit said as they all sat in the Armada back at the medical office's parking lot.

Gannon turned and looked at the dark-haired woman where she sat curled up in the back seat. She was pouting and staring at the handle of the back door.

The only things they knew about her after ten minutes of asking were from her license. It said her name was Megan Kraft and she lived in Casper three blocks away.

"I get that," Kit said. "But we're just trying to find out what's going on."

"And we're running out of time and patience," Gannon said, dabbing sweat off his face with a napkin as he drummed his fingers on the wheel.

"I don't know," Megan finally said. "I don't know if I should even say anything. Maybe I need a lawyer."

"Why would you need a lawyer, Megan?" Kit said calmly as they watched a maintenance pickup from the college park beside the soccer field. "I've already told you you're not under arrest. I just want to know why you ran out of the office."

Megan did some more pouting and staring, then she finally sat up.

"Okay," she said. Her hair was in a ponytail and she grabbed it and draped it over her shoulder and began twisting the end of it nervously with her fingers.

"Okay," she repeated. "There's no other way to say it. I was having an affair with Dr. Fletcher, okay? That's why I was in there."

"An affair?"

Her fingers twirled at her hair.

"Yes," she said. "I used to work in the office as a receptionist and I knew he was married but I don't know. He made me laugh and we just hit it off."

"You're not the receptionist anymore?" Gannon said.

"No," Megan said, giving him a funny look. "See, that's it. This was last year, about fifteen months ago. His wife found out about six months in. Or maybe she just suspected. Whichever. She demanded Gary fire me.

"But I wasn't really fired. I didn't show up anymore for work, but he was still paying me, see? He knew I had a daughter. Plus, he wanted to still see me. Besides, he was loaded.

"Anyway, it was driving me crazy all week because, well, see, I'm married, too, and my husband has no idea. He's deployed in the military and coming home next month and…"

"And what?" Kit said calmly.

"I didn't know if Gary's witch of a wife would make a stink about it because of the money. Sue me or something. She's a real bitch on wheels. I knew it was wrong, but I was crazed about all of it, so I thought I'd go in with everyone off at the funeral and see if I could take a look at the books to cover it up or something."

"Wait, wait. Go back," Gannon said. "Funeral? What funeral?"

Megan's fingers ceased in mid-twirl.

"Gary's funeral. Who do you think I'm talking about?" she said.

Gannon and Kit looked at each other in shock.

"Dr. Fletcher's funeral?" Gannon said. "Dr. Fletcher is dead?"

"Yes. Isn't that why you're here? Aren't you investigating his death or something?"

"How did Dr. Fletcher die exactly?" Kit said.

"He committed suicide," she said. "Last week. He did that thing with the hose in his garage. You know? Left the car running and pushed the hose into the tailpipe and the window? The carbon monoxide thing. It was a shock to everyone. Gary was an upbeat guy. Fun-loving. A runner and big-time skier. He had a house in Breckinridge. No one saw this coming."

Gannon and Kit stared at each other again.

"What day was this?" Kit said.

"Last Friday."

Kit tapped at her lip as she peered at the dashboard.

"Megan, how did you get into the office?" she finally said. "Do you have the keys?"

"Yes, Gary gave them to me. I used to meet him there sometimes when the staff was gone."

"Okay," Kit said after taking a breath. "I see the position you're in here. I'm sympathetic, so why don't we make a deal? I'm looking for the name of one of Dr. Fletcher's patients. I have the serial number for some breast implants he, um, installed. Do you think if I gave you the number that you could get me the name of the patient associated with it?"

"Sure," Megan said sitting up even straighter. "I could do that. In fact, I'm probably the only one who can."

"Why's that?" Gannon said.

"His files are gone. Or at least the official files. I checked when I went in. Somebody must have come in with a hand truck. All the paper is gone and the half the computers, too."

49

A long beat of silence took over the car as Kit and Gannon thought that news over.

"His wife's lawyer took them maybe?" Megan finally said.

"Maybe," Gannon said, looking at Kit wide-eyed.

Megan shook her head.

"I wouldn't put it past that greedy bitch," she said. "But it doesn't matter because Dr. Fletcher did some funky accounting, if you catch my drift."

"How's that?" Kit said.

"I've seen docs play loose with the Medicare billing, but Fletch was on another level. He had a backup file of all the regular stuff plus the funky stuff on a laptop computer he kept in a hole in the wall of the office supply closet. And she missed it, the dope. I was going through it when you knocked."

Megan stopped talking suddenly.

"Hey, what happens after I get you what you need?"

"We never saw each other," Kit said.

"Can I keep the laptop?"

"What laptop? Did you say something?" Kit said.

"I like this deal," Megan said with a smile.

Gannon turned the engine over as Megan came back out of the building ten minutes later. As she shifted the iMac laptop from one hand to the other, they could see there were printer pages on top of it.

"It's right there," she said as she handed the pages in through the passenger window. "Everything you're looking for came up right away. I even printed out the photos."

"Photos?" Kit said, shuffling through the pages.

"Yes. Gary would do before-and-after photos of the patients for his website. It was an option he would give some of the cuter ones. He would reduce the fee on enlargements if you agreed to model for him."

"What a guy," Gannon mumbled as Kit looked over the papers.

"Is that good? Can I go now?" Megan asked.

Kit nodded her head without looking up.

"You did great. Thanks, Megan. You can go."

Gannon watched Megan jog over to a silver Honda at the other end of the lot. She put the laptop into the trunk before she backed out and sped away out into the street.

"So we actually have a name?" Gannon said.

"Sure do," Kit said. "Our Jane Doe's name is Tracy. Tracy Marie Sandhurst."

"Is her address here in town?" Gannon said.

"No," Kit said as she took out her own laptop. "It looks like we need to go to... Cheyenne."

"Can I see the pictures?" Gannon said.

Kit gave him a look.

"The face, Kit. Just the face," Gannon said. "I want to see what she looked like before she was murdered."

Kit folded the paper and showed him.

Gannon looked down at Tracy Sandhurst. He looked at her Barbie-pink lipstick and her dyed bleach-blond hair with darker eyebrows.

She still had a little acne and there was a little girlish gap in her front teeth but she was actually very nice-looking. She was maybe twenty-two or -three.

"How, Kit?" Gannon said, shaking his head as he remembered the horror movie stills of her crime scene photos.

He winced as he stared into Tracy Sandhurst's soft blue eyes.

"Just how?" he said.

50

Seven miles south of Washington, DC, the Washington & Old Dominion Railroad bike and running path started in Shirlington, went up northwest through Falls Church and ended nearly fifty miles away in Purcellville.

Saturday morning at nine thirty, the FBI's Behavioral Science Division's newest section chief, Francis Sinclair, pulled his new Subaru Forester off the Dulles Toll Road into the leafy town of Vienna that was midway on the path.

Three minutes later, he came upon the bike path access he was told to report to. Just in off the road he noticed the shell of a tiny old-fashioned rail station along the path now serving as a rain shelter. He parked in the grassy shoulder behind it, making sure to bury his car deep under the shadows of the trees.

It took another five minutes to walk from the car

to a footbridge down the path where he'd been told to wait.

He dabbed a bead of sweat off his forehead as he looked through the bridge's chain-link down at a sluggish brown-green stream below. He thought to check his phone for the temperature but then remembered that he had left it at home like he'd been told.

He looked north up the desolate curving path, at the trees and transmission towers and telephone poles.

Then he closed his eyes and remembered the night he'd been compromised the year before.

It was in a cop bar that he'd gone to with an old classmate from Holy Cross who worked at State. His friend's brother was a DC cop, and it had been his birthday and they had actually closed the bar down as a bunch of strippers came in. He hadn't even wanted to cheat, but he was drunk and this one half-Spanish, half-Chinese-looking stripper was super hot, and she took him back to the room where they put all the empty bottles.

The camera that had recorded him must have been one of those low-light night vision ones.

He'd been able to mostly forget about it.

That was until they asked him to come for a meeting over at Justice the morning he flew back from Jackson after visiting Agent Hagen in the hospital.

Francis was still sweating against the fence several minutes later when he noticed some movement to his left.

Just to the north of the bridge, something large suddenly emerged from the undergrowth.

It was a horse.

Sinclair felt his jaw loosen as he recognized the stiff-backed haughty-looking woman riding it.

"Hello, Francis," Dawn Warner said as Sinclair approached.

He looked up at her. At her tight white T-shirt, her tight dark riding pants, her black leather boots. Her riding helmet was one of those English bobby-hat-style ones.

Sinclair stared at the horse. He knew nothing about horses. This one was brown.

"You live around here?" he said, puzzled.

"Not too far," Dawn Warner said as she dismounted with surprising agility. "My daughters were all equestrians at a stable about a mile from here, and I still come out here and ride every now and then. I find that riding in the woods is a great way to clear your head. What do they call it? Forest bathing? Why don't you bathe with me a little, Francis. Walk me back down the trail here so we can talk."

51

Sinclair stayed on the right of the assistant attorney general as she expertly walked the horse back down a slope of tall grass to a crushed bluestone bridle path. He almost bumped into her as she suddenly halted at the entrance of the tree line.

"Francis, could you pull up your shirt and turn out your pockets for me?" Dawn Warner said.

A chatter of insects started up as he followed her instructions. The humid breeze on his bare stomach suddenly made him feel sick and filthy like he was doing something illicit.

Which made sense, he thought. Since he was doing something illicit.

"Excellent," she said. "Hate to even ask but one can't be too careful with being recorded these days. Nice abs, by the way, though a tad pale. You need to get some sun before the summer's over, Francis, or what's the point?"

"What can I do for you?" Sinclair said.

"Where is Special Agent Kit Hagen?" Dawn Warner said with a curious tilt of her bobby-helmeted head.

"At home on leave where I sent her the way you told me to," Sinclair said.

Warner made a disappointed sort of sigh as she reached up and took out an iPad from a saddlebag.

"Watch this, please," she said, handing it to him.

Sinclair cupped his hand over the screen and watched.

"Isn't that funny?" Warner said as the video showed Kit Hagen walking along a corridor. "That looks like Hagen, doesn't it?"

"Yes. Where is this?"

"Wyoming," Dawn Warner said.

"Wyoming?"

"Yes. Casper, Wyoming. Yesterday she went into a college and flashed her badge. Said she was looking for a person of interest. Isn't that odd?"

"How did you find this out?"

"The security head at the college there used to be DEA in Denver. He put in an inquiry. Didn't feel completely kosher, he said."

"Is that right?"

"Do you know this man with her?" Warner said pointing. "Could this be a boyfriend?"

"Maybe. I've never laid eyes on him."

Which actually didn't mean much, Sinclair thought. Unlike himself, Kit was sharp enough to keep her personal stuff personal.

"Well, he was with her. Can you explain why she is in Casper, Wyoming?"

"No," Sinclair said.

"I think I can," Dawn Warner said, staring at him. "Which is the reason why we're having this conversation."

"I don't—" Sinclair started.

"Rein her in. And I mean yesterday, Francis. She's veering into a no-fly zone of extreme danger. I'm not kidding. This isn't me talking. If you care about her—or your promotion—you need to get her back here to DC pronto."

"But how do I do it? I call her and say what?"

Dawn Warner squinted at him as she took a riding crop from the saddle and began to stroke the horse's nose with it.

"You know the difference between you and this rented horse here, Francis?" she said, smiling. "This rented horse is smart enough to never ask me how to follow orders. Which part of 'get Hagen back here by Monday' is eluding you?"

"I'll take care of it," Sinclair said, wiping at the sweat on his brow.

"You better, Francis," Dawn Warner said, giving Sinclair a good long view of the back of her immodestly tight pants as she tucked the crop back in the saddle.

"Have a great rest of your weekend, now," she called as she led the horse away down the path. "And please say hello to your better half for me."

52

They set out at nine that morning from the Casper Best Western after the complimentary hotel breakfast, and it was coming on ten when Kit, at the wheel of the Armada, saw the low-gas indicator light flash in the dashboard display.

She drove on for another mile before she spotted a blue-and-white gas pump symbol on the sign for the next exit. As she hit the clicker, she yawned.

"What's up?" Gannon said, yawning himself and sitting up from where he'd been half snoozing in the passenger seat.

"Gas," Kit said.

The station was down the exit and under the highway overpass to the left. It had a sun-bleached white clapboard old general store attached to it with a dirt road alongside it that led back to an empty fenced field.

A plastic sign tied to the wood slats of the fence said Welcome to Glendo, Friend-o.

Kit shook her head at the lonesome prairie farmhouse store. She half expected Ma and Pa Ingalls and Half Pint to step out as she slowed before the dusty pumps.

She had just pulled to a stop and was looking around for tumbleweeds when she got the call. She went into her bag and lifted out her vibrating iPhone. She was surprised that there was service.

"Shit, it's my new boss," she suddenly said.

"Your new boss?" Gannon said.

"Sinclair."

"He call you regularly?"

"Never," Kit said. "This is a first."

Gannon reached over and killed the engine for her.

"You should probably see what he wants," he said.

Kit chinned the phone, opened the door, got out and grabbed the phone again in her free hand. She kicked the door shut behind her as she thumbed the Accept button.

"Hello," she said.

"Hey, Kit. How are you?" Francis Sinclair said.

"Great, Francis. Never better," she said as she wandered slowly past the pumps toward the grass highway berm. "What's up?"

"Where are you? In a wind tunnel?" he said.

"Out on my deck," Kit lied as she glanced back at the car. "There's a breeze. I'm repainting one of the Adirondack chairs."

"Wow. Ambitious."

"Why not?" Kit said, squinting as she came to the

edge of the station's worn asphalt. "It's not like I have anything else to do, do I?"

"Well, that's why I'm calling, Kit," Sinclair said. "Great news. You can put the paint can away. I went to bat for you, and I hit one into the bleachers."

"What do you mean?"

"I've got a buddy who works for the deputy director and he told him what was going on—about you being mothballed—and he really flipped his wig. I don't know the details, but he must have pulled some major strings.

"Last night, I got an email straight from the seventh floor to turn the investigation back on with you as the lead. Congratulations, Kit. Things are back to normal. You're back on the case."

"Francis, thank you," Kit said, smiling. "This is awesome. When can I come back in?"

"Immediately."

"Monday morning?"

"Yes. Monday morning eight o'clock sharp, I want you at your desk. And Kit, even better news. I just got an email from the lab that says the DNA results on the Grand Teton Jane Doe are coming in, so there's going to be a meeting."

Kit looked out at the empty cattle field, wondering if she should mention she already knew that the victim's name was Tracy Sandhurst and that she already had her address in Cheyenne.

Kit looked up the berm at the highway as a tour bus went by heading west.

She decided not to. Not yet. She needed to think about it. Let things settle a bit. She knew she needed to unravel this whole crazy thing with care.

"By the way, what are your plans for tomorrow? We're having a barbecue. The whole gang is coming," Sinclair said.

"Thanks, Francis. But I've got too many things to wrap up."

"So you'd rather watch paint dry. I guess I deserve that," Sinclair said and laughed.

Kit laughed with him.

"I'll see you at the office Monday at eight."

"Eight sharp it is," Kit said.

53

After Kit hurried back to the car and told Gannon the good news, he stood staring at her steadily with his slate-blue eyes.

"Are you feeling all right?" he finally said.

"What are you talking about?" Kit said, hurt.

Gannon was filling the tank. When the pump clicked, he ripped the nozzle out of the car and rammed it savagely back into the pump holder.

"First they say go away and you go away," he said as he capped the tank and slapped the cover shut. "Now they say come back and you want to go back? Sort of brings to mind that old Elvis love song. What was the name of it again? Oh yeah, now I remember. 'Puppet on a String.'"

He got in behind the wheel.

Kit peered at him coldly as she slowly sat down in the passenger seat beside him.

"I got my job back. I thought you'd be happy for me."

"Okay," Gannon said. "Whatever you say."

"You think I can't affect this case more efficiently by officially being in charge of it?" Kit said slamming her door. "You think it's better for everyone if we illegally skulk around some more?"

"Yes," Gannon said, nodding emphatically. "That's exactly what I'm saying. Our illegal skulking around is the key to our success. It's the only reason we've gotten anywhere at all."

"Gee, Mike. Don't hold back. Tell me what you really think."

"Your beloved team members are burying this case down a bottomless pit," Gannon said. "You know it and I know it, too. Going back to Washington reeks of total bullshit, especially now that we're actually getting somewhere."

"I see. Now we're into conspiracy theories."

"You want a conspiracy theory?" Gannon said. "I'll give you a conspiracy theory. The eight-hundred-pound one we've been dancing around since Casper. Where's the autopsy report?"

Kit thrust the manila envelope into his chest.

Gannon slipped it out and peered at the top of the first page.

"I knew it. See? Here's the printout of the email Dr. Thompson sent to your office along with the report. What's the date at the header there?"

"Monday of last week. So what?" Kit said.

"The FBI receives the lead on the breast implant ID Monday. Massive lead. But they sit on it for some mysterious reason. Then four days later on Friday, Dr. Fletcher, swinging tata king of Casper, Wyoming, out of the blue takes a sudden dirt nap and all his files go missing. That's some crazy coincidence there, don't you think?"

"You're out of your paranoid mind," she said. "You really are crazy."

Gannon took a breath.

"I get it, Kit. You're in it, so you can't see it. It's understandable. But to my objective eyes and ears, this bird's not only waddling and quacking now, it's linking arms with Mickey Mouse and dancing out in front of Epcot Center."

She stared at him as she pointed at her phone.

"So you're saying my boss, Sinclair, is lying now?"

"Listen to me," Gannon said. "Here's what's going to happen. When you go back to DC, you'll go to this useless meeting and then this lead we have right now becomes the hardest dead end you ever saw in your life. That's what I think. And then the case will be over. Over and out.

"Somebody must have noticed your keystroke entries or whatever, and they know you're out here snooping and now they want you back in DC on a tight leash where they can see and control you."

Kit looked down at the floorboard of the car. She was biting her lip.

"This guy killed your partner," Gannon said. "And Owen and the sheriff. Not only that, he shot you. He put a bead on you with his rifle and pulled the trigger and put a round through your back and chest like you were a fall season deer. He didn't do that to them, right?

"None of them got to feel what it's like to get a hole blown through them. None of them got to horrifically live through their own personal episode of *I Shouldn't Be Alive*. Not your boss, Sinclair, not Dawn Warner. Only you, Kit. You're the one owed justice on this. You. The only living person anyway. The important question is this. You want it or not?"

"Of course," she said with a sudden flash of anger in her eyes. "Why do you think I'm doing this? What are you saying?"

"I'm saying how about me and you keep on this trail like we've been doing. We're getting closer, Kit. I can feel it."

"What do I do though? I said I'd be back."

"Yeah, well, looks like you came down with the flu," Gannon said. "These summer ones are the worst."

They sat for a minute. There was a pop and a low rumble and Gannon looked up the berm as an old leather-vested biker went by on a panhead Harley, his gray hair streaming behind him.

"You're right," she finally said quietly. "They really do want this case buried, don't they?"

Gannon nodded.

"Well, screw that," Kit said, suddenly clicking on her seat belt. "Cheyenne, here we come."

"That's the spirit, partner," Gannon said, smiling as he turned the engine over. "Cheyenne, here we come. That sounds like a country-and-western hit to me.

"I'm sorry, by the way. I'm told I can be blunt."

"Blunt? You?" Kit said, peering at him.

"This is what I hear," Gannon said, leaving dust as he peeled out of the station.

54

They pulled into Cheyenne two hours later and went straight to Tracy Sandhurst's apartment building.

It was in the east part of town down a kind of cul-de-sac centered between an auto parts store and some railroad tracks. Her apartment was 2B and they parked and got out and went up the set of breezeway stairs and knocked. And knocked again. Even after five minutes, there was no response.

A freight train loaded with rusty shipping containers was clacking past on the tracks beyond the parking lot as they came back down to the ground floor. Around the side facing the auto parts store, they found a door with a "manager" sign on it. A young man with buzz-cut black hair answered it. He was barefoot and had on a Cheyenne fire rescue T-shirt and a pair of boxer shorts. He looked like he'd just woken up.

"Hi, we're looking for Tracy Sandhurst. Lives up on two," Gannon said.

"What are you guys? Police?" he said squinting at them.

Kit showed her badge.

"FBI?" the black-haired manager said, suddenly wide-awake. "What on earth did she do?"

"She died," Gannon said.

"Died? No! What happened?"

"That's what we're trying to find out. Could you let us into her apartment?"

"Yeah, I could do that," the man said, staring at them. "I mean, if this isn't some kind of trick or something? Like you're not pulling a sting on her, are you? You're serious, right? She's really dead?"

"You want to see the autopsy photos?" Kit said angrily, glaring at him.

"Wow. No," the guy said. "Sorry. Let me get the keys, then."

The train was still clinking past as they went around and up.

"Her rent was due three days ago," the manager said as he unlocked the door. "I was going to knock on her door today in fact. She usually slips it under my door on the day."

"How long has she been living here?" Kit said as they went in.

"Year and a half," he said.

"You own this place?" said Gannon.

"No, I'm a fireman in the city. My uncle is the owner, but he lets me stay for free to keep an eye on everything."

"Where was Tracy from? Here in town?"

"No. I think she was from Pine Bluffs. I saw her at a football game there once back in high school. She was real pretty then, a cheerleader, I think. Almost positive it was her, though I never asked. My uncle's office might know. They do all the application stuff. You want me to call them?"

"Maybe," Kit said as she went inside. "You can hold off for now."

The one-bedroom apartment was messy but not excessively so. College kid messy. There was plenty of food in the fridge. They examined the door lock, the window that faced the breezeway. There was no sign of a break-in or struggle.

Gannon went into the single bedroom. On the wall opposite the window on the other side of the bed there was a photograph collage board. He looked at the pictures tucked into the crisscrossing lavender ribbons.

They were mostly from high school. A blond pretty Tracy with a bunch of her pretty friends. At football games, at concerts, at a beach. A lot of laughing and smiling. Tracy with a nice-looking red-haired college football player. The last one on the bottom showed the two of them giving a beautiful baby a bath in a sink.

He looked around the room. No baby stuff. No toys.

"What happened to you, Tracy?" he whispered as he opened the closet door.

It was full of clothes hung up and neatly folded. When he got down on the floor, he spotted a knapsack under the bed. Inside of it was a couple of thousand dollars in cash along with a bunch of prescription pill bottles and about half a pound of marijuana in a

Ziploc bag. He shoved it back where he found it and came back out.

"Is her car in the lot?" he said to the manager standing in the doorway.

"I don't know. Let me see," he said, stepping away.

"No," he said as he came back a second later. "She drove a blue Toyota, a used one. A Camry, I think. I don't see it."

"This happened almost three weeks ago. You didn't notice her gone that long?" Kit said.

He shook his head.

"No, I'm not the prying type. And people go on vacation in the summer, right? I thought maybe she went on vacation."

"You ever know her to go out to Jackson, Wyoming, for any reason?" Kit said. "Or Grand Teton National Park? She do any camping?"

"Jackson? No, she wasn't a skier or a camper. Tracy wasn't the outdoor type, or even the go-out-during-the-day type. She was real skinny especially of late. I think she might have been a drug addict," he said.

Gannon shook his head as he thought about the picture of her with the Gerber baby at the sink.

"Did she have a boyfriend?" he said.

"Not that I know of," he said, shaking his head. "But wait. You said Jackson? That stuff on the news? Those cops that were shot? Holy crap. Tracy wasn't the girl who was murdered by this NATPARK killer, was she? That was Tracy?"

"That's what we're trying to find out," Kit said.

"This is just bonkers," the manager said, staring

at the floor. "Bonkers. You know Tracy was a stripper, right?"

"No," Kit said. "Where? Here in town?"

"No, it's called Dynamite Dolls," the manager said. "It's off I-25 right by the Colorado border."

55

Dynamite Dolls didn't open until four on the week-ends, but after they called the number on the website, the owner, Rollie Dettmar, agreed to immediately meet them there.

As they pulled into the lot, they saw a bald biker type of about sixty with a lot of tats sitting in the open door of a cherry-red Dodge muscle car. He had on a Metallica concert tee and was talking on his phone. He hung up when they pulled in beside him.

"Oh, my," Kit said as the man stood and they saw that Rollie Dettmar had to be six-foot-five.

"Ditto on that," Gannon said as they got out.

"I appreciate you meeting us, Mr. Dettmar," Kit said after she showed him her credentials.

"No problem," the large man said, closing his door. "You said on the phone this is about Tracy?"

"Yes, I'm sorry to tell you but she's deceased," Kit said.

The completely collapsed look that immediately overcame the TV-wrestler-sized man's weather-beaten face was as heartbreaking as it was unexpected.

"No," he said. "No, no, no. How?"

"She was murdered," Gannon said. "About three weeks ago."

He put his elbows atop the roof of his car and covered his face with his huge hands. They watched as he wept openly.

"We're really sorry, Mr. Dettmar," Kit said.

"Oh, I knew it," he said, snuffling loudly as he wiped at his eyes. "I knew it. Tracy was sweet. She would have called. She wouldn't have just left. These girls get into such crazy things."

I wonder why, Gannon, thought getting a bit tired of the big man's sob routine.

"I was going to give it a few more days and head by her apartment."

"When was the last time she worked?" Gannon said.

"I'm not positive," he said, wiping his eyes with the edge of the concert tee. "But I can check. The time sheets are in my office."

The inside walls of the large open barnlike building were painted all black like there had been a fire. They stepped past mirrors and black leather seats. The dark laminated mirror-like surface of the pole stage was so glossy it looked slippery.

Gannon counted six security cameras as they followed Dettmar through the warm stuffy air.

"Okay. We're looking at the second," Dettmar said as he sat with a binder in his lap in the back office. "Tracy's last night was August second. That was a Tuesday. She worked first shift which goes two to ten."

"She got out at ten on Tuesday the second? You're sure?" Kit said as she gave Gannon a look of confusion.

Gannon was perplexed himself.

The Grand Teton shooting had happened on Wednesday the third, he thought. How could Tracy have been at work at ten o'clock Tuesday night and then be found dead Wednesday morning up on top of a mountain four hundred miles away?

"Could she have left early?"

"Like, I don't remember specifically, but my managers keep the records real sharp. If it says it in the book here, it happened."

"How long do you keep video? A month?" Gannon said.

"Yep, a month," Dettmar said as he clicked at his computer. "You want to see inside or the parking lot?"

"Try the parking lot first," Kit said.

Dettmar brought up an array of screens and clicked his mouse and began fast-forwarding.

"Right there, see? Ten fifteen and there she is. That's her leaving after her shift," he said.

They stood looking as Tracy stepped out into the gray-toned parking lot. She looked skinnier and meaner than the photos of her Gannon had seen in her apartment. The lot was empty of people and there were about ten cars in it.

"Is this Tracy's car here in the corner?" Kit said, pointing at what looked like a Camry.

"Yep, the Toyota right there. That's her blue Toyota."

They watched her cross toward it and get in and close the door. She was in there for a full minute, then two, and then the brake lights on the car flashed and it began to back out.

"That's it. She left. I'm sorry I can't help you with anything else," Dettmar said.

"Can I see the part where she gets into her car again?" Gannon said.

"Sure," Dettmar said, rewinding slowly.

"Now stop it there. Pause it," Gannon said as he watched Tracy open the door.

"What is it?" Kit said.

"The dome light doesn't go on when she opens the door," Gannon said. "The interior dome light should go on."

"You're right," Kit said.

"Can we rewind some more?" Gannon said.

Dettmar started rewinding. Tracy went backwards into the building and then there was just the car.

The time stamp said it was nine thirty-five when they saw her car door open and the figure emerge from her car walking backwards.

"There was somebody already in the car!" Kit said. "Pause it! Pause it!"

Dettmar paused the video and they looked at the darkly dressed man on the screen standing there in the lot. He had a ball cap and a hoodie on. Facing away from the camera, his features weren't visible. He didn't look tall, but it was clearly a man because his shoulders and back were almost bodybuilder wide.

"Look, he's wearing gloves," Gannon said, pointing.

Dettmar hit Play and they watched as the hooded

man walked with his wide back to them toward the car. As he approached the driver's side door, both hands went to the front of him. He did something with his hands and the door popped open, and then he climbed in and closed the door.

"He slim jimmed it," Gannon said. "He waited in her car until she got off her shift."

Kit took out her cell phone and brought the video app up on it and turned it on.

"Do you think you could roll that footage again for us, Mr. Dettmar?" Kit said.

56

"You notice the way the guy walks to the car?" Kit said as they sat back in the Armada in the parking lot, watching the footage again and again.

"Yeah, he has like a prison yard hop roll thing going on. You think he's a gangbanger or something?" Gannon said.

"No," she said. "I don't think that's it. I've seen that kind of shuffling before on another case. There's a name for that. I forget what it is but it's a type of gait that people with prosthetics have."

"You think he lost a leg or something? Like a soldier maybe?"

"Maybe," Kit said. "It's definitely something to keep in mind. And I definitely think she was taken in the car. Just as she sits right there, he's in the back behind her and he gets a cord around her neck. Then when she's dead, he moves her over and drives out."

"Then only nine hours later she's found up on Grand Teton elaborately carved up and bound?" Gannon said.

"Something doesn't exactly add up with the time there, does it?" Kit said. "How the hell does he get her up there that quick? It's a seven-hour drive just to the base of the mountain."

Gannon put the car into Drive.

"Let's start driving back and see if we can find her car on any more surveillance cameras," he said.

They got back on I-25. Five minutes later, Kit pointed ahead at a gas station at the bottom of the first exit ramp.

"Let's start there. That station looks pretty new," she said.

The old black woman they found behind the counter inside had to be eighty if she was a day. She was named Jessie, according to the plastic name tag on her vest.

"Glad to help ya, of course," she said after carefully studying Kit's credentials through her thick eyeglasses.

The sharp-as-a-tack lady locked the front door before she led them past the chips and drink coolers into the back.

"This is a really great camera system, isn't it?" Jessie said as she showed them her computer. "These cameras just keep getting better and better. My husband, Bob, was a cop in Colorado Springs and he insisted we get the best system we could when we decided to open a new station."

"Wait, wait. Hit Pause," Gannon said two minutes later.

Kit tapped the mouse and the screen froze to show Tracy Sandhurst's blue Camry on the exit ramp.

"Hot dang! You nailed it, Kit. There's her car. Press Play. Let's see where it goes," Gannon said excitedly.

The Camry pulled down to the red light and its left clicker went on. The light turned green and the car went left.

"Come on," Gannon said, leading them back out of the closet-sized room. "Let's go left and see if we can find another camera."

Gannon pulled the Armada back out of the station onto the exit ramp and quickly made a left under the highway overpass like the Camry had done.

As they got out on the other side of it, he suddenly slowed as he saw there was something unusual in the road ahead.

There was some kind of black-and-white-striped barrier across the road and beyond it some sort of tollbooth and a high fence.

"What in the *hell*?" Kit said.

There was a large sign in the grass off to the right of the road, and Gannon and Kit both stared up as they pulled alongside it.

It said:

Francis E. Warren Air Force Base
RESTRICTED AREA
PHOTOGRAPHY PROHIBITED
HAVE IDENTIFICATION READY
NO TRESPASSING BEYOND THIS POINT

57

Seventeen hundred miles almost exactly due east along the beach in Osterville, Massachusetts, there was a whir and *fwump* and a crisp *pock* followed by the squeak of sneakers on hard court.

Dawn Warner's tennis whites glowed in the sunset dimness as she wiped sweat from her brow. She waited with knees slightly bent as the machine *fwump*ed out another ball, a lob this time. She groaned as she crushed it down the baseline hard enough to make the chain-link edging the beach sand jingle.

That's it, she thought as she jogged over and checked her steel-and-gold Rolex lady's Oyster beside her towel. She had to stop now or she'd be late to meet her husband, Neil, at the club for dinner.

Coming around the net to turn off the machine, she stopped for a moment as she heard the soft hum of a motor.

She turned out to look at the water, laughing softly to herself as a large catamaran skimmed past a quarter mile out.

For some people, it was the scent of suntan lotion or maybe the taste of saltwater taffy that flipped the endless summer nostalgia switch.

For her, out here on her father's old family vacation compound, it was the jolly purr of the Hyannis Port ferry heading out to Martha's Vineyard.

At least some things didn't change, she thought to herself as she clicked off the machine.

She heard the thump of bass coming from the pool house as she came across the cobblestone walkway a moment later. It was her brother's oldest twin boys, she knew. They were going to be seniors in high school now and were as rambunctious as that implied. She wondered if Auntie Dawn should knock on the door and get them to turn it down a tad.

No. She'd let it slide, she thought as she went into the side door of her seven-thousand-square-foot cedar-shingled beach house.

This time.

After her shower upstairs in her sumptuous master suite, she went into her vacation office in her robe and put on some Brahms. As she waited for her iMac to power on, she looked at the photographs on her wall. She and her daughters on a hike in Kenya. She and Neil at an art gallery in Stockholm. Her youngest daughter's wedding on the beach in the Galápagos the year before.

The email she was waiting on wasn't there, so she found her phone.

"Control," said a voice.

"Yes, this is Dawn Warner. Harris was looking into something for me. Is he still there?"

"He left but there's a note on his desk. Let me see here. Something about flight logs leaving out of some regional airports in… Wyoming, is it?"

"Yes. Flights from there to DC. I'm looking to see if there's a Kit, I mean, a Katherine Hagen on any of them."

"Hmm. Let's see. No. There's no Hagen."

"Okay, thank you."

"You got it," Control said.

Her new section chief had failed, Dawn Warner thought, shaking her head as she went back into her bathroom.

"Shocker," she said to herself as she took some skin cream out of a drawer.

They'd covered their tracks pretty well in Casper, she thought as she cracked the lid of moisturizer.

Lotion splattered the base of her makeup mirror as she slammed the bottle onto the counter.

"Shit," she said.

But maybe not well enough, she thought.

What if Hagen was in Cheyenne right now?

She took a deep breath as she stood and went to find her phone again.

She had to do it. It meant heading back to DC early but that didn't matter. There was no other choice.

One last grisly push and then they'd be home free.

She dialed the number.

The line picked up.

"Westergaard," said a voice.

58

The rest stop was near the Colorado border and as the sun set, Kit and Gannon were sitting at a concrete picnic table, eating ice cream.

They'd stopped to get gas and were going to get a burger when they saw that the tourist center ice cream shop had gelato.

"Funny, I've never had double scoops of chocolate chocolate chunk in a waffle cone for dinner before," Kit said.

"I'm seriously considering finding out how well it pairs with a bottle of Jack Daniels after making that left turn under that overpass," Gannon said as he bit into a chocolate chunk.

"I hear you," Kit said, nibbling the edges of her waffle cone. "So you're thinking what, Mike? Free association time. Start chucking out whatever you got. Wild speculations. I don't care. What the hell do you think this is? Some serious upper echelon top-secret-clearance behind-the-curtain shit that involves both FBI pressure to get me off the case and now even the military?"

When Gannon pulled his face out of his waffle trough, it was comically chocolate-covered.

"Hey," he cried. "You really can read minds."

Kit laughed.

"I think Tracy was flown up to Grand Teton from that air force base. That explains the time crunch. And she was flown up by someone with clearance. That's an actual nuclear weapon silo base that no one can get onto unless they have the right colored badge."

"I was thinking the same thing," Gannon said. "Now, how are we going to find out who drove in at 10:27 p.m. that Tuesday night? Ask the guard? Good luck with that."

"I know," Kit said. "Maybe we should put off trying to open that can of worms right now. I think we need to shift focus. And I think I know the perfect way how."

"You do, huh? I have to hear this," Gannon said, wiping some chocolate off his chin with a napkin.

Gannon watched as Kit chucked the remnant of her ice cream into the trash bin and came back.

"I never did it before, but Dennis did it once," she said. "He knew a guy in the NSA, and one time Dennis called him and he got Dennis some stuff. Some intel stuff. It was against every rule known to man but he did it anyway."

"What kind of stuff was Dennis looking for?"

"A facial recognition scan on one of the most dan-

gerous serial killers we ever caught. His name was
Rodrigo Vargas and he preyed solely on kids. We
had him on a liquor store security video in Rhode
Island but we couldn't identify him because he was
totally off the grid, totally in the shadows. Turned out
he was a woodsman from South America. He lived
under overpasses, along railroad tracks."

"Then you caught him?"

"Yes. The file Dennis got from his NSA friend
said Vargas was in Mexico. In Juarez living in a run-
down hotel. Dennis and I went down by ourselves
and found him and brought him back."

"How'd that happen? Finding him I mean. NSA
satellites or something?"

"No, I don't think they need satellites anymore,
Mike. They have facial recognition technology that
is scary and it's tapped into not just the internet but
virtually every public or private video feed on earth
with a connection to the internet."

"Comforting," Gannon said. "Then what happened?"

"Vargas hung himself ten minutes before his arraignment."

"Uplifting story. So what are you thinking now?"
Gannon said. "Give the NSA guy another call?"

"It's a violation of the highest order but since we
hit a dead end with Tracy, I could call him and ask
him to put the photo of the first victim, the Asian
woman, into the NSA facial recognition system."

"What are you hesitating about? Let's do it. Full
speed ahead. Call this NSA spook."

"I will but there's a glitch. If he has the info, I'll

need to be in a SCIF to receive it. You know what a SCIF is?"

"An intel top secret room, right? A cone of silence room for super-duper extra-sneaky spy bullshit. They had them in Iraq."

"Right. Well, every major FBI office has one. There's actually one in Denver. That's the closest. We could go to the one in Denver."

"So, what's the problem?" Gannon said as he bit off the bottom of the cone. "Denver's what? A half day's drive south?"

"What's the problem?" Kit said, shrugging. "Take your pick. First, I need a pretense to go in there. Second, I'm supposed to be on leave. Also, I'm supposed to be in DC tomorrow morning for that meeting, lest we forget. And you said that we're probably already on their radar.

"Mike," she said, looking him right in the eye, "this NSA backdoor move is highly, highly, highly illegal. I get busted, I'm not just getting fired. I'm probably going to jail. Dennis's friend, too, probably."

"You did say this is the Denver office though, right?" Gannon said. "Rocky Mountain High town? Think about it. The Bureau's greatest minds are in Denver? Not likely. Besides, you're a hotshot profiler. The one in the paper who was recently shot no less. And don't forget, you're quite an attractive woman, which tends to open doors all by itself for some strange reason, at least when men are around. We can come up with a story to get you in and out of there."

"I hope you're right," she said. "But it certainly won't be easy."

Gannon looked out as a restored old fifties pickup went past, the sleek silver skin of the Airstream camper behind it glittering in the sunset.

"Denver it is," he said, winking as he lapped at the ice cream that began dripping off his wrist. "This is some summer road trip, huh?"

"Oh, yeah. The best," Kit said. "Serial killers to the right, some mysterious corrupt government cover-up situation to the left. Who needs Disneyland?"

"Exactly," Gannon said with a wink. "This is more kicks than Route 66."

PART THREE

THINGS TO DO IN DENVER

59

The fourteen-passenger Dassault Falcon 900LX left out of San Francisco International at a little after seven o'clock in the morning. Heading due east, it seemed like it had only just reached its 50,000-foot cruising ceiling when it began its long bullet-like parabolic descent into Cheyenne Regional.

They were beginning to taxi in off the main runway when Westergaard got the beep on his laptop.

He was laid out half-asleep in one of the aircraft's aft cabin sofas, and he sat up and looked out the porthole window.

The text that he read quickly said the target wasn't in Wyoming anymore. The satellite had picked up Hagen's rental car on the move over the border in Colorado. The ground support team out of the base in Colorado Springs was already rerouting the vehicles to Denver.

Westergaard rose from the sofa and quickly came forward. Snoozing in the luxury jet's bespoke club chairs he passed by were the four other men in his unit. Large and broad-shouldered with headphones on, they could have been a professional sports team resting up before an important away game.

"Change of plans," he said to the pilot. "We need to head south now. Can you get us to Denver without refueling? Time is of the essence. We need to move as quickly as possible."

The Falcon's pilot frowned up at Westergaard with his scruffy flabby round face. Hollywood liked to show American pilots as charming devil-may-care masculine types but this one was much more Tom Arnold than Tom Cruise. He gave a walrus yawn as he checked his electronic instruments.

"Yes," he finally said with a sigh. "We can do that. Let me call the tower."

Westergaard yawned himself and spread out his lanky arms as he walked back to his seat. Tall and slim as an Olympic swimmer, the thirty-five-year-old South African had to duck to keep the top of his six-foot-two head from brushing the jet's low bulkhead.

"What now, Chief? What's up?" said Maniscalco as he sat back down on the couch.

Westergaard resumed his repose and took a deep, even breath as he closed his eyes.

"Boss? Yoo-hoo? Boss?" Maniscalco said.

Even with one leg, Maniscalco was brutally efficient in action. Especially with nip-and-tuck dirty work, which he actually seemed to enjoy.

But the New Yorker's nervous energy before an operation was a constant irritant in the extreme, Westergaard thought. *Why couldn't he just sleep like the rest of them?*

"Chief?" Maniscalco said, chewing away at some gum now. It was Nicorette, of course. When the jittery fast-talking mercenary wasn't smoking or chewing something, he was jiggling his leg or aggravatingly tapping at things.

Westergaard listened to the incessant chewing for as long as he could and then finally opened his eyes and looked over at the man with disdain.

Blond and pale and clean-shaven with slightly bulging brown eyes, Westergaard's stern yet refined countenance looked on virtually everything with a kind of arrogant disdain.

"What's the word, Skip?" Maniscalco said, blowing a bubble.

Instead of answering him, Westergaard lifted the tablet with the text on it and handed it across the aisle.

"Where now? Denver?" he said, chewing away.

Westergaard didn't reply.

He was already back asleep.

60

On I-25 driving south with the traffic north of Denver, Gannon rolled his neck as he slipped his coffee out of the drink holder.

There was early-morning rush hour traffic around him on the wide three-lane highway, and it was getting fuller and fuller by the moment.

A glossy black glass generic corporate office building went past on his right, then some indifferent high-rises. Except for the immense line of Rocky Mountains in the close right-hand distance, they could have been on the New Jersey Turnpike, he thought.

He looked over at Kit busily texting on her phone.

Overall the plan seemed to be coming along pretty good so far.

Kit had made contact with Braddock's NSA buddy the night before at their motel. The man's name was

Ian Parker and despite Kit's worrying, the senior intelligence analyst had been surprisingly receptive about helping them. Especially when Kit had told him truthfully that the facial recognition ID on the first victim they were looking for had to do with getting to the murky bottom of Braddock's death.

After that Gannon had gone out and done a little shopping at a Walmart to get a knapsack and a few hardware items to put inside of it. Kit wasn't the only one who liked to be prepared. His just-in-case emergency pack was sitting on the floor of the back seat.

There had also been another spot of good luck. After doing some research, it turned out Kit actually knew someone in the Denver office, another female agent named Amy Cargill who Kit had worked fairly closely with in LA.

The current plan was for Kit to call Cargill when they got closer. It would be far easier and less suspicious for Kit to get inside the facility if she had a friendly established face to smooth things over at the front desk.

Gannon clicked the blower fan on a little higher as he listened to Kit text. Then he clicked it back. He thought about switching on the XM radio but then decided not to. He drove in the center lane, listening to the steady hum of the tires all around until he couldn't take it anymore.

"So how we looking?" he finally said.

Kit thumbed at the screen with a loud release of breath and put down the phone. She rubbed at her eye with the heel of her hand.

"All I need is to get into the SCIF and type in the code Ian just sent me and the info will show up on the SCIF screen," she said. "Since I already downloaded the encrypted format protocol for the thumb drive he sent me last night, we're looking good to go."

"Okay, it's all set, then. Good," Gannon said. "We'll get to the city and you call your friend Amy and get in there and we're ready to rock."

"Sure we are," Kit said without much enthusiasm. "If I get into the SCIF, that is."

"You'll get into it, Kit," Gannon said. "Just play it the way we've set it up. Just follow the plan. Keep it short and keep it simple."

She stared out at the mountains for a moment. Gannon looked with her. The sun out from behind a cloud was on the snowcapped peaks now and the vista was stunning, majestic, celestial.

It didn't look like the Jersey Turnpike anymore, Gannon thought, blinking.

"Easy for you to say," Kit finally said as she lifted her Starbucks.

She took a sip of coffee and set it back down.

"You're not going inside," she said.

61

Dawn Warner's corner office in DC was on the fifth floor of the neoclassical Department of Justice building just under the base of its southwest pediment.

At thirty-three minutes after ten Eastern Standard Time she stood at its window and looked out between the fluted columns over Constitution Avenue at the Smithsonian Museum's scalloped dome.

Then she shut the big heavy drapes.

On the way back to her desk, she popped the two Excedrin gel tabs in her hand, dry swallowing them. She didn't know if maybe she wasn't drinking enough water or something before takeoffs, but she'd acquired a nice sharp altitude headache on the plane coming in this morning from the Cape.

She took off her jacket and hung it on the back of a tufted leather chair. She buzzed her secretary, Roberta, to let in Fitzgerald and Harris.

"We're in here," Warner said, pointing over at her suite's conference room.

Littering the long varnished mahogany table were computers and secure phones and cords. Behind them on the back wall of the dim windowless room was a whiteboard bookended by the two huge and bright American flags Dawn Warner used as background for her TV appearances.

She kicked shut the door as they all slipped on their hands-free mics. Her FBI men took off their own jackets before they all sat before the glowing terminals.

"Do it," she said to Patrick.

The tall FBI man nodded as he leaned forward and pressed on the speaker of the secure link phone.

"Red team, bring me up to speed," she said.

"We are inbound from Denver International ten minutes," Westergaard said.

"Las Vegas, are you there?" Warner said.

They had a UAV over the city now. Eighteen thousand feet above Denver, a high-altitude surveillance MQ-9 Reaper was traveling slow and steady in a wide east-west ellipsis. She could see the slowly moving feed of it on Fitzgerald's computer screen.

"Yes, ma'am. Right here," said a deep Southern voice.

"Good. How's the weather report around the city looking?"

"Crystal clear all day, ma'am. Perfect conditions."

"What's your name, Las Vegas?"

"Jhett."

"Jhett," Warner mouthed, rolling her eyes at Fitzgerald and Harris, making her FBI men chuckle silently.

"You're all linked up with the red team there, um, Jhett? Everybody has a good connection?"

"Audio and visual is clicked tight here," Jhett said.

"Red team, confirm," Warner said.

"Affirmative. Looking good on this end," Westergaard said.

"Okay, good," Warner said, looking from screen to screen. "Give me a look in, Jhett. Zoom in and show all of us the car."

The reaper feed went down and down and then there was a white Armada flowing on a highway.

"That's Interstate 25, yes?" said Westergaard.

"Affirmative," Jhett said. "Southbound."

"Where do we think their destination is? Any clue? The city?" Westergaard said.

"We have no idea," Dawn Warner said. "Hagen is running wild so get on them as quickly as humanly possible."

62

It was half past nine when Gannon brought them off the interstate at the Park Avenue exit into downtown Denver.

The sloping ramp of the exit passed up over the opposite lanes of the highway and some freight train tracks and then came down alongside Coors Field, the Colorado Rockies baseball stadium.

There was already some more commuter traffic where it dumped them out onto 22nd Street, and they had to slow to enter it and then slow again as they came to a red light.

At the next block to the left of where they waited was a cluster of people and tents lined along the sidewalk in front of a brick building. Gannon thought it was some kind of line of customers waiting for something —a new phone or concert tickets—until he noticed the shelter sign above the brick building's front door.

As he watched, a ragged bearded man sitting out on the sidewalk stood and began hopping on one foot as he pushed a junk-piled shopping cart. He seemed to be yelling at the sky.

When the light turned, they went through the intersection and at the next block, they made a right onto Arapahoe Street. They passed a new five-story residential building with terraces, a gym, an outdoor parking lot.

They had to slow on the next block into a single lane as they passed a cordoned-off line of idling cement trucks about to pour a foundation for yet another new building. Gannon stopped to let a couple of hardhats cross before they made the left onto 19th Street.

They'd only come one block south when Kit turned and pointed out the windshield.

"There it is," she said.

When Gannon put on the clicker, a horn honked behind him. He pulled over behind an already parked UPS truck.

She didn't have to point, Gannon thought, looking up at the behemoth of the white stone federal building a block to the east.

It was twenty stories tall and a block wide. The ugly Excel grid of windows in its pale facade gave it a look of a storm drain carved from a block of marble.

What was the name of the architectural style? Brutalist? Gannon thought. It was brutal all right. The

looming white stone structure looked like a mash-up
of a giant Rubik's Cube and a mausoleum.

"I don't know if this is going to work, Mike," Kit
said as they sat there listening to the clicker tick. "I
really don't."

Gannon opened his mouth to say something. Then
he closed it.

Just pregame jitters, he thought.

He looked out at the passing traffic. When he
looked back up at the building, the bright white
clouds in the cyan-blue sky above it looked unreal-
istically perfect, like they'd been drawn by a Pixar
cartoonist.

He put the transmission into Park and then folded
his hands and put them in his lap.

"Can I ask you a question, Kit?" he said.

She looked at him.

"Remember that stuff you told me about human
nature when we were driving to Casper?"

"Yes," she said.

"That wasn't just your partner who came up with
all that. A bunch of that was you, right?"

Kit looked down at the footwell.

Gannon nodded.

"It's because you care, Kit. Care about doing your
job right. Someone kills someone else, you ain't sitting still until something's done about it no matter
what. You care about what's right. And you care about
what's wrong."

Gannon reached over and held her hand.

"Me, too, Kit," he said. "That's why I'm here with
you. All I know is that you're in the right here. You're
doing your job. It's your bosses that are pulling some

kind of shenanigans. You and me are just here to un-pull them."

Kit finally squeezed his hand back and let it go.

"Short and simple," she said and then pulled open her door.

63

"And target one is on foot," Agent Harris said.

"Yes, I see, Harris, since I'm standing here beside you," Dawn Warner said. "But thanks for the running commentary anyway. Your eye for detail is unerring."

On the screen Warner watched Kit crossing 19th Street.

"What the hell is she doing?" Warner said as she began pacing between the two flags. "Where is she headed? What's that building there?"

"That's a Greyhound bus station," Fitzgerald said.

"What in the hell? She's going to ride the dog now?"

"No, look. She's heading south," Harris said.

"Las Vegas, zoom back a tad," Warner said.

The slowly panning camera of the reaper backed up.

"What else is around there?" Warner said to Fitzgerald. "Are those courthouses?"

"Yes, there are several courthouses," he said, clicking at his computer. "And let's see. It says there's an army recruiting center nearby."

"Wait, look. She's on... What's that? Champa Street? Now she's crossing west. She seems to be heading to that white building there."

"Holy shit," Fitzgerald said. "That's the federal building. That's the FBI Denver office building."

Dawn Warner felt her headache spike up through the top of her skull as she watched Kit walk the length of the block and go inside.

The three of them, still staring at the FBI building, suddenly jumped as there was a soft knock on the conference room door.

Warner sped across the room.

"What is it?" she said, cracking it to see her secretary standing there.

"It's Francis Sinclair," she said, handing in a phone. "He wants to talk to you."

She snatched the phone and banged the door closed.

"What is it?" she said.

"Hagen is texting me," Sinclair said. "She's saying she's in Denver at the FBI office."

No shit, Sherlock, Warner thought, closing her eyes.

"And?" she said.

"She wants to know if we can set up a Skype so she can still attend our 'meeting.'"

Dawn Warner squinted.

What the hell was this? Was Hagen on the level? Was she really coming in? Or playing more games?

Well, she was definitely playing some kind of game or why the hell was she in Wyoming poking around?

But maybe she'd hit a wall in Cheyenne, Warner thought.

They'd covered their tracks there. They could have gotten lucky.

But then again, she'd seen Hagen's records. Her law school grades. She seemed pretty clever. Especially for a field agent. Was it just some kind of a bluff?

Warner stared at the slowly panning reaper footage over the FBI building with her steady brown eyes.

Shit, she thought. There was no way to know.

"Hello, you still there?" Sinclair said.

"Set up the meeting. Set up the Skype," Warner said. "Keep me posted moment to moment. Do you understand? Moment to moment. Use two phones. I want to know exactly what's going on."

"Las Vegas, do we have eyes on the Armada?" Warner said after she hung up.

"Yes. I have the other camera on it. It's just sitting there. I'll mark it on my GIS map so you can track it."

As she watched the screen, a blue box appeared around the SUV.

"Excellent," Warner said. "Red team, where the hell are you?"

"Inserting into downtown. We see the marked Armada on screen. We will have eyes on it in a moment."

"Jhett, can you mark the red team on the GIS map, as well?"

Warner looked on screen where red boxes appeared around vehicles heading off the interstate. There were three of them. A Mercedes Sprinter van, a Chevy Suburban, and an ambulance.

She smiled at the sight of the white-and-orange ambulance. Nothing on earth beat an ambulance for discreetly taking a subject off the street.

"Okay, good. I see you. I want two cars on the Armada like static cling. You get me full court press. And Westergaard, you set up an over watch perimeter around the FBI building."

"An over watch around the FBI building?" Westergaard said.

"Is there an echo in here?" Dawn Warner said.

"Understood," Westergaard said.

64

The conference room off the white-collar squad bull-pen on the FBI building's eighth floor was decorated with generic office inspirational prints about team-work and perseverance.

"Amy, I can't thank you enough for all this," Kit said as she laid her bag down on the table.

Her old friend, Amy Cargill, flicked on the over-head light, then took a silly bow.

"Your wish is my command," she said.

Kit smiled. She had always liked Amy. Unlike most agents, she hated the field and actually loved account-ing and took every back-office gig she could grab.

She'd gained some weight in the three years since they'd last seen each other, but it seemed to suit her. She definitely seemed happier.

"Your boss really wants you at this meeting, huh?" Amy said.

"Apparently," Kit said, slipping out her Mac Pro.

"On your break from a shooting? I mean, really? He sounds like a real jerk."

"Well, now that you mention it," Kit stage-whispered back and they shared a laugh.

"Coffee?" Amy said.

Kit lifted the navy blue YETI travel cup in her hand.

"No, I have my yucky kale smoothie right here, thank you very much."

"You can take the girl out of LA, huh," Amy said, giving her a wink. "I already gave you the Wi-Fi. Anything else, Kit?"

"No, I'm set. You're the best, Amy."

Kit smiled at her old friend's back as she left, feeling somewhat guilty. She hated telling a lie. She looked down at her phone vibrating atop the cheap table and saw it was Sinclair calling back.

Well, at least to a good person, she thought as she picked it up.

65

"Kit, hey. Skype is in the building here. How's things on your end?" Sinclair said.

"Getting there," Kit said, folding open her laptop and plugging it in.

"Great," Sinclair said as Kit typed in the office Wi-Fi password Amy had given her.

Kit clicked on the link that was waiting on the website and suddenly Sinclair appeared on the screen, waving at her from behind his desk. She looked at his tie. His hairstyle was even shorter and blander now. He'd gotten it cut, she realized.

"There you are, Kit. Ta-da, the magic of modern technology, huh?" he said.

She looked at his eyes. There were bags under them. He was aging right before her eyes.

"Woo-hoo," Kit said quietly, turning off her phone as she sat.

"So tell me," Sinclair said, putting his chin on his palm. "How the heck did you end up in Denver, Kit? Last time we spoke, you had your head in a paint tray at home or something."

"I'm glad you asked, Francis," Kit said, grinning as she stared into his eyes. "It's a funny story. The second I hung up with you, an old girlfriend of mine called and asked me to be her maid of honor. She lives over here in Colorado Springs, and her original maid of honor bailed at the last second. Pain in my butt, but an hour later, I was on a plane. I thought I could get back in time, but I missed my flight. Can you believe all that?"

The blank expression on Sinclair's stressed face seemed to indicate a no to that one.

But he liked to lie, too, didn't he? Kit thought. *Through his shiny perfect teeth.*

"Get out! A last-second maid of honor? That's something else. But wait, you weren't invited to the wedding originally?"

"Oh, I was invited, but I decided not to go what with getting shot and all," Kit said, nodding. "But she was a good friend once and she was in a bind."

She looked Sinclair in the eye.

"You know how important that is, right, Francis? Loyalty to friends?" she said.

"Of course. I get it," the weasel said, looking away.

Yeah, right, Kit thought. *You don't get shit.*

Sinclair checked his watch.

Not a Rolex yet, she noted, but he was trying, wasn't he?

"Listen, Kit. Turns out you're not the only one running late to the meeting. It's actually going to be another half an hour before the rest of the crew gets here."

"Perfect," Kit said. "I'll grab a cup of coffee. Reconnect at, let's say, nine forty-five? Or text me if it's sooner. How's that sound?"

"Um," he said.

"Um what, Francis?"

"Nothing. Okay. Perfect. Half an hour," he said. "I'll text you."

Kit stood and took a deep breath.

Phase one, check mark, she thought.

Now for the fuzzy part.

Amy wasn't at her desk when Kit got to it, but when she turned she saw her friend coming down the cubicle lane with a new ream of printer paper in her hands.

"Hey, Kit? What's up?"

"Amy," Kit said checking her watch. "I hate to bother you even more, but it turns out there's actually some classified information my team needs to share with me. You guys have a SCIF here, right?"

Amy blinked at her. There was a puzzled look on her face.

"Yes, I think so. I heard it's up on fourteen next to the SAC's office. Your case is going that deep, huh? Counterintelligence deep?"

Kit nodded.

"What's the protocol for using the SCIF? Do we need to talk to the SAC or something? I've never even been in one."

"I have no idea," Amy said. "I never had to use it myself. Let's stick our heads into my boss's office and see."

66

Down on the street on the corner of 17th and Champa, Gannon sat at a red light, lightly drumming his fingers on the Armada's wheel.

He watched as a young bearded dude pedaling a city rental bike went by in the crosswalk followed by a nice-looking young mom in yoga pants pushing a stroller. Beyond them on the southeast corner, a helpful city worker in a neon-yellow jacket was changing out the bag on the corner trash barrel.

"I could live here," Gannon said to himself with a nod as the light went green and he wheeled a slow turn past a corner pool hall.

Declan and I could buy an apartment here and move in and never look back.

From the moment Kit had gone into the federal building, Gannon had started looping and re-looping Denver's central business district, and he was actually quite impressed. The light was spectacular, for one thing. It was extremely clean and easy to move around, and there was parking everywhere. It was mostly new buildings, but if you liked architecture, there was an old opera house and several old hotels and banks and the courthouses.

The square grid blocks reminded Gannon of his old stomping grounds of Manhattan, only with about ninety-eight thousand percent less traffic. It had all the shopping and the feel of a real city but unlike his old hometown, it wasn't falling apart at the seams. He didn't spot even one rat.

He was on 14th Street coming along the opera house pavilion when he lifted his cup and noticed he was out of coffee. He was right by the opera house entrance and when he looked forward, he saw the neon sign of a coffee cup in a shop window up ahead.

"You have to be kidding me," Gannon said as he saw there was an actual free parking spot right out in front of it.

Gannon laughed as he parked and got out, trying to imagine the odds of finding a free parking spot on Broadway out in front of Lincoln Center in the middle of a workday.

He was heading back out of the coffee joint with a large paper cup of Italian roast, still marveling at how clean the restroom was, when he looked through the glass door and suddenly halted.

Then instead of heading out, he turned on his heel and decided to get back on line again.

Because something was wrong.

Across the street, there was the guy in an EMT uniform and there was something not right about him.

He was a short broad-shouldered guy just standing there with his wide back to the coffee shop.

Gannon had to stop himself from snapping his finger as he suddenly realized it.

"Can I help you…again?" said the same coffee clerk he'd dealt with two minutes before.

Gannon stood there wide-eyed, staring at him. Then he glanced out of the corner of his eye again back out through the glass.

It was his build, Gannon thought. Five-seven or so with the same broad shoulders and the hunched way he stood. It was him. It was actually him.

The guy from the strip club parking lot video he and Kit had watched over and over again.

"Sir? Can I help you?" said the clerk again.

Why in the name of all things holy is Tracy Sandhurst's killer across the damn street?

"Yeah, uh, you guys have donuts?" Gannon said.

"Sure do. What kind?" the clerk said.

"Forget it," Gannon said as he turned and headed quickly out the door.

The fake EMT guy started moving just as Gannon came back out the door. He began to walk in parallel with him across the street.

Every and all of Gannon's doubts were erased as he watched him walk in his peripheral vision. He had the same slight hitch-and-roll gait, the same slight sideways swing of his right foot.

Gannon was climbing back into the Armada when he saw Tracy's killer get into the white-and-orange ambulance across the street to his rear on the corner. The ambulance had just pulled past him and he was just about to pull out behind it when he glanced back into the mirror and noticed the idling silver Suburban on the corner of the next block directly behind him.

There were two formidable-looking men in the front seat. The black guy driving had a full beard and a Detroit Tigers ball cap and next to him was a square-jawed bald white guy.

Gannon looked at the white guy's no-nonsense expression. His bald head resembled that of a ball-peen hammer. They were both wearing sunglasses so you couldn't tell where they were looking.

Couple of heavy-duty customers, Gannon thought, taking in their aura of menace. Plus at least two more in the ambulance. Two teams.

If not more.

Gannon tapped his fingers on the wheel, feeling an actual chill in his spine as he realized what the hell he was in the middle of now.

"Here we go again," he said as he turned the Armada's engine over with a roar.

67

Maniscalco had just Zippo-ed up another Marlboro when he got the beep from Westergaard.

"Where are you now?" his South African boss said in his snotty accent.

"We're in Canada," Maniscalco yelled as he clacked the Zippo closed. "Where do you think? Did the link go down? Me and Davies are in front of him back near the highway. Patchell and Davenport are behind him. We keep leapfrogging him. He just keeps driving the hell around."

"Wait, he's slowing down," Davies said from behind the ambulance's wheel.

"He make you?" Westergaard said.

"Give me a second with all the questions here. Jeez," Maniscalco said, turning as they pulled over.

"Shit, you're right. He's stopping now. What is that place, Charlie?" he said to Davies.

"I don't know. There's a neon cross," Davies said. "A church? No, it's a homeless shelter. Look, he's parked right out in front of it. Now he's getting out."

"What's this clown doing?" Maniscalco said as they watched him head inside. "Making a fricking donation?"

"Get back out on foot, Maniscalco," Westergaard said.

"Me again? On foot. I only got one! Get Davies to do it. I'm the gimp, remember?"

"Manny's right. Send in Davies," Davenport said from the other car that had pulled over across the street from the shelter. "Davies could pass for a stumble bum easy."

"Hold up," Maniscalco said. "None of us can go in. Are you kidding me? It's all bums in there. He'll see us in a second."

"Shut up," Westergaard commanded. "All of you. I don't care. One of you get the hell in there now."

"I got this," Patchell said in his Texas accent from the Suburban.

"That's the spirit, Patchell," Maniscalco said. "Show us how it's done."

They watched the six-foot-three bald mercenary get out of the Suburban and cross the street and head inside. He wasn't in there two minutes before they saw the people running out. There had to be twenty homeless men yelling and laughing as they ran.

"What in the hell did you do, Patchell?" Maniscalco said. "Flash your johnson at them? Why are they all running?"

"How should I know?" the Texan said.

Maniscalco hopped out of the ambulance and entered into the fray of the running men on the sidewalk. He almost clotheslined one of the homeless guys as he rode him down to the concrete against a fence.

"What the hell, man? What the hell?" the bum said.

He was a skinny little man. He was about sixty years old and smelled like piss and had maybe two teeth.

"PD," Maniscalco said. "What the hell are you doing? Why are you all running?"

"For the money, man," the bum said.

"What money?"

"White homeboy just came in the shelter handing out hundreds if we race around the block. Whoever wins gonna get two thousand," he said.

"You have to be shitting me," Maniscalco said, letting the guy go. "You picking this up?" Maniscalco said. "You watching this skid row marathon with that eye in the sky? I'm not Sun Tzu like you, Westergaard, but I'm thinking this is some sort of diversionary tactic here."

"Manny's right," Patchell said from inside. "He made us."

"How can you be sure?" Westergaard said.

"Because there's some drunk old dude in here wearing the target's gray suit jacket," Patchell said.

68

Dawn Warner sat at the conference table staring at her phone.

"Hello," Sinclair said from it.

"What's going on?" she said.

"I'm still waiting for my team here to get the meeting going."

"Where's Hagen?"

"She went to get a cup of coffee."

"You don't have eyes on her?"

"Not right this second."

"Is the Skype connection on?"

"Yes, but it's just showing her empty chair."

"For how long?"

"Ten, twenty minutes now. Why? What's up?" Sinclair said.

"Moment to moment, remember, Francis? Moment to moment! Twenty minutes? Are you crazy?"

"I'm doing everything you said," Sinclair said. "I can't have a meeting without my team, can I? First you said she wasn't coming, so I told my guys to forget the meeting. My closest guys are up in Baltimore, and they're stuck in traffic coming back."

Warner felt it in her gut then. Something was off. Hagen was bluffing them. The bold little bitch was doing something, playing some kind of game. What kind she didn't know. Only that it was bad news.

"Get on her now, Sinclair. Call her. You need to maintain eye contact with her in that building at all freaking times."

"Why?"

"Because I said so. Listen closely to the words that come out of my mouth and do what I say. That's your job. I want her in front of that Skype camera now."

"Okay, okay. I'm texting her."

Dawn Warner picked up a whiteboard marker and began stabbing its cap into her palm as she paced back and forth.

"What's up, Boss?" said Fitzgerald sheepishly.

"Screw it," Dawn Warner said as she began to stab the marker repeatedly into her thigh.

Her gut didn't lie. Had never failed her. Twenty minutes was too long. Her gut was telling her they needed to talk to Denver. Dicey or not, they needed to bring Denver in on this.

She suddenly flung the marker across the conference table as hard as she could. It sailed off the other end and clicked off a filing cabinet before it landed in the corner wastebasket with a bright clang.

She hit the button on the phone for her secretary. "Yes?"

"Roberta, get me the Denver Special Agent in Charge now."

69

The claustrophobic inside of the bright antiseptic white-walled SCIF had the feel of a high-tech confessional.

Or a high-tech prison cell, Kit thought grimly as she clicked shut the thin metal door behind her.

She turned back and stood for a moment looking at the desk against the SCIF's glowing white wall. There was a wide-screen iMac computer on top of it, and in front of the desk was a cheap black leather rolling office chair.

It seemed normal enough. She tried to reassure herself. It looked fine, like a cubicle.

In the belly of a flying saucer, she thought, trying to tamp down her rapidly building panic.

She forced herself to walk over and sit in the chair. As she looked down, she saw there was a wastepaper basket under the desk with two empty Poland Spring water bottles lying in it.

She tried to piece together the significance of them and, failing to do so, finally reached out and slowly laid her fingers atop the wireless mouse in front of the iMac screen.

She instantly lifted her hand off the mouse as the NSA eagle and key logo appeared, filling the wide screen.

She sat examining it closely. She'd seen the logo before, of course, but for the first time, she'd noticed how angry the expression on the eagle's face was. And how sharp the talons that gripped the silver key seemed.

Beneath the seal, along the bottom of the screen, there was a black box. It had a blinking white cursor inside of it, and beside the box on the left, it read,

DESIGNATION:

Shitting bricks, Kit thought as she took out the paper she had written on that morning.

She typed in the code Dennis's NSA friend, Ian Parker, had given her.

Then she squeezed her eyes shut as she placed the pad of her right forefinger to the slick white plastic of the mouse and slowly pushed down until she finally heard the click.

When she opened her eyes again slightly, the NSA angry eagle and DESIGNATION screen were gone. They had been replaced by a new white screen with the word PROCESSING in the top left-hand corner followed by several blinking black dots.

She stared at the flashing dots, feeling like Alice free-falling down the rabbit hole.

It was connecting to the mother lode, she thought. *All the data on earth.*

Then suddenly as she watched there was a flash, and a grid of small photograph boxes began filling the screen. On each one was their first victim with a box around her face. There were dates along the tops of them. GPS coordinates.

Kit felt hot and like she was going to vomit. Then the grid finally stopped.

There were about twenty pages of images and she scrolled down with the mouse until she got to the last, most recent one.

In it was the victim with someone. It looked like a man, but the image was small so she wasn't completely sure.

She felt her heart begin beating harder and faster when she saw the date on it was three days before the body was found.

She clicked the image to enlarge it and saw that it was in fact a man with their victim.

"Holy fricking shit!" Kit said as she stared.

Because it was a man Kit recognized.

In fact, it was a man everybody in the world recognized.

70

"Hi, Harry," Dawn Warner said as the Denver SAC got on the line.

His name was Harry Wheaton and his file said he was a former Mississippi college football player and former marine helicopter pilot. She looked at the man's picture from his file now on her screen. He was forty-two and square-jawed and was actually quite attractive.

I wouldn't toss that out of bed for eating crackers, Warner thought.

"Thanks for taking my call right away, Harry," Warner said. "I hope I'm not keeping you from something."

"No, not at all," Wheaton said. "Glad to talk to you. What can I do for the Department of Justice this morning?"

Wow, he didn't even have the Walmart hick accent she was expecting, Warner thought. He sounded normal.

"I'm glad you asked, Harry," Dawn Warner said pleasantly as she stood and started a loop around the conference table. At the other side of it, she knelt at the wastepaper basket and picked out the whiteboard marker.

"Harry," she said as she began to twirl the marker between her fingers and continued her walk. "I'm trying to, well, I guess I'm trying to get your take on something. On an agent I believe is in your offices today. Special Agent Kit Hagen."

"Kit Hagen?" Wheaton said. "Yes, she's here. She was just in here with me a minute ago."

Warner's antennae, already up, went suddenly way, way up.

Why would Hagen be talking to the SAC? she thought.

"She's an impressive agent, especially after that tragedy in Wyoming," Wheaton continued. "I mean, to bounce back like that so soon. Truly, I tip my hat to her."

"Well, Harry," Warner said. "This is confidential, extremely confidential, but Special Agent Hagen is acting somewhat erratically. She's supposed to be home on leave here in Washington, DC, but obviously she's not. She's, well... She's sick, Harry. Mentally unbalanced. We think she's suffering from PTSD from the shooting."

"You've got to be kidding me," Wheaton said. "She seemed absolutely fine. I spoke to her not five minutes ago. What the hell is going on?"

"It's bad, Harry. Trust me. A family member contacted us yesterday. He said Hagen drove over to his house out of the blue and that she was acting very strangely. She told him she wanted him to have her apartment and car if anything were to happen to her. He asked her what the hell was she talking about and she took off. We spoke to a Bureau psychologist, Harry. They think Hagen's risk of suicide couldn't be at a more critical level."

"This is a shock," Wheaton said. "Agent Hagen was just in here. She said she had to receive some classified information. She's in our SCIF right now."

The marker dropped from Warner's hand.

In the SCIF! Warner thought.

That was it! The NSA files. Hagen was going through Echelon. Going through the files for something. And in the damn SCIF!

"Hello? Are you still there?"

"Some classified information?" Dawn Warner finally spat out.

"Yes. I mean, I guess. That's what she said. But that isn't true? She's mentally unstable?"

Warner closed her eyes. They needed to grab her. They were right outside. They needed to grab her right now.

"Yes," she said. "It's worse than we thought. Harry, listen. Do you know if she's armed?"

"I don't, but I would assume so."

"And she's still in there? I mean, she didn't leave the SCIF, did she?"

"No, she didn't leave. It's right around the corner near my office and I would have noticed. Let me ask my secretary. Hold on."

Please, Warner prayed as thcy waited.

"No," Harry said. "My secretary says she's still in there."

Thank you, Warner said to herself, pumping her fist.

"What do you want me to do? Do you want me to get some agents and get her out of there?" Harry said.

"No, Harry. She's armed. Don't go near her. When she comes out, just act like everything is fine. Just stall her and keep her in the building. I'm actually getting on the horn right now with the Bureau doctor. We already called the nearest military hospital. They have a team on the way.

"They have people for this, Harry. Specialists. Kit needs to be hospitalized but we need to do this delicately. Let the professionals handle it."

"I don't know what to say," Wheaton said. "This is just…"

"Tragic. Exactly, Harry. But it's going to be fine. Just keep your personnel away from her and give the specialists I send in as much latitude as they need. They'll be arriving in the lobby forthwith."

71

The thumb drive with all the photographs on it was tucked in beneath the plastic of Kit's temporary ID pass as she came out of the SCIF room into the corridor of the federal building's fourteenth floor.

She held her breath. The hall was empty. Silent. She let her breath out slowly, then looked up at the black plastic bubble camera above her.

She stood for a moment, rooted there. Wondering who was watching her, wondering if they knew, wondering how much time she had.

Move! she thought.

She went left down the hall through the dead fluorescent lighting. She suddenly noticed all the grids everywhere. The grid of industrial carpet tiles. The grid of acoustic ceiling tiles.

It made her feel like she was actually inside a computer. Like she'd become a rebel data point that was now trying to escape the boxes of a malevolent spreadsheet.

She stopped again for a moment when she turned the corner. She could see the elevator way down at the other end of the hallway. Between her and it were several office doors on each side. One of them on the right was the SAC's office, she knew.

Her stomach felt like liquid as she stared at it. The bump of her heart was like a hammer tapping slowly against the inside of her chest.

Doesn't matter, she thought. *Move!*

She swallowed dryly and started moving for the elevator. She'd taken three steps when she saw the door for a stairwell on her left.

She stopped and glanced at the elevator again.

Then she stepped back and went left into the stairwell, taking out her phone as she entered through the door.

The buzz of her calling Gannon mixed with the clop of her heels on the descending concrete. The metal stair railing brushing her elbow felt cool as she came down as fast as she could.

"Come on, come on, Mike. Pick up!" she said.

"What's up?" Gannon said.

It was loud where he was. It sounded like he was on foot maybe.

"I have it. I got it, Mike. I'm coming out."

"Kit, what's wrong? You sound panicked," Gannon said.

"I am panicked," she said truthfully. "I'll tell you why when I get out of here. It's bailout time. I need to get out of here now."

"Is someone after you? You need to be careful. There's—"

Then Kit stopped in her tracks as the stairwell door on the landing below her blasted open.

72

Men were there.

Ten steps below, two men, two strong-looking men, stood there in EMT uniforms looking up at her. Kit stood frozen, staring back at them with her mouth agape.

A radio suddenly went off, the tinny squawk loud off the concrete walls.

"We got her," the shorter of the two men said with a wild-eyed grin as he lunged onto the stairs and headed up.

Kit's phone slipped from her hand and clattered off down the stairs as she backpedaled. She actually came out of one of her shoes as she turned and started back up.

This can't be happening, she thought as she struggled up the stairs. *Not again. Please, not again.*

She'd made the top of the landing, dizzy and shaking, when the man grabbed her ankle and yanked her feet out from underneath her. Black stars of pain flashed in her vision as her bad shoulder smacked into the hard landing.

As the evil medic hovered over her, she screamed as she swung with her good hand for the man's balls with everything she had.

But at the last second, he shifted his hip gracefully and it felt like her pinkie broke as her fist smashed his thick thigh instead.

"Scrappy, huh? I like scrappy. Tomboys are my favorite," he said in his New York accent.

Then he open-palm slapped her across the face hard enough to make her nose bleed.

She fell over on her side, her face on fire, dazed. She scraped her fingertips on the rough concrete floor. One of her nails snapped as she scrabbled with her free hand to get away.

"Help, Mike!" she screamed when she looked down the stairs and saw her phone at the bottom.

"Help! They got me! They got me! Two men. EMT uniforms!" she screamed.

The short man laughed as he threw a hard forearm up under her jaw. Terror pulsed through her like live voltage as there was a pinch on her backside. He was sticking her with something, she saw as she glanced down.

No!

"Help me, Mike! They're drugging me! Help!" she yelled again.

"On second thought, Mikey, don't worry. We got her," the short brute called out loudly as he pressed the plunger.

Kit felt the liquid going into her, hot in her veins.

"False alarm, Mikey. We'll take it from here," Kit heard the man say with a cackling laugh as the lights began to dim.

73

Maniscalco tore away the blister pack tin foil with his teeth, then popped another Nicorette into his mouth as the federal building's steel garage door in front of him began to clank upward.

"Boy, oh, boy, do we got her, Boss," he said into his phone. "Yeah, uh-huh, she had a thumb drive on her. Yep. Davies got it, and she's wrapped up in the back on the stretcher with a bow. No. No one said shit to us. The lobby security guy even held the door for us, the helpful dope. We're coming out now."

The shutter had just stopped its clatter, and he was tucking the phone into the pocket of his fake EMT jacket, when he heard it.

From the street came a sound. A loud sound, a kind of industrial bellowing horn. Maniscalco squinted, listening. It almost sounded like a fire truck but not exactly.

The horn sound stopped as he pulled up the ramp, but as he paused at the ramp's apron before the street, he heard it start up again.

It was nearer and louder now. Definitely some kind of horn rapidly gaining in volume somewhere to his left.

The truck appeared at the corner just as Maniscalco flicked the transmission to Drive. It was a large Mack-style construction vehicle, and horns from other vehicles blared along with it as it blew the light and swung with a dangerous wobble the wrong way down the narrow one-way Champa Street.

"What in the hell?" Maniscalco said, swallowing his gum.

The truck growled again and a billowing cloud of exhaust from its cab stack rose into the air behind it as it just missed hitting a Prius head-on.

Maniscalco had just put it together that there was one big-ass problem and was scrambling to put the ambulance into Reverse when the speeding truck struck the high curb ten feet to the left of the ambulance.

"Shit!" Maniscalco screamed.

Then the massive gray grill of the sixty-five-thousand-pound fully loaded cement truck embedded the driver's door into his sternum.

Sailing sideways and puking blood in the roar and diesel stink, Maniscalco was still alive to watch the guard in the booth beside the ramp wisely dive out its front door a split second before the crushed metal missile of the shrieking T-boned ambulance slammed the booth off its foundation.

Then the booth and Maniscalco's skull exploded

into splinters as the cement truck plowed everything
into the cold stone base of the federal building with
a sound like a bomb.

74

The ba-booming sound of the wreck was still reverberating through Gannon's own skull as he unclipped his seat belt, swung open the smoking cement truck's cab door and jumped down to the rubble-strewn sidewalk.

Kit's backup Glock was in his just-in-case pack, and he reached back and put it in his hand as he walked into the street and back alongside the truck through the cloud of dust.

The mixer was still spinning, and as he arrived on the other side of it, he stopped for a moment, coughing into his fist, as he surveyed the wreckage.

The cab of the ambulance was lost entirely from view under the rubble of the building, but the rear of it was still accessible. One of its bright orange rear doors had actually swung open in the crash, and

Gannon hurried over and peeked in over the barrel of the Glock.

Over the mess of spilled-out cabinets and broken glass, beyond a pair of overturned oxygen canisters, he saw Kit on the emergency medical stretcher with her eyes closed.

On the pebbled steel floor almost beneath the stretcher lay a thick-necked white guy facedown in a pool of blood. He was strapping some kind of machine gun over his shoulder.

Gannon jumped up and in and grabbed the gun. Then he lunged farther in over the stretcher and checked Kit's pulse at her neck.

"Kit! Kit! You okay?" he said.

There was no response but her heartbeat and breathing seemed fine. He scanned for head injuries. Though the stretcher was half knocked over, she'd been belted in with three tight straps so she actually seemed to have weathered the crash pretty well, all things considered.

At first, he thought to unstrap Kit from the gurney, but then thought again. Instead, he kicked the fallen debris out of the way, yanked the stretcher loose and slid it out onto the street.

When he was done, Gannon took a quick look at the gun. As he lifted it, he saw it was a Heckler & Koch G36 short-barrel carbine.

He popped out its magazine. It was filled to the brim with 5.56 NATO bottleneck full metal jackets. He slapped it back in and when he looked back into the ambulance, he saw that the fake EMT had a bag with two more mags of 5.56.

Gannon hopped back inside and took those as well before he began rifling through the guy's pockets.

"Bingo," he said as he found Kit's thumb drive in the man's back left pocket beside his wallet.

He was squaring the guy's fake EMT ball cap on his own head when he heard the hissing.

He looked down and saw the tactical hands-free headset radio rig the fallen man was wearing, and he stripped it off and traced the cord down to the push-to-talk unit and then down another radio cord to the Motorola radio on his belt.

Gannon quickly re-clipped the rig onto himself as he hopped back down onto the sidewalk.

Then he grabbed the bottom of Kit's stretcher bed, and they were rolling north out in the street beside the crash through the dust, giving the truck's still rotating mixing drum a wide berth as they passed.

75

The tires on the Mercedes Sprinter cargo van squealed as Westergaard booted the gas, reversing it up the parking garage's ramp. He listened patiently to the panicked report from Patchell and Davenport of the startling events taking place down on Champa Street.

"Well, we'll just have to deal with it, gentlemen," he said calmly into his own hands-free microphone as the Mercedes roared out onto the open top level of the garage, still in Reverse.

"Wait and watch on the corner of 20th there. Yes, on the corner. Look sharp now. You're closest. My bet is he'll be coming out to you."

This level of the parking garage was almost completely empty. Westergaard rocketed backwards toward the northeast corner, shrieked to a stop, put it in Park and ripped open the little low door in the cab behind him to the van's rear.

In the back was a prone shooting platform that he had designed himself. It had a comfortable gym-mat-like padded surface and hydraulic lifts worked by a joystick controller to raise and tilt the platform into whatever position that was needed.

His Accuracy International AW, the most accurate sniper rifle on earth, was already seated on a bench rest at the back of the platform, aimed out the rear door.

Westergaard climbed in, slammed the cab door shut behind him, lay down onto the platform beside his gun, took the joystick and buzzed it up and up.

He took a few seconds lowering only the front of the platform just right so he could get a nice downward angle to either his left or right. As he did this, he put his eye off and on the Bender scope to get things as comfortable as possible.

He had a clear open firing lane north down Stout Street now. To his left was the side of the huge federal building, and past it, down Stout across the street, there was an open municipal parking lot. Davenport and Patchell had the north and west corners covered. If the targets came south or east, they were dead meat.

When Westergaard was done, he lifted the already loaded magazine beside the rifle and took out the top round of .338.

The Lapua Magnum round was cold against his fingertips and then cold against his lips as he kissed the copper jacket of it.

He clicked the .338 into the chamber, closed the bolt and snapped in the magazine.

Then Westergaard zipped down the van's wide tinted rear window with a flick of the joystick and looked down the street beside the federal building, breathing calmly to center himself as he waited and watched.

76

Gannon walked out into the street, pushing Kit before him north up Champa.

There had to be a lot of activity inside the big white block federal government building beside him, he thought, glancing at it out of the corner of his eye.

But thankfully none of it had reached outside as of yet.

Through the dust he could see people and traffic were still crossing through the intersection of 20th Street.

Gannon watched as a bearded pudgy Hispanic man clutching a coffee got out of the driver's door of a white Ford Focus that was parked by the corner ahead on his right.

"What's up? Was it terrorism?" he said. "Man, I heard the bomb. I work at the courthouse, bro. Are we under attack?"

Gannon ignored him as a pickup turned off 20th onto Champa close by them. The driver was a wide-eyed woman with blond hair, and she slowed her truck as she stared at them and the crash behind him. When the pickup had passed on his left, Gannon glanced across the street.

Then it was his turn for his eyes to go wide.

It was one of those moments where everything slowed. The flow of motion. The flow of time.

Catty-cornered to where they were, a figure stood in the gutter of the street in front of the silver Suburban. It was the broad-shouldered ball-peen-hammer-headed white man, and he was putting a pistol grip shotgun up to his shoulder.

Gannon grabbed the Hispanic man and rammed him into Kit and the gurney and pushed all of them behind the rear of the parked car as the first explosion of double-aught buck shattered the Ford's windshield.

The second shot came as Gannon hauled Kit's stretcher half up onto the sidewalk behind the car. He was collapsing it down when the next blast disintegrated the driver's side glass and side view mirror. The left front tire exploded as he grabbed up the carbine beside Kit on the gurney and thumbed it on full auto.

Gannon knelt in the tight space between the curb and the car as the Hispanic man wisely took off somewhere. When he crawled up a little and peeked out past the Ford's right front fender, he saw the second one, the black guy in the Tigers cap, out in the open of the crosswalk. He was running full-out for the other side of Champa with his own carbine to flank him.

The deafening eruption of automatic gunfire that

came as Gannon opened up on the running figure with the H&K caught even his breath. The violent deafening *pow* and *pow* and *snappa pow pow pow pow* of the powerful 5.56 rounds crackled off the metal side of the sedan he knelt beside.

One of his rounds skipped off the asphalt and another hit the front panel of a U-Haul truck parked at the corner, and then Gannon finally tucked in right to left and cut the Tiger fan in two. He put one through the guy's abdomen right above his groin, then another in his sternum, and then a third that hit him dead in his right cheekbone.

The guy's hat went flying and his rifle clattered to the asphalt as he face-planted and came to a skidding stop against the curb.

Still on his knees, Gannon reared back and changed out the mag as three more blasts of double-aught buckshot ripped into the hood of the Ford from the opposite diagonal corner.

He waited a second, then quick-peeked and ducked back as another shot came.

When he looked again, the big hammer-headed white fella's dropped shotgun was in midair as he went for a sidearm.

Gannon leaned up against the bumper of the Ford and aimed through the reflex sight.

Then he opened up and the shooter slid left with his head flung back from the three-round burst Gannon drilled into the T-box of his face and chest.

77

Gannon leaped up with his head on a swivel, checking his spots, went back to Kit, popped the stretcher up again, grabbed its back rail and rolled forward.

Pushing off the corner over the ringing in his ears, he heard the first fluttering squeal of an approaching siren. The traffic had stopped completely by the time he made it halfway across the street.

Of course it had, Gannon thought.

With the rifle slung over his shoulder, he looked like the most dangerous crossing guard who'd ever lived.

Gannon bumped them up over the curb onto the sidewalk at a wheelchair ramp. There was a large open municipal parking lot beyond the sidewalk, and he lowered the rifle as he pushed the stretcher into it along the rows of cars.

He walked as calmly as he could, not looking behind him. The people with guns would make themselves known in a moment, no doubt. He pushed the stretcher in a zigzag pattern diagonally across the lot toward Stout Street. He kept his eyes leveled forward at the other side of Stout. There was a tire store there where he was planning on acquiring some transport.

He'd made it near the lot's southeastern end and was coming along a building wall for the sidewalk when the brick a centimeter above the top of his skull spontaneously disintegrated.

Gannon recoiled from the explosion. Blinded and blinking at the stone dust, he turned and ducked and collapsed the stretcher again as he retreated back into the lot.

He searched and searched, and two rows over to his right he found what he was looking for. It was a late 2000s maroon Town & Country minivan, and he shattered its front passenger window with the butt of the carbine and reached in and opened the door. From his just-in-case backpack, he removed the hammer and chisel-like screwdriver he'd bought from Walmart the day before, and he hammered off the ignition cover and rammed the screwdriver in and turned the engine over.

He unstrapped Kit from the gurney and laid her in the back of the van and closed the door back over her. He'd come around to the driver's door and was about to get in and tear ass out into the street when he slowed himself down with a breath and assessed the pumpkin-sized hole in the brick wall.

He looked to the right north up Stout Street where the shot had come from.

An over watch position, Gannon thought. Some-where on the opposite side of Stout.

He'd get a bead on them. Would have at least two shots. With some heavy firepower, too. Turn the van into Swiss cheese, he thought. His noggin, too, prob-ably. Or worse, Kit's.

He took out his phone and brought up the Google map of downtown Denver. Right away he saw it. A multilevel parking garage a block back across on the other side of Stout.

"Shit," he said.

78

Gannon slung the rifle across his back and left Kit where she was in the already running van as he ducked down and headed west along the parked cars. As he approached 20th Street again, he made sure to keep the federal building's corner between himself and the elevated garage.

As he hurried forward, he heard the first police car arrive a block to his right. He could see its blue-and-red strobe light on the pale facade of the federal building.

Ignoring it, he turned up the Motorola's volume, then keyed in the push-to-talk.

"Calling asshole," Gannon said. "Come in, asshole. Over."

He smiled at the silence of chatter that followed his announcement.

That had gotten their attention, hadn't it? he thought.

"That was a nice shot, buddy," Gannon said as he reached the last row of cars.

He looked left and saw something on the sidewalk corner that just might work.

"I'm not kidding. Truly a pucker factor of eleven," Gannon said as he ducked down and slowly began to make his way back toward Stout.

"You just missed a hair high," he said. "If I had to guess, your assumed zero is off. You didn't factor in the elevation change, did you? The air's thinner up here in the Mile High City, dummy. You forgot to consider the decrease in drop. But I admire the attempt at a head shot. Go for broke or why bother. I'm with you, bro. I'm the same exact way. They must have taken you down from the top of the shelf."

There was a pause then.

"Thanks for the tip," came a voice.

It was a foreign voice, Gannon thought as he strapped the gun onto his back and knelt down and began to crawl now behind the row of cars closer to the corner.

German maybe? he thought as he crawled more slowly now. Some mercenary or something. Were the assholes bringing back the damn Hessians now? The fricking Nazis?

He stopped as he came past the last car and spotted something on the corner. It was the meter box where drivers paid to park. It was just large enough to scrunch in behind, and on the other side of it, he would have a shot north up Stout.

"Anytime, stranger," Gannon said. "I'm full of

good advice. Here's some more. Pack it in. You're backing the wrong team here. You need to stand down."

"Is that right?" the foreigner said in his earbud. "Or what?"

"Or you're going to be assuming room temperature like those four little Indians over on the next block," Gannon said. "You do know how the end of that song goes, right?"

"You're some real badass, huh?"

Gannon got to a crouch and turned the gun around in front of him as he stepped behind the meter box. He got his back on it and edged himself up slowly against it until he had his feet back under him a little better.

He took out his phone and turned on the video. Quick as a card trick, he stuck it out the other side of the box and back and then smiled as he froze the still.

Five stories up at the top corner of the garage was a large white van backed up against the edge.

He studied the phone and put it away. Then he adjusted his weight and got his feet completely right as he tucked the rifle butt high and hard and deep into his shoulder.

He took a deep breath. He would only have a second, he knew.

But a second was all he would need.

"Deep breathing now? Making you nervous, am I?" the foreigner said.

This is it, kemosabe, Gannon thought to himself. *Put the devil in a body bag or die trying. All in with the chips. For all the marbles.*

"I thought you were a badass," the mercenary taunted.

"Well, put it this way. I'm not a helpless stripper or even a park ranger," Gannon finally said as he rose up until his head was just under the metal box's top.

"No?"

"No," Gannon said as he put the rifle to his cheek and stepped right in a balanced lunge.

He saw the top of the Mercedes center into his scope pretty as you please just as he came to a solid wide-legged stop.

"I'm smarter than your average grizzly," Gannon said as he buried the trigger.

79

Westergaard had just caught the firework flash of a muzzle low in the reticle when the van window shattered apart in his face.

He jolted back as something struck his cheek. As he landed, he hit the joystick at his elbow and the shooting platform canted violently to the right and down, spilling the rifle with a clatter.

He reached up and felt something warm and wet.

How? he thought, looking in wonder at his blood there on his fingertips.

Westergaard patted at his head. A narrow gouge had been stripped across his ear. As he probed the wound, it flapped disgustingly almost in two. The bullet had cut the back end of it above the lobe neatly almost in half.

He looked down at the rifle where the scope had been destroyed.

The scope? He'd hit his scope, he realized. *How?*

Something strange happened then. A cocktail of feelings he hadn't felt in a very, very long time pulsed through him.

Envy mixed with fear.

"What's up with your heavy breathing now, buddy?" the American said in his ear. "I know I'm pretty sexy, but I hate to break it to you. I'm just not that kind of guy."

Westergaard sat up and looked out the shattered back window. Down the street a block beside the building where he'd just missed the American, he saw a maroon minivan drive out of the parking lot onto Stout.

"No!" he yelled as he lunged over to his right and grabbed at the rifle. Then he screamed as it wouldn't budge. It had become stuck somehow in the tilted-over platform.

"My, my, you sound upset," the American said. "Let me guess, your little sister won't lend you her clothes anymore? No wait, one of your girlie man soccer teams lost again?"

Westergaard gritted his teeth as he screamed again.

"Yes!" the American said. "That's a sound I like. Music to my ears. Sounds to me like you're bleeding. Please tell me I nicked something good. Strike a gusher, did I? Well, I warned you. We have a saying in these here parts. Sometimes the bear gets you."

"You've made a mistake," Westergaard said very evenly as he watched the minivan depart. "A grave mistake."

"Au contraire," the American said as a hand shot

out the minivan's driver's side window, middle finger extended skyward.

"Drawing your blood is what I call a good start," he said. "You like round one? Let me assure you, round two is going to be a real Sunday church barbecue. Ta-ta."

80

The forty-five minutes after the shoot-out were the busiest in Dawn Warner's life. Never had she needed to move so many pieces and to make so many crucial decisions in so little time.

At thirty minutes post-shooting, the first live-feed Denver newscast began. The optics were not ideal. Helicopter shots showed the cement truck and the crushed ambulance clear as day half sticking out of the destroyed corner of the federal building.

It was another fifteen minutes after that when Denver SAC Harry Wheaton called.

She stalled Handsome Harry while they got the last details nailed down. Then she and Fitzgerald and Harris all headed from her office into the main floor conference room, where they had the big board for important interoffice videoconferencing.

"Harry, how are you? I'm watching the report. Are all your personnel safe?"

"What in the hell just happened?" Wheaton said.

"We're watching it on TV just like you, Harry. We're trying to put it together ourselves. They said the truck looked like it hit the ambulance deliberately? How can that be right? This couldn't have been just an accident or something?"

"An accident? Ten witnesses saw it veer straight for the ambulance the wrong way down a one-way street. The shoot-out on the corner started a minute later after the crash. I've got a witness that said one of the participants was the cement truck driver, and he had a fully automatic machine gun."

Dawn Warner nodded, her eyes in a half squint as if she were using all of her mental powers to process the information.

"We've got another two shooters, both dead, one with a machine gun and another with a combat shotgun. No ID on them, of course. Then there was more shooting before a van was stolen from the lot across the street. This cement truck driver put Agent Hagen in the back of it, they said."

"You're saying Hagen's been kidnapped?" Dawn Warner said.

Wheaton peered at her furiously from the screen. "Looks like it."

"Wait," Dawn Warner said. "There was a man with Hagen. An old boyfriend, we think. We're still trying to nail that down. Maybe it was him?"

"What are you talking about?" Wheaton said. "She came in alone."

"Maybe the boyfriend was waiting outside and

overreacted when he realized Kit was being brought to the hospital," Fitzgerald tossed in.

"In his cement truck?" Wheaton said. "Armed with a fully automatic weapon?"

"We don't have a lead on their whereabouts?" Warner said, turning and giving Fitzgerald a glare to shut his trap.

"We have an APB on the stolen minivan but so far nothing."

Good, Dawn Warner thought. The last thing they needed was for them to be picked up legitimately. They'd get back on track their own way.

And at least she had Denver snowed on the ambulance thing. The two mercs in the ambulance were still not being scrutinized. She'd already sent in two more of their recon teams and they'd already gotten the bodies out of there.

"What do I tell the press? They're already showing the ambulance on the news."

She held up a finger and began tapping it to her temple.

"I think the best play is to simply say there was an accident. We needn't talk about Hagen. At least not yet."

"And the shooting?"

"So far you think it was a road rage incident involved with the accident. You don't know fully but will keep them updated. You're investigating. Stonewall them," Dawn Warner said.

81

Wheaton took a long, loud, deep breath as he leaned back in his office chair.

"Okay, you've had your say, Ms. Warner," he said.

He placed his palms flat against the desk in front of him as he suddenly leaned in closer to the camera.

"Now it's time for you to listen to me," he said. "Special Agent Hagen in no way, shape, or form seemed to be anything but completely cognizant when I spoke to her. So don't even try going there again. Then you send in some so-called experts and it's Dodge City on my front porch.

"Now, I know you guys there in Justice sometimes quarterback counter-intel stuff, right? Hagen was in a SCIF. You guys got yourselves some top secret counter-intel troubles over there in Justice? Is that what this is?"

"Intelligence?" Dawn Warner said, acting confused.

"Dawn, stop insulting mine by playing dumb, would you please," Wheaton said. "Be straight with me. Tell me what's up. Because I'm getting to the bottom of this one way or another."

Dawn Warner turned to her left. Through the glass of the door out in the hallway she could see her secretary, Roberta, standing there.

She gave Roberta a questioning look. Roberta nodded rapidly.

"Harry, there's someone here that needs to talk to you."

That's when they brought in their secret weapon, the nuclear option.

In walked the new FBI director, Thomas F. Foldager, himself.

"Harry," the six-foot-seven friendly-faced man said as he walked in smiling. "I know you're steamed, but I was just at the White House, and I'll tell you what they told me. This is an internal security matter. Play ball. Whatever script they want, it's their game. And Harry, no leaks. They're cracking major stones over this."

"Over what?" Wheaton said.

"Your guess is as good as mine, Harry. Ours is not to wonder why."

"No," Harry said. "No way. This is bullshit. You want me to lie to the public? Tom, we're friends. You know me. You know I can't do that. Ain't in my DNA."

"That your final say?" Director Foldager said. His Mr. Rogers-like face was still smiling but his eyes were not.

"Honestly, be careful, Harry. I'm not joking," Fold-ager said. "I'm giving you a direct order."

"I don't care what you're giving me. Actually, I know what you're giving me. The answer's no. I won't do it."

"Then you're relieved of duty immediately," Fold-ager said coldly. "Get off my screen and send in your deputy."

"Send him in yourself, Tom," the Denver SAC said, giving the director the finger.

They stood watching as Harry Wheaton hovered the bird over the keyboard and then inverted it and pressed down.

Director Foldager turned to Warner as the screen went dead.

"Any suggestions, Dawn?" he said. "I'd like to help you guys out, but you really screwed the pooch on this one. Harry's a straight shooter."

"We don't have anything on him," Dawn Warner complained. "No leverage at all."

"On Harry?" Foldager said with a frown. "No, you're digging a dry hole there. Got a silver star in Afghanistan. Married his high school sweetheart. Got seven kids. Eucharistic minister at his church. The Little League team he coaches lost the national world series three years ago by a run. I've never seen him walk on water but you never know. You know he's going straight to the press."

"Let him," Dawn Warner said. "We have a line into every network. They already know the script."

The director shrugged his shoulders.

"Okay. Well, as usual, I'll leave it to you guys, then."

He gave her an air kiss.

"Hit me on my personal phone if you need me. I have to head back home early today to help my daughter pack for college."

"Is that right? Emmy?"

"No, Gwen."

"My goodness, the baby? Time flies. Where is she headed? Brown?" Dawn said.

"Dartmouth."

"Perfect," Dawn Warner said, smiling. "Give her my love."

PART FOUR

THE RUBBER MEETS THE ROAD

82

When Kit woke up, Gannon was driving and they were on a two-lane country road.

A sign for US 385 flew past the passenger window. The country beyond it was a flat, wide-open landscape. It looked like Wyoming except the mountains were gone.

She felt woozy as she sat up. A pleasant woozy like a beer buzz.

A trailer home went past. Kit saw a kid, a cute blond little boy, on a swing in the dirt yard beside it. In a pen behind the double-wide on the other side was a foal.

"Oh, look, a little baby horse," she said.

"How are you feeling?" Gannon said.

"Tired. Where are we?"

"Oklahoma," he said.

"Oklahoma?"

"Yep."

She looked up at the big sky above, gray and over-cast, like it was about to rain. The land was shadowed off to their left. It looked to be near sunset.

As she looked out the window, what had happened started to come back slowly. She remembered the FBI building. The horrible EMT man. After that there were just snapshots. Being strapped to a gurney. The sound of shooting. She remembered lying on her back next to a car in a parking lot.

She couldn't put the rest of the pieces together. She wasn't sure she wanted to. She patted at her numb face.

"Wait, is this the rental car?"

"No," Gannon said. "I acquired another one. An-other two, actually."

She looked at the steering column then. It was cracked open and there was a screwdriver handle sticking out of it. The seats and the rest of the inside of the vehicle seemed really big.

"What is this? A truck?" she said.

"Yes. It's a dumpster truck," Gannon said as he cocked a thumb toward the back. "Beggars can't be choosers. How are you feeling?"

"Groggy."

Gannon laughed.

"You look groggy. I got you a Gatorade. You need to hydrate. Try to flush your system."

She carefully lifted it out of the cup holder. The sports drink was the red fruit punch one. She labo-riously opened it, then sighed after she took a long cool sip.

She dropped the bottle back and wiped her mouth.

"That tasted good. This is a great drink holder," she said.

Gannon laughed again.

"I know!" he cried. "I thought the same thing. The tongues on it really grip, don't they? This thing corners like a cinder block and guzzles gas like crazy but the drink holders are amazing."

"Are the cops after us?"

"No," Gannon said. "I saw the news in the gas station. No APBs. No video stills. We're in the clear so far. I guess this Warner woman is covering this up somehow. Besides, those guys back in Denver weren't cops."

"Mercenaries? Special Forces guys?"

"Yep," Gannon said.

"Like you?" she said.

"Yep," Gannon said again. "Like me."

"No," Kit said, shuddering as she remembered the troll-like man who'd slapped her. "No way, you're not like them at all."

A minute of silence followed. Kit looked out at the empty land. Since the setting sun was on the left, they must have been heading somewhat north now. She felt an odd elation as they drove, a teenager on her first road trip. It made no sense but there you had it.

"What do you think they gave me? Was it Oxy-Contin or something?"

"No, ketamine, probably."

"The club drug?"

"Emergency rooms use it as a sedative. Intelligence services, too, because it induces memory loss. You're feeling it, huh?"

"Got a kick to it. What now?"

"Take a nap. You'll be okay."

"Okay," she said curling up by the door.

"You're a gentleman, too, huh?" she said after another second.

Gannon laughed.

"You think so?"

"Sure. Gentlemen save damsels in distress, right? Gentleman, ass-kicker, funny, smart, cute. You cover all the bases. A girl could fall for a guy like you, Mike. Even in a dumpster truck. You oughta be careful. Where are we going anyway?" she said, half-asleep.

"Back to Barber's ranch," Gannon said.

"That's in Utah. Isn't Oklahoma the other way?"

"I called John. There's an old airfield nearby. We're going to meet him there. He'll fly us back."

"Perfect," Kit said, smiling with her eyes closed.

"I have one more question," she said sleepily after a moment.

"What's that?" Gannon said.

"You really do have a navy SEAL frogman tattoo somewhere, don't you?" she said.

Gannon laughed and then laughed again a moment later when he heard her snoring.

He leaned over as far as he could and bent as low as he could toward her ear.

"Yes," he whispered into it. "Yes, I do, Kit. I really do."

83

Westergaard was ordered to head northeast out of Denver to a town called Kersey.

The designated motel was on a stretch of road up from a Family Dollar directly across from a car wrecking yard. He parked the Hyundai Sonata he'd stolen in the back of it and opened the door and painfully stood. In the cool of the evening, he walked slowly around the cheap structure of the motel to the sound of crickets. The key for room 17 was under its mat. He opened it and went inside and locked the door behind him.

He looked out the window through the gap in the curtains as he shuffled stiffly toward the bed. It gave a view across the road into the center of the dump, where dozens of cars were strewn about in various states of destruction.

"I wonder if someone is trying to tell me something," Westergaard mumbled as he sat and gingerly worked his bloody ear bandage free.

When the knock finally came at the door two hours later, it was pitch-black outside and Westergaard was half-asleep with fever. He left the gun under the bed as he stood with a bloody towel turbaned around his head.

To say that the figure on the other side of the door did not look very encouraging would have been quite the understatement. He was tall and soft-bellied and homely with curly blond hair. Westergaard looked at the individual's thick eyeglasses. He was maybe twenty-five.

"You're Bob, right?" the American said. "I'm Duane."

"Aren't you too young to be a doctor?" Westergaard said as he stepped aside before shutting and locking the door behind him.

"I'm actually an RN and an EMT, but I'm about to get my certificate as a physician's assistant," he said as he unslung his backpack.

"My lucky day," Westergaard said as he staggered back toward the bed.

"I get it. You're hurting, fella, aren't you? Tell you the truth, you don't look so hot. Let's take a chair into the bathroom and get a look at you."

"Ahhhh!" Westergaard yelled a few minutes later as Duane dug with his tweezers into the meat between his right ear and eye again. He stomped at the tile with his big foot as the medic finally pulled something loose.

The bathroom tile was blotted with his blood. There were blood canals in the grout. There was blood everywhere.

"You need more meds, I got em," the medic said in his annoyingly soft Midwestern singsong as he lay the shard of glass from his face into a medical pan.

Westergaard cried out again as his stainless-steel facial began anew.

"Seriously, bro, more meds. What's the issue? If it hurts, it hurts."

Westergaard looked around the depressing room. The mint-green bathroom tile. The shower curtain that was the color of piss. He looked at his blood all over everything. Then he looked back at the American butcher.

"Okay, okay," Westergaard said. "You're right. I need more."

Westergaard shook his head as he swallowed the pills he was handed. He'd been wounded several times and was usually quite stoic but not this time. This time was new. Even he was surprised at how unglued he'd become over this.

It was Maniscalco, he thought as he bent over, catching his breath. The fact that Maniscalco had been killed had spooked him to the core. Maniscalco had survived the bloodiest violent conflicts the world had to offer, had been a military advising mercenary in the Congo for two years.

How could Maniscalco be dead?

Westergaard sat back up and glanced over at the Vincent van Gogh portrait staring back at him from the bathroom mirror.

"I won't lie. This part's going to hurt a little now," Duane said as he laid down the tweezers.

"Now?" Westergaard said as the EMT suddenly pulled his head wound agape with his big rubber-gloved thumbs. The saline wound wash he sprayed in a moment later felt like he was being murdered with a Black and Decker drill bit dipped in lemon juice.

"Stings a bit, I know," the medic said as Westergaard shuddered in agony. "Let me bandage you up now."

"Why am I sweating so much?" he said, snuffling. "And why the hell won't my nose stop running? I'm drooling like a bloodhound!"

The medic began wrapping gauze around his head.

"There's a nerve between your ear and your eye. It's called the auriculotemporal nerve. It regulates the saliva and sweat glands. It looks like it took some damage from some of those splinters I took out. It's not critical, but you get a chance, you should see a specialist about it."

"You're saying I'm just gonna be leaking spit, snot, and sweat until further notice?" Westergaard said.

"Some over-the-counter cold medication might help for the mucus, but in sum, yes."

Westergaard turned and dropped his forehead down until it was resting against the cold porcelain top of the toilet tank. A warm drip of snot hung from the end of his pointy nose, then plopped onto the thigh of his bloody jeans.

"I know, fella," Duane said, patting him on the shoulder. "I know."

84

On his Hotel Juliet Bravo ranch, John Barber had a heavy-duty professional outdoor shooting range fronted by a small field house with a lean-to roof. Inside of the barnlike building were gun lockers and regular lockers and benches and an armor-plated clearing trap beside a card table by a window overlooking the range.

At nine o'clock in the morning on the day after the Denver shoot-out, Gannon was in the gun barn standing by the card table with John Barber, looking out where his son, Declan, was lying prone on the macadam with a Savage Arms .30-06 deer rifle.

Down the desert range were markers and hanging steel targets at various distances of up to 1,200 yards. Through his binoculars, Gannon could see that Declan was consistently hitting the target at the 700 mark. As he calmly let off rounds, John Barber's daughter, Stephanie, sat cross-legged beside him, wearing earmuffs, also looking downrange with binoculars.

"He's been up here ever since you left," John Barber said as Declan cracked off another round. "He's actually getting pretty good, Mike."

"You really think so?" Gannon said proudly as he heard the faint clink of a target in the distance.

"Okay, I'm all set up," Kit Hagen said from where she sat at the card table beside them.

Gannon lowered the binoculars as they both turned.

Kit was wearing a plaid shirt and shorts and some flip-flops she'd borrowed from John Barber's wife, Lynn. She looked a hell of a lot better after some sleep and a shower and their big pancake breakfast.

The Denver SCIF thumb drive was sticking out the side of the laptop she was typing on. She suddenly stopped typing and turned the screen toward them.

"Okay, first thing I wanted to show you is this, Mike. It's a surveillance camera still that my friend Amy just sent me from the Denver parking garage."

The guy he'd had the gunfight with in Denver was lanky and pale and younger than Gannon would have guessed, maybe in his early thirties. Gannon looked at the intensity in his eyes. He had a kind of nose-in-the-air polished viciousness to his expression.

"He even looks like a Euro weenie, doesn't he?" he said. "We got a name?"

"No, not yet. He's not in the system. But it doesn't matter. That's only the appetizer. Now for the main course," Kit said, clicking a button.

It took a moment for Gannon to realize the multiple photographs on the screen were of the first unknown female victim from Grand Teton.

Fully clothed and alive without bite marks, the young Asian woman Owen Barber had videotaped was quite cute. In two of the photos she was wearing khakis in what looked like maybe Africa. In one of them she held hands with a little smiling child on a crowded market street and in another she was hugging and kissing a baby in a dirty hospital. There was something almost elfin about her features, something sweet, a palpable sort of innocence, a childlike caring.

He had pegged her as some kind of charity doctor or something until he saw one shot along the bottom where she was dressed to the nines wearing a metallic Tiffany-blue gown with a glittering diamond choker, standing on a red carpet somewhere.

Gannon suddenly recognized the face of the thin bland man of about thirty-five with salt-and-pepper hair who was wearing a tuxedo beside her. At least vaguely. Was he from a business cable TV channel or something? he thought.

"The man there," John Barber said sitting up. "Isn't that…that's that internet company guy, right? That billionaire. What's his name?"

"Weber," Kit said. "Yes, that's Ethan Weber. He worked at Apple before he started the smartphone behemoth Sonexum. Remember, they did a movie about him on Netflix last year? He's the eleventh richest man in the world."

"Holy shit!" Gannon said, grabbing his head as he stood. "One of those internet billionaires from that damn conference in Jackson, right? Only someone with unlimited sway and cash could even dream of attempting all this bloody insanity."

"So you're saying our missing victim one is some billionaire Silicon Valley dude's girlfriend or something?" John Barber said.

"No," Kit said, looking at him steadily. "Victim one isn't Weber's girlfriend. This is Lisa Weber. It's his wife."

"No!" Gannon cried. "His wife?"

"Yes. They met in college at MIT. The reason we didn't recognize her straight off the bat from Owen's video is because she's reclusive and notoriously camera-shy. Especially in the States. The only time she does any PR at all is for their philanthropic foundation, which is run out of Italy and based mostly in Africa and Southeast Asia. Her parents are actually from China."

"And Weber killed her," Gannon said. "Or hired someone to do it. Had to be. And all this, the shooting, switching out the victims, all of it was part of a cover-up."

"You've got to be shitting me," Barber said.

Kit nodded.

"That's what it's looking like," she said.

"Walk me through it," Barber said.

"Here's how I think it probably went down," Kit said, standing. "Like Mike just said, there was a bunch of Silicon Valley computer execs staying in Jackson for a mogul conference. Ethan Weber was the keynote speaker. His speech is actually on his Facebook page. I'm thinking at some point he and his wife are bored at the hotel, so they decide to head up to Grand Teton for some reason. Do a little glamping under the stars or something. Who knows? And he kills her."

"But come on, he ripped her apart. Why?" John Barber said.

"We don't know. Why do husbands kill their wives? She was cheating on him? Going to leave him? Or she confronted him about an affair and he snapped? Whatever it was, we can assume Weber doesn't want to suffer the consequences, so he snaps his globally connected billion-dollar fingers and voilà! His goons and Assistant Attorney General Warner go to work and the cover-up begins."

85

"But if Weber wanted to cover up his wife's murder," John Barber said, "why the hell did he leave his wife out there in the open for my brother to find?"

"There must have been a lag between when Weber killed her and when the cover-up started," Kit said. "Maybe it was a spur-of-the-moment thing and after it happened, Weber got scared and left back for the hotel and didn't go into cover-up mode until he calmed down and got his bearings.

"And in that lag is when Owen finds the wife. Thinking quite rightly that he's looking at some sick psycho ritual murder, Owen remembers our FBI bulletin about serial killing in the parks and calls it in. And thinking it's our NATPARK killer, Dennis and I flew straight to Wyoming."

"And as you were on the way," Gannon said, "word of your imminent arrival somehow got back to government-connected Team Weber, who had just started the cover-up."

"Exactly," Kit said. "Once they realized we were on the way from DC to see a NATPARK victim body, they knew they needed to get one and quick."

"Which is why they snatched Tracy Sandhurst in Cheyenne," Gannon said, snapping a finger.

"Right," Kit said. "They grabbed her and they killed her and then they flew her up to Grand Teton from the Warren Air Force Base."

"From a covert nuke missile base?" John Barber said. "Isn't that a little too far of a stretch?"

"Is it?" Kit said. "Not only does Weber obviously have Dawn Warner in his back pocket, Sonexum, like all the rest of these big tech companies, has multiple joint R & D projects with the military. I read that Sonexum is actually in the lead now in terms of the global artificial intelligence race, and they just bumped out Google to score a top secret contract for the NSA and NASA and the Pentagon.

"You think getting IDs and clearance at that level is a problem? Or dropping bribes to make people look the other way? These losers have literally unlimited amounts of money. How much money would a base guard take to switch off a camera and go get a cup of coffee for fifteen minutes? A hundred grand? That's too low. How about two? Don't like that? How about seven? No stretch is too far."

"Good point," Barber said.

"So some hired mercenary killers go to Dynamite Dolls," Gannon said, "and snatch the first stripper they can get their hands on. Then they race from the air force base up to Grand Teton, hoping to beat the FBI profilers. But they must have been a little too late."

"Then what?" Barber said.

"As Kit headed in from DC," Gannon said, "one of Weber's security guys—the sniper—must have snuck past Owen somehow and waited for the rest of his team to arrive with the body. But Kit and her partner and the sheriff got there first. Knowing that Weber's wife being identified is a no-go, the sniper goes to plan B. He shoots Kit and everybody else and then they do the switcheroo to blame all of it on this crazy NATPARK killer."

"And *then* they all flew the hell out of there with Weber's wife?" Barber said, shaking his head.

"Yes, but not before they meticulously prepared Tracy Sandhurst's body," Kit said. "They knew all the details about the NATPARK killer's victims through Warner, is my guess. She has top-echelon data access. She must have snatched up our NATPARK file for the deets on the killer's modus operandi and given it to Weber's goons in order to snow us."

"I get it now," John Barber said. "Talk about the cover-up being worse than the crime. But it fits. All of it fits. This computer geek, Weber, and his crew actually killed my brother."

"They might have even gotten away with it, too," Gannon said, "except they missed something. They didn't count on Owen already having filmed Weber's dead wife on his personal phone."

"Or the fact that our NATPARK suspect—the real killer, Ketchum—was already in jail," Kit said.

"Okay, so now we probably know what happened," Barber said. "What now?"

"Now I start making some phone calls," Kit said.

"Are you sure about that?" Gannon said. "When you went into work there in Denver, it didn't turn out so hot."

"Warner's obviously insanely compromised, but not everybody in the government is on the take, Mike," Kit said. "At Dennis's funeral, I met some of his old partners and old students who begged me to tap them for help. Some of Dennis's old friends are super connected people high up in the Bureau who are chomping at the bit to find out who gunned him down.

"With Owen's video and all the rest of it, we've got Weber by the short hairs. Not just him either. I hope Dawn Warner has her stylist on speed dial for the cameras that are going to be camping out in front of her house. Because it's nailing corrupt murderous assholes to the floorboards time."

86

Dawn Warner had meetings all day in town. It was so late when she got out, she had to hustle her driver along with a promise of an extra day off to run a few red lights so that she could catch the last Acela Express to New York City.

The floodlights on the Metropolitan Museum of Art grand classical facade came on as she arrived in her Uber from Penn Station. Growing up on the Upper East Side, she'd been coming here since she was a child. On a summer Friday this late, the great temple-like Fifth Avenue steps were mostly gray and empty. Clopping up the steps in her Louboutins, she passed only a few tired Asian tourists and a pathetic old mumbling homeless woman surrounded by a half dozen can-filled bags.

It was dim inside as she passed beneath the oculus skylight domes. As she waited on line to get her pin at the reception desk, she yawned, looking around at the ancient Greek statuary. Back through the deserted corridors, her eyes kept getting drawn to one piece in particular. It was the great marble of Perseus proudly holding the head of Medusa aloft.

From the desk, she quickly made her way into the north gallery. It took her two minutes of walking through the Ancient Egypt wing to get to its main attraction, the Temple of Dendur.

It was actually closed off with a velvet rope, but she stepped over it as she had been instructed. Beyond the doorway in the stunning cavernous installation space, a figure was facing the temple, sitting on one of the stone blocks by the pool.

Ethan Weber smiled as he turned around.

With his salt-and-pepper buzz cut, the famous billionaire had an almost George Clooney thing going on.

But he seemed thinner than the last time she'd met him six months before, Warner thought as she got closer. She'd read in a *Fast Company* article that like some other Silicon Valley moguls, he'd recently been on a stoic philosophy fasting kick.

She really didn't think it was doing a lot for him, she noted as she arrived in front of him. Always thin, he now looked sort of skeletal. In the dim museum lighting, his shadow-filled eyes were like skull sockets, and when he yawned, she couldn't help but think of Munch's *The Scream*.

"Do you actually know why this structure is here, Dawn?" the billionaire said to her, casually crossing his legs as she sat beside him.

"You mean the temple itself? No, not really," Warner said.

"It was a gift to the United States from Egypt after the assassination of J.F.K.," Weber explained. "With the gift, they especially cited their condolences to Jacqueline. She actually lived across the street here on Fifth Avenue and could stare down at it from her apartment window with John Jr. and Caroline."

"Noble gesture," Warner said.

"Yes, quite," Weber said, gazing up at the magnificent sandstone behemoth. "Most widows are lucky to get a casserole. But that's not the reason I come here. I come here because of him."

He pointed to an Egyptian figure carved into the stone.

"He looks like a pharaoh, doesn't he? But he's not. It's a trick. He's actually Augustus, the Roman emperor."

"I didn't know that," Dawn Warner said.

"Augustus Caesar was perhaps the greatest Roman emperor of all. Rome ruled Egypt during his long, happy reign, and this temple was originally a gift from him to the people of Egypt."

Ethan Weber crossed his thin arms.

"Some think Augustus was great because of how clever he was. He was as much and perhaps even more of a military dictator than Julius Caesar, who had preceded him, but unlike the glory hound Caesar, he was smart enough to hide it. To cloak his ruthless will to power behind the grand facade of service to the Republic.

"And he did serve it," he said, cocking his head up at the figure. "Despite all his devious machinations, and I would claim *because* of them, the Roman Empire lasted several, maybe even as much as five centuries, longer than it would have."

Ethan Weber sat and silently stared at the temple.

Warner was deft enough a bureaucrat to say nothing when the powers that be were in guru mode.

Then after a minute or two, he sighed.

"How's our friend?" he finally said.

"He's fine," Dawn said. "Much, much better. He has the senator's estate all to himself like I told you. There's a small golf course. A lake. He goes out in the morning and feeds the ducks. Gandalf is doing much better."

"Gandalf?" Ethan Weber said, puzzled.

"That's his code name. Security needed a code name for him. He chose it himself."

"Oh, he must love that," Ethan Weber said with another sorrow-tinged sigh. "I'm glad he's doing okay. I really am."

Dawn Warner resumed silent mode. She didn't touch that one. Not with a hundred-thousand-foot pole, she thought.

"I assume you're doing everything you can to staunch the shitstorm in Denver, so you needn't mention it," Weber said. "I asked you to come because I wanted to invite you to the meeting. Considering our situation, I managed to reschedule. We're on for Monday evening."

"Back in Wyoming?" Warner said.

"No, in San Francisco. They'll be leaving from the airport right after."

"Do you really think that makes sense for all of us to be there? It's a bit, um, overt, isn't it?"

"I know, Dawn. It is a bit. I wouldn't even ask but here's the thing. They're not stupid. They have people in the same places we do. We have to assume they know everything that's going on. The bit of a bind we're in. You know as well as I do how much it's all about saving face for them. If you are there, it will comfort them that there is no law enforcement risk on their end. No risk of embarrassment. That the matter is being handled smoothly by all their partners."

"I see," Dawn Warner said. "Okay. Of course. That actually makes a lot of sense. If you need me there, Ethan, then I'll be there. I'll make it happen."

"Thanks, partner," Ethan said, standing and offering his hand. "We'll keep it between you and me, then."

"And Augustus," Warner said, tossing a chin at the temple as they shook.

87

Westergaard was home at his town house in Ventura when his eyes opened in the dark.

Was it the alarm? he thought. No. By the faint glow on the barrel ceiling above, he knew that he'd just received a text on his work phone.

To his right on the bedside table beside his phone was an old-fashioned mechanical clock and he listened to it tick. He turned and looked out the big picture window beyond the table. There wasn't any light in the sky over the water yet.

He turned left to his perfect blond wife. Elena always slept in the buff, and he reached out and softly laid a hand to her stunning bare back. He listened to her soft, measured breathing. Then he passed a finger down her spine and over to the valley upslope of her men's magazine model hip and smiled.

He'd met her in Las Vegas a year before at a crazy

casino bar where all the bottles were stacked two stories high up a kind of climbing wall. For hours he sat and drank glass after glass of wine, mesmerized by Elena and two other beautiful bartender girls in bikinis as they were hoisted up on climbing harnesses to get the bottles.

He'd only gone for the weekend to gamble with Maniscalco but two whirlwind weeks later, Elena had moved into his hotel room. It was two weeks after that that she'd told him she was pregnant.

After the announcement, that very night he found himself drunkenly standing at an altar. He'd been unable to contain his laughter as the Elvis preacher thanked him very much before he asked him if he had brought the ring.

He'd brought the ring all right, Westergaard thought, looking at the bulge of her belly. Bought the ring and bought the farm. Their kid was due in only a month and a half now.

A father, Westergaard thought, shaking his head.

He thought about his own father back on the farm outside Mutare in Zimbabwe that he'd bought them after being a lawyer in Sun City. He'd always thought him a simple fool, the serious way he'd pore over his planting schedules. Like an accountant over a spreadsheet.

But maybe not, Westergaard thought with a glance at his phone.

Why not cash it in like his father had done? he thought as he lay there. Get out of the city. Live simply. Maybe get a farm. Hell, with the money he had squirreled away, they could do anything. Or nothing at all. They could get a trailer out in the country, have one of those cheap pools in the back. Watch the sunset from it. Watch his kid learn to swim.

His new American daughter, he thought, smiling.

He pretended he wanted a son, but he secretly wanted a daughter. He'd had three older sisters back in South Africa who'd always been so nice and kind and loving toward him.

Well, at least before the rebel soldiers came that New Year's night when he was seventeen and raped and hacked them to death, then hung them up in the barn with barbed wire beside his mother and father.

If he hadn't been away at Danie Theron Combat School at the time, he would have been up there with them himself.

Westergaard listened to his phone buzz again.

He put a hand to his bandaged ear.

The man they'd been up against in Denver was, like himself, quite obviously a professional. A dedicated professional.

He pictured the American. Pale and broad-shouldered and square-edged. A block of marble, he thought. A stumbling block. A life-sized Lego man who one messed with at the peril of their life.

What had the American said the next round was going to be? A Sunday church barbecue? He didn't even want to know what that meant. And the authoritative way he had said it. Like he was really looking forward to it.

Did he really need that? Westergaard thought with another sigh.

He turned and stared at his wife's belly, her perfect ass.

Wasn't it time to hop off the gravy train with all his cash and prizes?

Westergaard lay between his pretty pregnant wife and his phone, thinking.

He touched his ear again.

One last time, he thought, and he leaned over and finally lifted up the phone.

88

It was coming on two in the afternoon when Gannon came out of a 7-Eleven on the concourse of the Salt Lake City Airport, walking along with the crowd.

The airport had been empty the week before when he had left with Kit to Wyoming, but it was packed now for some reason. Coming around a corner, he glanced up at a CNN news screen across the corridor and smiled when he saw it wasn't showing his face.

Perfect, he thought. So far so good.

Passing one of the other gates, he saw a service member with a shaved head, sleeping in a seat in the waiting area. He was a young marine, the brim of his camo cap over his eyes, his shaved head against his olive green canvas rucksack.

Gannon thought about his own deployments over the years and how he never thought to wonder on whose behalf he was being sent to wreak incredible amounts of violence. It had never occurred to him that the unseen hands signing his top secret orders were just a pack of incredibly connected corrupt criminals pulling global strings to pour more and more money into their multinational pockets.

"Keep your head down, brother," Gannon mumbled as he continued down the concourse.

Kit was talking on her phone when he arrived back, so he stood by the window. Right outside was a big white Delta airliner. He watched the orange jumpsuited mechanic on a scissor lift beneath its wing, refueling it.

The guy still wasn't done when Kit finally hung up.

"So?" Gannon said.

"It's on, Mike," she said. "Just heard back from everyone. It's on like Donkey Kong."

For the last twenty-four hours, Kit had been calling people. Her friend Amy Cargill had told her about how the Denver SAC was relieved of duty and how there was a huge dustup throughout the Bureau.

That coupled with some other calls she had made to the heavy hitters she knew in the FBI's New York office had prompted her to drop the entire mother lode of their investigation.

She had sent out Owen's video and the NSA match on Lisa Weber, and now an FBI task force was quickly being put together to do something about it.

Which was why they were at the airport. Kit was on a three o'clock Delta flight into Baltimore to meet up with the New York office team to drop the hammer.

"You sure about all of this?" Gannon said, wincing as her flight was called.

"I'm positive," Kit said, grabbing up her new carry-on.

John Barber stood.

"Here, Kit. I got you a going-away present," Barber said, offering her a plastic bag.

She reached inside of it and took out what looked like an old iPhone.

"Why, John, an old phone," Kit said. "You shouldn't have."

"It's actually a souvenir from my time in military intelligence," he said. "See the bottom here? The little thing that looks like a button? It's not a button. That's the receiver you point. You press this switch here, it'll work as a shotgun microphone. You press this one here, it'll pick up a cell phone conversation or any other radio signal you point it at. It eats battery like crazy so I included the charger. Downside is you have to be pretty close. A hundred yards is about the max range and you have a clear line of sight. Otherwise it'll get scrambled with other signals."

"Got it. Thanks, John, but this is for…?" Kit said.

He shrugged.

"Who knows? Might come in handy where you're headed."

"This isn't legal, John, is it?" she said.

"Not in any way, shape or form," he said with a grin.

He stepped away as Gannon came over. He had his hand behind his back.

"I got you a going-away present, too," he said as he handed her the Twix he'd bought at the 7-Eleven.

"Twix," she said with a laugh. "Who doesn't love Twix?"

He gave her a hug goodbye.

"Listen, Kit," he said, holding her for a second more. "I know what you said about these new friends of yours, but be careful. That Dawn Warner gets wind of your little plan, you know she'll be coming for you with her flying monkeys. Trust no one."

"Except you, you mean," Kit said in his ear.

"Now you're finally getting with the program," Gannon said as he winked and squeezed her wrist and finally let her go.

89

After Kit left, Gannon and John Barber got back into Gannon's pickup truck in the airport parking lot.

"Hold up there a second, would you, Mike?" Barber said, slipping a square of paper out of his jacket pocket.

Gannon looked down at the photograph. It was of several men smiling for the camera in front of the porch of a dusty old brick house. They were bristling with tactical gear, rifles on straps, and some of them wore goggles and earmuffs.

"Hey, wait, that's your shoothouse."

"Why, yes, it is. Let me ask you. Who does this fella remind you of?" Barber said, pointing.

"No," Gannon said shaking his head. "Come on. What the hell?"

There was no mistaking it. The hooded eyes, the arrogant expression. In the photo's top right-hand corner was the shooter from the Denver parking garage shoot-out that Kit had shown them. Or it was his twin brother.

"You know the Euro weenie?" Gannon said.

"I spent a week training him two years ago. He came through with some heavy-duty government contractor types who wanted to use the shoothouse to run simulations. I thought it was him straight off when Kit showed us. But I asked around the grapevine. I needed to double-check."

"You know his name?"

Barber nodded.

"Not only that," he said. "I know where he lives."

Gannon smiled.

"What's his name?"

"Clarence Westergaard."

"Clarence? Wow," Gannon said. "His parents should be charged with cruel and unusual punishment. What is he? Dutch?"

"South-African-born but moved to Munich in his teens before he joined up with the KSK."

"Hmmm. Clarence German-commando-trained Westergaard, huh? Very interesting, John. Let me guess. You're leaving Kit out of the loop because you're thinking maybe we should tackle this lead on our own? Maybe pay Clarence a visit. See what he's up to? See if we can persuade him to own up to his transgressions?"

"Had crossed my mind," Barber said. "Kit's certainly got enough on her plate tackling things with the Silicon Valley folks in DC."

"What's Clarence's address?"

"Ventura, California," Barber said. "We fly out of Moab at five in the morning."

Gannon looked over at his friend. How much it had to be weighing on him that he had probably helped train the son of a bitch who had killed his brother. How ripped up he had to be about it. How much he needed to personally set things straight.

Then Gannon looked back down at Clarence in the picture and remembered the brick wall in Denver exploding a centimeter above his own head.

"And if old Clarence doesn't feel like being persuaded?" Gannon said.

"Ah, don't be so cynical, Mike," Barber said, patting Gannon on the arm. "We're creative people. You and me both know there's more than one way to skin a cat."

90

Brady's Ale House, one of the oldest Irish pubs in Baltimore, was in an old redbrick building with stone trim midway down the slope of East Pleasant Street downtown near the courthouses.

Inside there were old whiskey barrels along the walls and red, white, and blue bunting above the hunter-green leather booths. On the old dusty wood-paneled walls above the booths hung yellowed photos of bare-fisted boxers and Charlie Chaplin movie posters and old liquor licenses in frames going back to the early 1900s.

At nine thirty in the morning in one of its back rooms, Kit, straight from the airport hotel, stood in the glow of a neon beer sign. Standing around the rear of the barroom with her was the FBI New York office head, Bill Ferguson, a dozen New York office FBI agents and a fcderal district attorney.

They were all standing before Bill's brother, Federal District Judge Joseph P. Ferguson, who was sitting in one of the booths.

On the old pinewood table where the judge sat was a half-full draft of Sam Adams lager, and beside that was a federal arrest warrant for Ethan Weber waiting for his signature.

Kit looked about the room as they waited for the judge to silently absorb all that Kit had just presented to him.

Her eyes locked onto a life-sized cigar-store-style wooden statue of Babe Ruth in the corner.

Come on, Babe, she prayed as she looked into the great Bambino's eyes. *Help us convince Judge Joe.*

When Kit glanced over, the judge was still positioned exactly as his brother had sat him down in the booth half an hour before.

With his arms crossed and with a very skeptical look on his face.

As Kit watched, the judge lifted his beer and drained it. Then he re-crossed his arms.

"That's all you got?" he said.

Kit rolled her eyes as everyone groaned.

"All we got? Are you listening, Joe?" Bill Ferguson said. "That's Weber's wife dead on Grand Teton there. I showed you the park ranger's video and the facial recognition pictures."

"Which are inadmissible."

"Who gives a care? They're real. A two-year-old can see it's the same woman. With his endless billions, this guy used a team of covert mercenaries to kill not just his wife but an FBI agent, a county sheriff, a park ranger, a stripper, and probably even a Wyoming boob doctor to cover it all up. We've got a kidnapping attempt on Kit here in Denver, and if that's not enough, it looks like we've got a rogue Justice Department assistant AG quarterbacking this nonstop insanity."

"I know," the judge said. "I've heard of Warner. She's from the deepest end of the pool. She's the one who scares me the most."

"You are a criminal law judge, right, Joe?" Bill Ferguson said. "You prosecute crimes, right? Crimes like cold-blooded murder?"

"Screw you, Bill. You didn't have to go to law school, did you? No, you get to drive around free as a bird all day playing G-man while good old Dad made *me* follow in his footsteps into the courts."

"And that's not even it in terms of evidence," Bill Ferguson said. "We have a guard at the Francis E. Warren Air Force Base that positively ID'd three of the men who were at the Denver shoot-out. He puts them arriving there by Black Hawk helicopter right before Tracy Sandhurst was abducted and then taking off right after. We also have another of the shooters on a doorbell video near the house of Dr. Fletcher on the morning he supposedly committed suicide."

"Fletcher's who again? The boob doctor guy?" the judge said.

"Yes, Joe. The *dead* boob doctor guy," Bill Ferguson said.

"This seems like an intelligence thing," Judge Joe said, shaking his head.

"Who cares, Joe!" Bill Ferguson screamed. "It's

illegal! Killing American people is against the fricking law even if you're in the CIA!"

"It's going to be a shitstorm."

"So what. Let it rain. Remember what Dad used
to say? Let justice be done though the heavens fall.
Remember?"

"He's right, Your Honor," Kit said. "I don't know
about you, but covert military psycho killers flying
around abducting American citizens and killing them
to cover up for wife-murdering billionaire software
developers isn't a world I feel too comfortable living in."

"Exactly," Bill Ferguson said. "If this isn't shit you
sign arrest warrants for, we need to hang a closed sign
on the courthouse door. Who cares who we piss off?
They shot Dennis. You loved Dennis. You owe him
big-time! Get a spine."

"I'm going to be needing a new one probably,"
Judge Joe said, not moving his crossed arms a centimeter. "What happens after I sign this? What's the
next step?"

"Weber's coming to Congress for a hearing about
social media censorship at two," Kit said. "We're
going over to Capitol Hill and we'll arrest him as
he's coming in to testify."

"On the Capitol steps? It'll be all over the news!"

"Yes, we know. That's the point, Joe. It'll be the
frog march to end all frog marches. Your brother's
cuffs here one day will end up in the Smithsonian
along with that piece of paper in front of you. *The
Ferguson Brothers Save America!* It'll be a Broadway play. You'll go down in history."

"A Broadway play," Judge Joe spat. "We'll go down all right but not in history."

"Fine, Joe," Bill Ferguson said. "Fine. Forget it. Give me the warrant back. We'll go to plan B."

"Plan B?" the judge said. "What's that?"

"I march over to Capitol Hill and when Weber gets out of the limo, I take out my gun and I avenge Dennis by blowing the son of a bitch's brains out."

"Fine, you crazy son of a bitch," Judge Joe said, taking out a pen. "Just fine. You satisfied, little brother? My career is done now, you know that. Hope Dee and the kids like the couch in Mom's basement at the over fifty-five in Orlando."

"Cry me a river, Joe. Your house is as big as a Home Depot," Bill Ferguson said as he picked up the document.

Kit had experienced a lot of great feelings as an agent, but coming out of the dark of the beer-smelling bar into the bright morning light of Baltimore with the good men around her to arrest Ethan Weber took the prize far and away.

"Thank you, Babe," Kit said, patting the Sultan of Swat on his pin-striped shoulder as they all left.

"We're doing this, Dennis," she whispered to her dead partner as she stared down the old-fashioned narrow street.

She was piling into the back of Bill Ferguson's lead Suburban when his phone rang.

"What's this? Hold way the hell up. I'm getting a text from my buddy. No, this can't be happening."

"What?" Kit said panicked. "Weber's gone? He fled the country?"

"No," Bill Ferguson said. "He's still here. Right here. In fact, he's waiting for us."

"What?"

"Ethan Weber apparently just turned himself in. He's over at the J. Edgar Hoover Building in DC."

91

Despite a near constant headwind almost the whole way west, it took exactly four hours to land at the tiny Santa Paula Airport in Ventura County, California.

Hertz had already sent over the Cadillac Escalade they had requested, and they piled in their bags and found Highway 126 and took it southwest. They saw the ocean for the first time when they got on the 101 Pacific Coast Highway north forty minutes later.

When they got off at the next exit, they came over an overpass and parked at the deserted dead end of a road by the beach. Gannon, behind the wheel, flicked up the AC another notch as Barber unpacked the food his wife had made for them out of a blue cooler bag.

"What did you tell Lynn we were doing anyway?" Gannon said as Barber handed him a plastic bottle of iced coffee along with a tin foil package. Gannon smiled as he saw the sesame seed bagel brimming with cream cheese.

"Hunting," Barber said.

Gannon chuckled as he took a bite.

"You tell her what we were hunting?"

"Didn't specify."

Gannon chuckled again.

"Clever," he said, munching. "John Barber and George Washington: the only two Americans who never told a lie."

After he had demolished his bagel, Gannon got out and chucked his napkins into a trash bin. He stood for a moment, stretching and gazing out at the water. The white break of waves along the curve of the inlet, the long pier on their right, the high desert hills drab-colored and rumpled in the haze beyond. A couple with a golden retriever was playing with a stick by the water's edge, and their silhouettes were like something out of a love song music video from a more innocent time.

When he came back, Gannon accepted the second coffee John Barber had already opened for him along with a binder. Inside of it were tactical maps and a blowup of a mission-style house with a Spanish tile roof and a pool.

"This is up in the hill above the town, right?"

"Uh-huh. This is a condo place in front of it," Barber said, pointing at a yellow stucco building. "But it looks pretty private with this hedge."

They both looked up as a jogger went by on the sand, followed by a scraggly guy with a metal detector wand.

John finished his coffee and burped loudly as he tossed the empty plastic bottle into the back seat.

"Okay. You ready?" he said.

"What? No goodies?" Gannon said.

"Goodies?"

"In Lynn's bag there. You know, like pastries or cookies?"

John Barber reached into the back seat and grabbed up a duffel bag and unzipped it in his lap. Inside of it was a cut-down M4 fully automatic carbine rifle along with some balaclavas and radios and similar bric-a-brac.

"I got a goodie for you right here," Barber said as he took out a brand-new Colt Gold Cup Series semi-automatic .45 and handed it over.

Gannon took a look at it. The bright satin stainless finish. The black rubber grip crisp in his big hand.

"I was thinking something more along the lines of a Yodel or an apple pie," Gannon said as he tucked it into his shoulder holster. "But you know what, John? This will actually do."

They took side streets from the beach into Ventura town proper and made a right onto the hill up a wide palm-lined street. Gannon looked out at the soft California morning light on the pale stucco mission facades. There were bikes and surfboards in the windows of the pleasant old Spanish-tiled shops. They rolled past a funky coffee joint. Out in front of it, a dog slept lazily on the sidewalk beside a full-dress Harley.

Part beach town, part art deco old Hollywood, Gannon thought. It looked expensive.

"Nice little town, huh? Sleepy."

"Yeah, well," John Barber said, folding his arms. The just-risen sun gleamed off the dark shade of his sunglasses.

"It's about to get woke the hell up in a second."

Two minutes later, they passed the yellow stucco condo and then Westergaard's address without slowing. A few hundred feet up past it, they made a left into a public park with hiking trails and beautiful rolling hills covered in wildflowers.

It took them ten minutes to park and hike up high on a secluded spot on the hill overlooking Westergaard's house.

They squatted low in the undergrowth, staring down. When Barber handed him the binoculars, he saw they had a good vista into most of the backyard lanai and pool.

"Come out, come out wherever you are," Barber said.

"Can't believe it's actually come to this," Gannon said, handing Barber back the glasses.

"Come to what?" Barber said.

"Doing sneak-and-peeks in our own damn country."

92

"The damn puzzle palace. Just great," Deputy Director Bill Ferguson said as they arrived before the white tomb-like J. Edgar Hoover Building.

"That doesn't sound very encouraging, Bill," Kit said as they got out on 10th Street.

"Have you ever been here before?" Ferguson said.

"Just at graduation."

"Yeah, well," Bill said as they stepped up onto the sidewalk. "The New York office is nothing like this. Nothing too good ever seems to happen here."

At the top of the stone steps, the side door was propped open. Three feet inside, there was a white-shirted veteran DC Capitol cop standing by the security desk. His arms were folded across his chest.

"We're—" Bill Ferguson said.

"Oh, we know who you are," the guard said coldly as he thumbed them for the elevator.

The wiry bespectacled middle-aged female agent that met them on the other side of the elevator door on the seventh floor reminded Kit of the farmer's wife in that famous painting. She looked bitter as burnt coffee, like a mean first-grade teacher who'd run out of students to put in the corner.

"They're waiting for you in here," she informed them as she pointed at a door.

The conference room Special Agent Schoolmarm led them into was as plush as any Kit had ever been in. She looked at the glossy lacquered tables, the glossy leather chairs. The coffered ceiling had panels in bird's-eye maple. She glanced at the navy-colored grass cloth wallpaper on the walls. It had a faintly raised filigree of fleurs-de-lis.

After another step inside, on the other side of the slick mahogany conference table, Kit saw the famous Ethan Weber. Sitting contentedly, surrounded by his lawyers, he looked like the world's scrawniest quarterback protected by a pudgy foppish middle-aged offensive line.

This wasn't good, Kit thought, shaking her head. Weber getting the VIP treatment *wasn't good at all*.

The tan, prosperous-looking lawyer to Weber's immediate right looked vaguely familiar from cable news. The few remaining squiggles of hair on his large bronzed forehead gave him the look of a wealthy, arrogant Charlie Brown.

When she turned to the left, she saw a little mousy blond middle-aged man with bifocals sitting in the corner with a laptop on his knees. He was a legal stenographer there to record everything as if it were a deposition, Kit realized.

What in the hell was this? she thought.

"Four lawyers, Ethan. Wow. That's a lot," Kit said.

"I'll be representing Mr. Weber in this matter," Charlie Brown, Esquire, said. "Please direct your questions to me. I'm Attorney Fred Ingraham."

"Oh, boy," Ferguson said as he sat.

"My client," Ingraham said, "has become aware that there is some inquiry into an alleged disappearance you believe he may have been involved in. My client is a very busy individual who would like to get the matter cleared up, so if we could get started? Agent Hagen, is it?"

Kit nodded.

"Please, Agent Hagen, if you could begin by clarifying precisely what information you need. And if you could be expedient about it, I'm sure the United States Congress would be most appreciative."

"To clarify," Bill Ferguson interrupted, "we're not looking into a disappearance."

"No?"

"No," he said. "Our inquiry is into a murder."

"Exactly," Kit said as she passed over a still of the video Owen Barber had taken. "The murder of your client's wife."

Weber and his lawyers leaned forward in unison to look down at the photo. Then they leaned back, and there was a great amount of whispering as they put their heads together.

They finally sat back up normally as Ingraham cleared his throat.

"My client wants to know what he's looking at here," he said.

"Your client might want to look into a pair of glasses," Kit said.

"I'll handle this, Kit," Ferguson said. "There lies your client's wife, naked and dead as a doornail."

Instead of answering, Ingraham brought up his briefcase onto the table and opened it and took something out of it.

It was a thumb drive.

"In this drive," he said, holding it up before placing it on the table, "is security tape of the hotel my client was staying at in Jackson, Wyoming. You will see when you view it that my client went into his room and stayed there until his speech and then went back to his room, emerging only one last time to leave the following morning. You will also see from this tape that his wife was not with him on the Wyoming trip."

"Who said we were interested in Wyoming?" Kit said.

The attorney smiled weakly.

"Rumors abound," he said as he lifted a remote control from the table and turned and clicked it at the wide screen on the wall to the left of the conference table.

93

Everyone looked over as a woman appeared on the screen.

Kit started shaking her head.

She was an Asian woman in her early thirties with a very uncanny resemblance to Lisa Weber.

And she was very much alive.

"Hello," said the woman, waving at them from what looked like an outdoor table. She seemed to be sitting at a terrace with city buildings behind her. There was an older Chinese couple with her. They waved, as well.

"Hi, honey," Weber said, waving back.

"Whatever this is about," the Lisa Weber look-alike said, "these reports of my death have been highly exaggerated."

"Oh, you guys are funny. Real funny," Kit said, looking at Weber. "This is some production."

"I would like to present to you Mrs. Weber from her hotel in Chongqing," Ingraham said with a straight face. "That's Chongqin, China, where her parents live. She's been staying there for the last two weeks."

He took a slip of paper from his still open briefcase.

"For your records, here is the manifest of the flight she took that left out of San Francisco International on the eighth."

"Oh, I see," Kit said, staring at Weber. "You sent the body to China. Crafty, Ethan. She's dead already, then you fake that she's still alive and going on a trip using this look-alike. Where'd you put her body? In the luggage compartment?"

"But I am alive," the woman on the screen said.

"What is this, Ethan. The latest in deep fake?" Kit said, refusing to look at the screen. "One of your geeky friends whipped up a *Mission Impossible* mask for that hooker there. Is that it?"

"Kit," Ferguson said.

"Don't Kit me. You're falling for this? My wife's not dead, she's alive, but she's in China? Look, she's right here on a fake news video. That's even better than 'the dog ate my homework.'" Kit took a breath. "Actually, it's not."

"One more thing," Ingraham said, going into his briefcase again. "I just spoke to Judge Joe, your brother, I believe, Agent Ferguson? Well, I think this speaks for itself."

The lawyer showed them a piece of paper.

Kit looked down.

The arrest warrant had been rescinded.

When she looked up, Weber was giving her a queer smile from behind his lawyers.

"Smirk away, you ugly pencil-necked scumbag," Kit said.

Kit watched a hot flash of anger ripple across the placid calm of the young billionaire's face.

Apparently, people didn't speak to him like that.

94

"That's all, gentlemen," Ferguson suddenly said. "Thanks for coming in. Sorry for the misunderstanding."

"No, thank you, Agent Ferguson," Ethan Weber said, standing. "And you, too, Agent Hagen. I forgive you for your insults. I know how much you've been through."

"See that last little dig there, Bill?" Kit said. "That was in reference to Ethan having me shot. This son of a bitch had me shot. He killed Dennis Braddock and the others. Splattered them all over the top of Grand Teton and you're going to let him walk out of here?"

"We don't have a warrant anymore, Kit," Ferguson said as Weber and his phalanx of lawyers pushed past them out the door.

"I don't care. He killed her. That video on the screen is complete bullshit and you know it."

"I do, Kit. But would a jury buy that? They wouldn't. We need to retreat here a bit."

"Yeah, you're right, Bill. That computer freak is the only one allowed to do the buying around here, isn't he? He's the only one who buys things. Like senators, judges, district attorneys, FBI personnel."

"We don't have a body, Kit," Bill Ferguson said quietly as he stared down at his shoes. "If we had the body, we could do something, but we don't."

"Who is this then?" Kit said, lifting the paper. "Who is this dead woman? And let's not forget Tracy Sandhurst, mutilated and then draped like a party streamer up on Grand Teton to cover it up!"

"Chill, Kit," Ferguson said, standing with a sigh. "We're going to nail him but just not now. It's only a matter of time. He can't get out of it. He really can't. This is just a stall tactic. This is round one."

"Yeah, round one," Kit said as she stumbled out of the conference room. "A round one knockout."

She was coming by the director's office in the hall when she stopped.

"Kit, no!" Bill Ferguson said, hurrying after her as she walked inside.

"Excuse me, you can't go in there," said Agent Schoolmarm as Kit burst past her and threw open the door.

Inside, off to the left, Director Foldager himself was sitting at a dining table by the window, eating Chinese food and laughing with three other Brooks-Brothers-suited cronies.

"You must leave now," the agent said.

"No, no, Carol. Honestly, it's fine," said the photogenic father-figure-like FBI director, smiling.

He lay down his chopsticks as Kit walked over.

"Special Agent Hagen, is it?" he said. "Is there something I can help you with?"

"No, I'm here to help you, actually," Kit said.

"Oh, boy," said Bill Ferguson as he arrived behind her.

"Is that right?"

"Do you remember in the Old Testament where Lot tries to save Sodom and Gomorrah?" Kit said.

"Perhaps," the director said, shrugging his shoulders.

"See, God wants to vaporize the cities because of how foul and rotten-to-core they've become, but Lot bargains with God. Lot says, 'God, if there's just one good person left—just one—will you spare them?' And God says okay, but then what do you know? It turns out there isn't even one, so God nukes everything from orbit."

"Your point, Special Agent?"

Kit looked up at the coffered ceiling, then back level into the director's eyes.

"I'd stay the hell out of this place if I were you," she said.

95

"Mike, check it out. By the pool," Barber suddenly said.

Gannon rolled over from where he'd been dozing in the wild grass and accepted the binocs.

In Westergaard's backyard next to the pool, a shirtless guy was rolling out a yoga mat. He was tall and muscular with a bunch of tats down one arm and had his blond hair tied back in a man bun. Gannon peered at him. Then he smiled when he saw he had a bandage on the right side of his face.

"That's him, right?" Barber said.

"Oh, that's him," Gannon said. "You see that fanny pack in the grass next to him?"

"Yep, he brought it out with him. Imagine? You have to be one paranoid son of a bitch to pack beside your own pool."

"Well, what do you think? So far so good. Target of opportunity? Should we get the truck?"

"No," Barber said standing. "Let's just go now. I'll go over the driveway fence. You go high and swing in around back."

"Sounds good to me."

They came down the slope of the dry loose dirt hill and split up as they crossed over the road. Gannon went up high into the hill beside Westergaard's house and made a wide loop. He passed a firepit and a tennis court. He could see the fence for the pool over some hedges.

"In position," he said as he grabbed the top of the waist-high fence.

Gannon's boots had just landed on the cement pool deck with a scuffling sound when he heard John Barber yell.

"Freeze! FBI!"

"You do it, you're dead," Gannon yelled as he came slowly up behind Westergaard and saw him lowering his hand toward the fanny pack in the grass.

Gannon had closed half the distance to where Barber had him down putting on the first handcuff when there was a sound from the right.

It was the sliders on the other side of the pool, and a woman—a young pregnant blond woman—came out from its shadow yelling.

"Get the hell away from him!"

"Gun!" Gannon yelled, breaking into a full sprint as he saw the steel in her hand.

He and Barber were already lunging into the bushes around the corner of the house as the gun started popping.

"Shit!" Barber yelled as they watched Wester-gaard fly across the grass like a jackrabbit in his bare feet and scale the pool fence and disappear down the slope.

"I'm on him," Gannon said leaping up after him. "Get the truck."

"Careful. He took the fanny pack," Barber called at his back.

"Don't remind me," Gannon mumbled as he hopped the pool fence and came skidding down a hill.

At the bottom, there was a parking lot for the condo facility and across it, there was an apartment door open, and he bolted for it.

He'd just poked his head in when he sensed movement up the short set of stairs to the right. He dove back as a gun came over the bannister and blew apart the door frame beside his left ear.

A second later, there was a thumping and the crash of glass, and he plunged through the doorway behind his gun. He crossed a living room with a kitchen at the other side of it and through its broken slider, he saw Westergaard past the backyard in another parking lot, running for the street.

He'd just gotten to the street himself when a white convertible Jaguar came squealing around the curve in the street above. It was the crazy pregnant woman who had tried to kill them, and Gannon ducked down behind a car as it shot past him down the hill. It made another hairpin turn and was screeching to a stop about a block away beside a corner church when Gannon looked up. He was just in time to see Westergaard dive into its open passenger window. Then the Jag peeled out down the wide palm-lined street.

Gannon shook his head as Barber arrived in the Escalade a full minute later.

"What! Gone?" Barber yelled.

"We missed him. She picked him up in her car."

"No!" Barber yelled like a savage as he punched at the steering wheel.

"Screw it, John," Gannon said, getting in. "Let's get the hell out of here. The locals have to be on their way after those shots."

"No way. Not yet," Barber said as he began reversing the big truck at speed back up the hill. "We got a minute yet. I'm not leaving here empty-handed. It's pocket litter time."

They parked beside Westergaard's house and went back in through the open slider. In the room beside the master was an office, and they'd just grabbed a couple of laptops and a cell phone when the wall phone rang.

"Vinny's Pizza," Gannon said, lifting it up.

"You have no idea what's going on, do you?" Westergaard said. "Not the foggiest clue."

"If that's the case, why am I standing in your office, Clarence?"

"Two can play at that game, eh?"

"Not if one of them is dead. Besides, you started it up on that mountain, Clarence. Hope those big-pocket buddies of yours at Sonexum gave you a life insurance plan for the little lady and Clarence Jr. Because you tapped the wrong guy in that ambush, friend."

"Go to hell," Westergaard said.

"Your choices are down to two. You can turn yourself in right now and play ball with the law or we can do it the hard way."

"You're the one messing with the wrong guy," Westergaard said.

"The hard way it is, then," Gannon said.

"Is there any other?" the South African said and the line went dead.

96

Outside of the Hoover building, the gray street was hot and pale in the noon sun, the sidewalk baking. From the various federal government buildings, workers on their lunch break were pouring out onto the hot concrete like ants from a burning nest.

"C'mon, Kit. Let's get something to eat," Ferguson said as he was about to climb back into the SUV on 10th Street.

"I can't," Kit said as she went to the rear door and grabbed her carry-on. "I need to... I need to take a walk or something."

"I get it, Kit. Call me if you need anything, okay? I'm sorry. I know this hurts like hell but this is the battle, not the war. Okay? We're going to rebound," he said.

"Okay, Bill," she said, unable to look him in the eye.

The Suburban had pulled out and Kit made it as

far as the corner of Pennsylvania Avenue before she
stopped and covered her mouth with her hands as
she started crying.

She shook her head and bit at her lip as she looked
out at the rush of the traffic, the flow of the people.

Weber really had won. He'd killed Dennis, shot
her. And he was really going to get clean away with it.
Instead of being cuffed he was probably at the Capitol Building right now being greeted like a rock star,
getting seated by some name Congressman while
some intern asked him if he'd like a cup of coffee or
some water.

Justice was dead, she thought, stunned, as she
looked back at the Hoover building. It was official
now. After that meeting, it was official. She lived in
a country where there were two tiers of justice. One
for the rich and connected and one for everybody else.

Which made the purpose of her being in law enforcement what now? she wondered. To arrest only
the little people? Round up the dissidents?

What the hell was she going to do? she wondered
as she wiped at her eyes. *What the hell was anyone
supposed to do?*

She'd managed to compose herself as she grabbed
the handle of her rolling carry-on and was just about
to head across the street when the Range Rover pulled
up. She saw that its rear passenger window was already in the process of zipping downward.

When she saw who was inside of it, Kit's eyes shot
wide-open and something in her stomach dropped
like a cable-snapped elevator.

Her breath caught as she stood there rooted to the

concrete, thinking she was about to see the barrel of a pistol.

"Life's just full of surprises, isn't it, Kit?" Dawn Warner said.

97

Dawn Warner climbed out onto the street beside her.

"I was wondering if we could talk for a second," she said.

Kit said nothing as her heart started beating again. She began hurrying across the street.

"Kit?"

"No thanks," Kit said, moving quicker.

"Don't be silly, Kit. Just for a second."

Kit kept walking but Warner kept pace with her as they approached an open plaza.

"I heard about your tirade to the director," Warner said as Kit finally halted, glaring at her.

"And you tore Weber a new one, as well. That took some real fire, Kit. Bravo. You're fierce. You remind me of myself twenty years ago."

Kit shook her head, her face hot.

The plaza they'd stopped in was a memorial for

the US Navy with a huge fountain in it. Kit looked at Warner, then at the bubbling green water, wondering very seriously if she should do something right there and then. Split her nose open with her already balled fist. Grab her by her haute couture jacket lapels and get her over the fountain wall into the water and drown her. She had ten pounds on her and was two decades younger.

"Why are you here? What do you want?" she finally said.

"Can I tell you a story?" Dawn Warner said, looking her in the eyes. "When I was a teenager I knew a lot of kids from the Upper East Side of Manhattan. One of them was a close friend of a famous political family of a former president. One night I went to a beer party at their apartment. In this apartment there was a display of moon rocks—actual moon rocks from the Apollo mission—that had been gifted to the former president."

"Who gives a shit," Kit said.

"Listen. There was a drunken boy at this party, a football player from Fordham Prep. He decided to take one of the rocks as a joke. Two weeks later, this boy never made it home from football practice. He was found with two bullets in his back floating facedown in the Hudson River near Yonkers."

"I repeat," Kit said glaring at her.

"But that's not the kicker," Dawn Warner said. "The kicker is that the next time this girl went to the famous apartment for an event, the moon rock the boy had stolen was back in the display. That's the kicker."

Kit stood and looked at her for another beat.

"No," Kit said. "I think I know the real kicker."

"What's that?"

"The dead football player was your boyfriend and you shooting him in the back was how you made your bones."

The smile Dawn Warner gave was the first genuine one Kit had ever seen her make.

"Those claws, Kit. Like razors. That's why we're having this conversation. How would you like to be splendidly wealthy? Or have a post anywhere in the world? Or better yet, both?"

"How's that?"

"You're not going to beat us. You saw what happened in there. It's just going to happen again and again and again. There's just too much money at stake. We're not talking billions, Kit, but trillions. With a T. I'm telling you truly as a person with sympathy for you and with respect, you need to come into the tent where it's warm."

"Excuse me?"

"We're past being caught, Kit. We run it now."

"It?"

She made a gesture at the fountains, the buildings, the street, the sky.

"This town, this country, this planet. Everything, Kit. The computer tech and surveillance grid has delivered a paradigm power shift of historic proportions. It's the magic mirror from *Snow White*, Kit. It tells all. We see all and go where we want and do what we want. Nothing happens now without our consent. They say if you can't beat them, join them, right? Well, you ain't beating us. I could use you, Kit. Truly. You could be my protégé."

Kit reared back, staring wide-eyed. Then she started laughing. Really hard. Belly laughing.

"That's a no, I take it?" Dawn Warner said, giving her a half smile.

It was a cold half smile now.

"You're crazier than a shit house rat," Kit said mirthfully. "You and Weber and all of you. Run the world? You're on those Silicon Valley drugs, too, right? LSD microdoses? That must be it. At your age? You need to get off that stuff, Dawn. You're going to end up in the cemetery."

"*I'm* going to end up dead?" Warner said softly. "Well, I tried, Kit. You can't say I never offered you a chance."

"A chance to what? Be corrupt to the bone like you? Sell my soul to the devil? Screw over my neighbors and countrymen and their children? Gee, thanks, Dawn. That's real nice of you, but I'm good."

"I offered you a seat in the lifeboat, Kit. I can't help it if you're too stupid to take it."

98

Kit stood rooted to the concrete, listening to the bubbling of the fountain as she watched Warner walk
back to her car. She got in and slammed the door behind her. Kit thought the car would pull away. But
it didn't.

Kit scanned the sidewalk. Looking across Pennsylvania Avenue, she saw one of Warner's minion
agents, the tall, rusty-haired one. He was paying
a street vendor for a brown bag of something. She
watched as he carried it to the corner light and took
out his phone.

Kit froze for a moment and then began fishing
through her carry-on. She produced the surveillance
phone John Barber had given her and turned it on
and pointed it at Fitzgerald as she pretended to put
it to her face.

"No, honey. I can't talk now. Seriously, I'm

jammed right this second," said Fitzgerald's voice suddenly in her ear from where he stood waiting to cross the street.

"But you have to," said a woman's voice on the line.

"It's not happening. I'm right in the middle of all this. I can't," Fitzgerald said.

"How about at the airport? When are you leaving?" the woman said.

"In three hours."

"That's not acceptable," the woman said. "That coach might be gone by then. I'm not taking this shit anymore, Patrick. You know how embarrassing it is to watch your oldest son ride the bench game after game?"

"Fine," Fitzgerald said, annoyed around a mouthful of pretzel. "I'll try, all right. But if I can't catch him today, I'll call him first thing tomorrow from San Fran."

"Ooh-la-la. San Fran. The way you say it," Fitzgerald's wife said sarcastically. "All this jet-setting around with the elite is turning you so cool, Patrick. It really is. Can I have your autograph when you get back from San Fran, darling? After you hand me your dirty underwear."

Fitzgerald laughed at that.

"Alrighty then. Fun as this is, I have to go now, sweet pea."

"Wait. Is he still with you? He's testifying on CSPAN in twenty minutes they said. I just turned it on."

"No, billionaire boy isn't with us anymore," Fitzgerald said. "His security took him a second ago, but we have to pick him up from Capitol Hill in two hours. The witch is excited she's getting so much time with him on the flight."

"You need to follow her lead, Patrick. You need to kiss his ass like there's no tomorrow. I'm telling you, this is the chance of a lifetime. Weber could make us rich by sneezing on you."

"Yeah, right. When the witch hits the powder room, I'll just lean over and say, 'Hey, Ethan, baby. You need me on your team, bro.' Oh, shit. Gotta go. Broom-Hilda is back in the car. For real. She's waving at me. I'll call you tonight when we get in."

Kit slipped the illegal spy phone back into her carry-on and had her real one out before Fitzgerald made the Rover's door.

"Kit, hey. What's the scoop?" Gannon said.

"Mike, listen. I need help."

"Help?" Gannon said. "What happened? How many of them are there this time?"

"Very funny," she said. "We got blocked here in DC but I'm heading to the airport now."

"The airport?"

"Yes. I'm getting the next flight to San Francisco. You need to do the same."

"Why?"

"Warner is flying there this afternoon with Ethan Weber. Something is up. I can feel it. This isn't over yet."

99

Dawn Warner's suite was on the top floor of the Clement Hotel in Palo Alto. In the mirror where she sat doing the finishing touches to her makeup, she could see the jack-o'-lantern lights atop Stanford's famous Hoover Tower behind her through the window across the street.

The ice cubes in the vodka tonic rattled as she lifted it. She took a bracing sip and placed it back down.

One drink, she thought, laying down her lip primer as she smiled at herself in the mirror. Just one little stiffener to anchor her calm.

Her lips and then her mascara finished, she dotted on her perfume. It was Yves Saint Laurent Opium, and the courtly fragrance of it and the rose glow of the evening sky outside the window behind her suddenly reminded her of her childhood.

Her *glorious* childhood, she thought, smiling as she sipped at her drink.

She remembered her Brearley uniform, shopping with Mommy on Madison, birthday parties at the Waldorf Astoria, at Serendipity. She remembered being in her pajamas standing atop the curving staircase in their 67th and Park duplex as she watched Mommy and Daddy getting ready for all the fall charity week soirees.

Her tall daddy in his spotless Armani tux standing on the marble by the door, her model mother with her curly blond hair up, an Australian beauty in a black gown and heels.

She'd been born and raised on such Park Avenue scenes. Her father, a financier at a merchant bank, even had a limousine, a long hunter-green Lincoln that he would sometimes take her in to her piano lessons, if she was very good.

You're a princess, he would tell her as they rode hand in hand among the taxis and skyscrapers and crowds. *You're my little American princess*.

Then suddenly everything had changed.

It was her first year in high school when her mother and father divorced.

That's when she and her siblings had ended up in *Bronxville*, she thought with a frown.

Bronxville.

What a fall it had been, she thought, squinting. A Brearley girl at Bronxville High? Prometheus had hardly fallen lower when he was hurled from the top of Mount Olympus into Tartarus.

No more looking out over the storybook yellow-and-pink spring tulips on the Park Avenue median.

No more Mr. and Mrs. Carabante, the live-in couple who had been their butler and maid. And certainly no more limo rides with Daddy through Central Park.

Instead they'd lived above a dentist, their run-down building so close to the train station that her grimy bedroom window would rattle every time the Metro North train passed.

She thought of her pathetic know-it-all obnoxious father with his '80s Porsche and suspenders the occasional times he would deign to come by. The sniveling visits to go for pizza, where she'd given serious thought to how much life insurance he had and how difficult it would be to successfully poison a person.

But she had brought them back, hadn't she? Dawn Warner thought with a nod. She and her brother and her little sister. She had withstood it all. It was she who had gotten into Columbia and then graduated summa from Harvard Law. Her discipline, her tenacity, her steamroller ambition.

And it didn't stop when she'd scored the top slot at Justice. No way. That was the beginning. She'd gone hard at it for years making connection after connection, getting mentor after mentor to show her how things were actually done in the beltway.

It was also she who'd made all the proper moves to perch her brother, Charlie, back into Daddy's investment bank despite his horrible college career and trouble with the law. No one else.

Now with her guidance, her brother, Charlie, was VP in the multinational investment bank's mining sector. In this position, he was now at her obedient beck and call to instantly and conveniently connect with her newest branch of business, her ever-expanding contact list of overseas global friends and partners.

She laughed to herself softly. Who knew that one day the words *bismuth*, *nickel*, and *tungsten* would be so very charming to her. Because dug up from the Third World dirt by her busy bee multicultural partners worldwide, a generous percentage of these industrial metals were now, at this very moment as she sat there, being turned into electronic currency and shot across the magical under-the-sea high-tech glass fiber lines to be deposited at the speed of light at her pedicured feet.

How many offshore accounts was Charlie juggling now? Thirty-six? Most of them seven-figure, some even eight. Minute by minute, they increased like the debt clock in Times Square.

In her happy vodka tonic buzz, Dawn Warner smiled at the analogy. She closed her eyes and breathed in Yves's lovely Opium as her vision filled with a string of numbers, huge numbers that continually flickered higher and higher toward infinity as they burned brighter and brighter in blazing glowing neon red.

100

When Kit carded into room 811 at the Palo Alto Westin, John Barber was set up on the bed, working a laptop, while Gannon was by the window with a camera on a tripod.

She put down the coffee and sandwiches on the desk of the tight discount room and went over and huddled next to Gannon.

"How's it looking?"

"See for yourself," Gannon said, edging back the curtain.

Kit bent to the Nikkor zoom lens that was pointed at the window of Dawn Warner's suite across the street.

Its viewfinder showed a balcony, a glass door, and a portion of the suite's living room. Through the gap in the curtains the blown-up view in the ten-thousand-dollar spy camera was vivid enough to pick up the wood grain in the credenza.

Gannon and Barber had been at the airport with the surveillance equipment waiting for Kit when she landed. She already had the New York office head, Bill Ferguson, help her get a bead on Dawn Warner's whereabouts, so they had headed straight from the airport to the Clement.

They found an almost perfect surveillance vantage point at the Westin just across the street, and then Gannon had gone across into the Clement Hotel covertly. He'd managed to plant two bugs, one on her room's phone line from the basement and another audio bug in the hall just outside the room.

They still might do a counter-intel sweep for them but Kit didn't think so. From what they'd already heard they seemed to be very much in a hurry about something.

"I see steam," Kit said, looking through the camera. "Okay, there she is by the mirror scrubbing up, dress on the bed there. Gucci. My, my. This dinner they're heading to must be *très chic*. What's the name of this mind-blowing new restaurant again?"

"Flower Moon West," Gannon said.

"Flower Moon West. How…something."

"Upscale yet earthy?" Gannon tried.

"Stuck-up rich asshole?" John Barber said.

"There you go, John. You win," Kit said, laughing.

"Wait, I hear something."

"Is she speaking Chinese again?" Kit said.

That Warner had received two phone calls on the room phone from people speaking Chinese was quite shocking. But that Warner had answered them back also in Chinese was even more so.

Expert-level Chinese was quite a curious skill for a top-echelon US Justice Department official to have.

But it was all starting to fit, Kit thought. Warner, Weber, China.

Weber's interview in *Wired* magazine said Son-exum was going to be looking into making a bigger move into the Pacific Rim.

Also, what had Warner said in DC?

This is about trillions, Kit. With a T.

"No. No Chinese this time. Worse," John Barber said, leaning into the headphone. "She's singing again."

"What now? More vintage Whitney Houston?" Gannon said.

Kit shook her head. As Warner got ready, she was rocking her personal play list. It was heavy on eighties and nineties love ballads. A countdown of pure cheese, Kit thought.

"No, wait. Let me guess," Kit said. "Celine Dion?"

"'I'd do anything for love,'" John Barber sang dramatically in almost pitch perfect imitation of Meatloaf. "'But I won't do that.'"

Gannon and Kit burst out laughing.

"That's really good, John. I didn't know you had such a high and sensitive singing voice," Kit said.

"Yeah, a little too good, John," Gannon said.

"Heads up. Her room phone's ringing," Barber suddenly said, clicking the audio up on the laptop speaker.

"Hi," said a man's voice.

"It's the driver. Fitzgerald," Barber said.

"I told you not to use the landline," Warner said.

"I know. My phone died. I'm in the lobby."

"What is it?"

"I just wanted you to know he's here."

"Gandalf?"

"Yes, they just landed."

"How's he looking?" Warner said.

"Harris said okay. He's pouring coffee into him. He's going to make him shower at the hotel."

"He's got a suit?"

"Yes. He has one with him. He has everything with him."

"His passport everything?"

"Yes. Harris checked first thing."

"Passport?" Kit mouthed.

"And have him shave, too. That thing on his chin is vile. If I have to sit next to it during dinner, I'll be blowing chunks before the second course."

"He'll do what he can."

"And tell him to get a move on. Our guests don't do late. And charge your damn phone."

"I will. Sorry."

The line clicked off.

"Gandalf?" Kit said. "Who's Gandalf? Not Ethan Weber. He's already at the other hotel."

"Gandalf with his passport?" Gannon said, squinting. "I guess we're going to need to find that out."

101

Flower Moon West was southeast of Palo Alto on Loyola Drive across from the Los Altos Golf and Country Club.

More like a kind of compound than just a regular restaurant, behind the modern glass building was a patchwork array of tiered gardens that took up several city blocks.

The vehicle that arrived at ten minutes to nine o'clock was a shiny new Chevy Suburban in iridescent black with tinted black windows. Its big twenty-two-inch tires crackled off the crushed stone as it came up the sloping driveway.

As they stopped and Harris got out to open her door, Dawn Warner turned and spotted Ethan Weber right away in the restaurant's foyer.

"Hey, you," Ethan said, smiling warmly as he and the maître d' emerged out of the restaurant.

"Thanks so much for this," he said as the maître d' led them along a path away from the front door. "You look breathtaking, by the way. Everyone is here already. But Gandalf isn't with you?"

"No. A few minutes behind us," Warner said as the maître d' pushed open a gate and guided them toward a lit door.

On the other side of it was the kitchen itself, and they were brought past stoves and steel tables and busy kitchen workers.

Instead of taking them through into the restaurant proper, the maître d' parted some pocket doors just to the left of the swinging one.

Dawn Warner halted in the doorway as the two Chinese Communist Party officials who they were there to meet stood from the chef's table.

The older one was silver-haired and bland-faced and round-cheeked with a bit of a beer belly while the younger one was slender and wore John Lennon glasses and had thick black hair.

As the men bowed, Dawn Warner couldn't help but notice the perfect hang of their silk suits, the bespoke fit at the shoulder, the just-so break at the trouser cuff.

Savile Row, she thought, smiling approvingly. She loved Pacific Rim heavy hitters. Demure be damned. Why have it and not flaunt it?

"I am Bob," the older one said, smiling. "And this is my partner, Frank. So very nice to meet you."

Bob and Frank, Warner thought, almost laughing at the generic American car-salesmen-like cover names the agents had chosen. They certainly didn't look like any Bob or Frank she'd ever met before.

She assumed Bob was the head honcho, but you

never knew with these folks. These nosebleed-level party members didn't do obvious. They were always playing some kind of game.

"*Ni hao*," Weber said with a formal little bow in return.

Warner didn't follow suit with the formal Chinese greeting but merely shook Bob's hand.

As they all sat, she saw that Bob and Frank's aides-de-camp were both young and female and annoyingly wearing midnight blue couture cocktail dresses that looked very much like the one Warner herself was wearing.

Great, Warner thought, shaking her head as one of them smiled at her subserviently. Instead of a world-shaker negotiating in a new global era, she thought, with the other females at the table she could have been just another goofy airhead bridesmaid in a cheesy wedding party.

Gandalf slipped in through the pocket doors two minutes later just behind the table-side bartender.

"So sorry I'm late," the wiry, rumpled fifty-something said, shaking Ethan's hand before leaning over and giving Warner an air kiss.

The good news about Gandalf's looks was that he had a boyish face, she thought, watching him. The bad news was that with his weather-ravaged skin, deep-set eye bags and spiky dyed blond hair, it was the face of a homeless boy who was addicted to crack.

She'd never seen him in a suit before. Or in a shirt that had buttons, actually. He hadn't shaved the poodle-like chin goatee, but he was sober enough to stand without assistance, so that was something at least.

Gandalf's real name was Alex Novak and he was

Sonexum's resident supra-genius. From the gutters of Manchester, New Hampshire, he had graduated Brown at sixteen and by twenty-four was the youngest mathematics professor in Berkeley's history.

"That's one year younger than the Unabomber," he told people at parties.

An enfant terrible of the worst kind, the only thing that rivaled his mathematical intellect, they said, was his voracious, insatiable, rock-star-level appetite for drugs.

Novak's specialty was artificial intelligence, which was why he was there. If negotiations went the way they were expected to, Novak would be heading to China from the meeting on a two-year project to bring the Chinese government's AI project up to snuff.

"*Wo yao ning shei lai he yibei,*" Novak suddenly cried as he slammed a fist on the linen. He grinned at the party officials as he fired up a Marlboro Red with a Zippo lighter.

Warner fiddled with her napkin, pretending she didn't realize the stupid jerk had just asked two of the most powerful men on the planet who he had to screw to get a drink.

Across the table, the two grim-faced Chinese stared wide-eyed for a moment at the crazy American. Then their hard facades suddenly cracked as they let out roars of laughter.

As they did this, Ethan nodded over at Warner knowingly with his intelligent clear blue eyes. It was an all-systems-are-go look.

Whatever worked at this point, Dawn Warner thought as the tableside bartender uncorked the first bottle with a crisp pop.

102

The upscale restaurant had low white tables and a huge square fountain in the center and elegant curved walls of varnished bamboo.

Coming in from the garden after hopping the compound's wrought iron gate, Gannon saw that even the Calvin-Klein-clad waiters wore crisply knotted silk ties and perfect pocket squares.

The dishwashers, too, probably, Gannon thought as he slowly walked along the curve of one of the walls toward the corner bar.

Behind the four-sided bar, an arch-browed meticulously scruffy bartender with slicked-back hair stood staring suspiciously at Gannon's new Banana Republic jacket and Clark-Kent-style black-rimmed glasses.

"Talisker 18," Gannon said as he flicked down a hundred.

That seemed to smooth things over with the help,

Gannon thought as he watched the guy head to the other side of the bar.

Gannon took a look around the cavernous space. At the low tables sat long, slender young women with fine looks beside much shorter and older men without them. Between them processed waiters and waitresses bearing wine bottles and plates with the reverence of pagan clergy about to perform a sacrifice.

Gannon looked at one of the plates that went past. On it was a folded napkin and on the folded napkin was a single spoon covered in some yellowish-green goop.

Gannon stifled a laugh. But he had to admit, the restaurant actually smelled pretty amazing.

Gannon leaned back into the bar as he adjusted his glasses, making sure the lens of the spy camera embedded in its left front side wasn't obscured. As his eyes adjusted to the dimness, he could see there were two VIP rooms to the left of the front entrance.

A crashing sound of plates turned his head toward the kitchen to his right. He suddenly stood up straight as he stared at the large guy by the swinging door.

"Okay, heads up," he said into his lapel mic. "Large Asian guy with cropped hair, lantern jaw, and boxer's shoulders three o'clock of the kitchen's swinging door."

"Look at the size of him," John Barber said in his ear. "I didn't know China had a wrestling federation."

The bartender had finally arrived back with his scotch when Gannon saw the wiry American guy with the spiky blond hair come out of the swinging kitchen doors beside the big Chinese bodyguard.

Gannon squinted at him. His weather-beaten face. His scraggly goatee. He definitely didn't look like one of the Calvin Klein waiters.

"Who's that guy?" John Barber said.

Gannon noticed the Chinese security guy talk into his hand as the spiky-haired guy passed him. The guard didn't take his eyes off the guy. He seemed to be heading toward the bathrooms behind the bar.

That's when it clicked.

"It's Gandalf," Gannon said as he made a beeline for the men's room.

103

Another hundred-dollar bill was in Gannon's hand as he pushed quickly into the men's room.

He waved it like a flag at the white-jacketed attendant, who looked up from his basket of colognes. He was a white college kid of about nineteen.

"Hey, buddy, could you run to my car?" Gannon said quickly, thrusting the hundred at him. "It's a Bentley parked on the other side of the block. There's a pack of Marlboros and a bag of peanut butter M&Ms on the passenger seat. I need them like now."

"Sir, I'm sorry. I'm not supposed to leave here," the college kid said.

Gannon took out another hundred and shoved them both in the guy's hand.

"C'mon, be a pal, son. It'll only take a second. It's a gag gift for my brother. It's his birthday. But you gotta run," he said.

"Well… Okay. I guess, sir. Do you have the key?"

"No, it's unlocked. Get going," Gannon said, pushing him for the door.

After he shoved the attendant out, Gannon had just enough time to drape a napkin over his forearm and lift the hand soap before the spiky-haired guy came in a moment later.

"Good evening, sir," Gannon said, smiling as the guy walked over to the urinal.

Gannon smiled even wider as the man zipped up.

"Great weather we're having, isn't it?" Gannon said as Gandalf headed to the sink. "Hey, wait, you're that guy who works at Sonexum, right?"

Gandalf glanced at him in the mirror. A tense smile played on his lips.

"Do I know you?" he said.

Gannon tucked his nerd glasses away as he crossed the room and locked the door.

"What the hell?" Gandalf yelled as Gannon snatched the back of the guy's jacket and bent him over the sink none too gently. It took a split second for Gannon to chicken-wing him and to get the hand-cuffs ratcheted on him nice and tight.

"Get off me! What is this?" he squealed.

"His name's Novak," Gannon called into the mic after he removed the man's wallet. "Alex Novak."

"Who the hell are you?" Novak said.

Gannon smiled as he put a finger to his lips.

"Bingo," Barber finally said in his earpiece. "Oh, boy, Mike. This guy's some kind of world-renowned artificial intelligence guru. There's all this shit about cybernetics and quantum computing and infrared fiber optics and satellites. He works for Sonexum heading up some defense department project, it says. Some big R & D military contract Sonexum was picked for over Apple. It says Sonexum got the military contract because of that dude right there. The Albert Einstein of AI, they call him."

"He's right, Mike," Kit cut in. "This must be Gandalf. And they asked about his passport, right? Mike, I think they're about to hand this guy over to the Chicoms for AI supremacy. Tonight. That's why they're all here being so secretive. Why they're all in such a fuss. Must be. This is the exchange."

"Whatever it is we need to bust up their plan, Mike," John Barber said. "If he's their golden goose we need to bag him. Grab that jackass and get back to the truck now."

"Oww, stop! Who are you? My wrists!" Novak said as there was a knock on the door.

"Okay, working on it," Gannon said as he grabbed the computer whiz up by the scruff of his jacket.

He began to kick open the stalls. In the third one was a window with an air conditioner in it. The bottom of the sill cracked loudly as Gannon reached up and ripped it free. It shattered through the top of the toilet tank on its way down.

Gannon turned as the knock on the bathroom door became a pounding.

"Cut that chain at the north wall gate now," Gannon said as he grabbed Novak's belt and pushed him into the stall.

"We're coming out hot," he yelled.

104

"Let me out of this car now," Novak screamed as John Barber gunned their Cadillac Escalade rental down the suburban side street back toward Palo Alto. "Or I swear you're all going to jail!"

"It's all good, Alex, my friend," Gannon said calmly from where he sat beside the handcuffed scientist in the second row. "Thanks for cooperating. We just need to ask you a few questions."

"What the hell is this? A kidnapping? What are you doing? Who are you people?" Novak said.

Kit was sitting in the center of the third row, and she leaned forward and showed him her FBI credentials.

"My name is Special Agent Hagen."

Gannon watched the sudden wideness that came to Novak's eyes.

"I work for the Bureau's Behavioral Science Division," Kit continued. "Do you know what we investigate, Alex? Any clue?"

Novak stared at Kit's badge with his wide brown eyes.

"What happened, Alex?" Kit said. "It's time to tell us."

"Yeah, Alex," Gannon said. "What happened up on that mountain?"

"I'm…" the scientist said, looking down at the floor.

They watched as his right knee began jittering like crazy.

"Okay, I see. I'll tell you what I know but… I need a cigarette. Please, in my jacket. Can I please have a damned cigarette?"

Gannon went into his jacket and took out a pack of Marlboros and a lighter. He put one in Novak's mouth and lit it.

"I…" Novak finally said after he exhaled. "I want to talk to my lawyer."

Gannon reached out and snatched the cigarette out of the guy's mouth and then zipped down the window. Sparks flew off Novak's forehead as Gannon flicked the cigarette off his face into the night.

"Hey!" Novak said.

Then Gannon reached down between his feet and took a cut-down Sig Sauer P365XL 9mm from the gun bag and placed the carbon steel barrel of it between the scientist's bugged out eyes.

"Games are over, jackweed. The only thing you're getting is your genius brain blown out the back of your skull unless you start explaining exactly what the hell happened in Wyoming."

Beads of sweat appeared on his sunburned fore-head as he unsuccessfully tried to shy away from Gannon's gun into the door.

"But you can't do this. You guys are cops," he said.

"No," Gannon said, digging the barrel in beside his nose. "She's the cop. We're the friends of Owen Barber, the guy you scum murdered up on top of that mountain."

"And we're here for some damn payback!" John Barber yelled savagely from behind the wheel.

"Exactly. All that 'I want my lawyer, day-in-court' shit got nullified the second your billionaire boss, Weber, started bribing all the cops and judges."

"Now we're going old school, Hammurabi eye-for-an-eye shit, you son of a bitch," John Barber screamed.

"We already dug the grave, Novak," Gannon said. "Someone's going in it. You got a minute and count-ing to try to convince us that someone ain't you."

"Wait, wait, wait. No, please."

"Screw it!" John Barber screamed. "I'm sick of waiting. Do him, Mike. Do this piece of shit right now, then we'll go back and get the other ones."

"Fine," Gannon said, snick-snacking the pistol's oiled slide.

"No! Please stop! She fell. Lisa fell. We were camping, and she fell off the ridge we were camp-ing on."

"Fell my ass," Gannon said. "She wasn't wearing any clothes and had bite marks all over her!"

"I killed her, okay?" Novak said, staring down at the floor. "You're right. I killed Lisa Weber. Ethan did everything else. I'll sign a confession if you want. Take me to jail. Just please don't kill me. I don't want to die."

105

"Finally we're getting somewhere. Let's go with the rest. Now! All of it!" Gannon yelled, digging the gun into Novak's temple.

"We just went camping while Ethan did his talk," Novak said quickly. "Lisa hates these formal events so she and I went camping. We did it last year, too. Please, please put the gun down. It could go off by accident."

"Yes, it could. You better believe it could," Gannon said, tapping the barrel above his eye. "So you better keep talking quick before we hit a pothole."

"What happened next?" Kit said.

"We hiked up to Grand Teton. We got about halfway when the sun started to go down so we set up camp. We had a glass of wine at sunset, and then Lisa went into her tent. I stayed up by the fire. It was such a nice night. And after about an hour or so as the fire died down and I finished the wine, I took, um, this, this pill."

"A pill?" Kit said.

"It was a hallucinogenic that a friend of mine designed. He told me it was like a mix of mescaline, LSD, and DMT only different."

Alex began sobbing.

"It was the drug, man. It wasn't me. Please help me."

"What happened after you took this pill, asshole?" Gannon said.

"No, no. Help me. I can't breathe. I need an ambulance," Novak cried.

"You're going to need a hearse if you keep stalling," Gannon said, clicking off the safety.

"I raped her. Okay? I raped her. Honestly, I wasn't in my right mind. One second I'm tripping out and the next I'm on top of her. It was the drug, I tell you. I didn't mean it. I really didn't. Lisa was a friend. It was the drugs. Oh, please. I don't want to go to jail."

"You didn't just rape her," Gannon said. "We saw her body."

He shook his head.

"No. I hit her, too," he sobbed. "I flipped out, man. First with my fist. Then with a rock. A bunch of times. Then I think I bit her. I think. I'm telling you. It was like someone else was doing it. I, like, came out of myself. I became a caveman. It was the drug. I was watching myself do it."

Kit looked at Gannon wide-eyed while Alex exhaled deeply.

"When I woke up the next day, I saw her and I flipped out. I mean I just ran. I got lost. I almost fell into a ravine. But then I finally made it back to the car and I drove back to the hotel and told Ethan."

"Wait, what?" Gannon cried. "You told Ethan? Weber knows this? You told him you raped and killed his wife?"

"Well, not exactly," Novak said. "I mean I lied. I said she fell but I was high and didn't notice until I woke up."

"And he just accepted that?" Gannon said. "Why didn't he turn you in?"

"Because he's my friend. We worked at Apple together. I helped him to get Sonexum off the ground. I'm his main advisor. And well, also because of tonight, I guess. Tonight's been in the works for over a year."

"What's so special about tonight?" Kit said.

"The Chinese merger. For the last year it's been all about the Chinese merger. They need me for the AI. I'm the expert on the AI program. Without me there's no merger. I have to move to China now, Ethan said. I said before I wasn't interested but things are different now. Because if I don't, they won't be able to protect me. Either I move to China or I have to go to jail. That's the deal."

"You taping all this?" Gannon said, turning to Kit.

"Every word," Kit said.

"So Weber didn't kill his wife after all?" John Barber said from the front seat.

"No, his number one meal ticket here did after he got whacked out on his Silicon Valley goofballs."

"Weber just killed everyone else for the cover-up," Kit said. "How's Dawn Warner involved with the Chinese?"

"Who's she?" Novak said.

"That lovely woman with Ethan back at the restaurant," Gannon said.

"I don't know her," Novak said with a shrug. "She came with Ethan. I thought she was a lawyer on the merger. He has so many lawyers now. Am I going to jail now?"

"Mike, listen. Heads up," John Barber said as the throb of the Caddy's V8 engine suddenly went up several levels in volume.

Gannon turned.

"What is it?" he said.

"We've got company," Barber said tossing a thumb behind them.

106

There were three vehicles in the pursuing security detail.

The second of them was an incredibly fast Jeep Cherokee Trackhawk and Westergaard sat in the front passenger seat of it, looking out its windshield as they closed in on the rapidly accelerating Cadillac.

He looked down at his phone, consulting the map that showed the tracking device in Alex Novak's thigh.

Then he looked back at the Escalade.

"We have confirmation," Westergaard said over the radio. "Novak is in the truck."

He shook his head. He'd told Weber and Warner's people several times that his team should have a presence inside the damn restaurant. But did they listen to him? Of course not. They said that they needed to keep a low profile. That the Chinese would handle the inside.

"The Chinese, my ass," Westergaard mumbled.

If he hadn't personally insisted at great resistance on injecting the bio tracker into Novak, the whole lot of them would already be up shit's creek.

"I think they made us," Westergaard's new team member, Stackhouse, said from behind the wheel beside him.

"I know they did," Westergaard said as he looked up from his phone.

Including Westergaard, his new team consisted of seven men. Stackhouse and Addison were with him. Coleal and Hardwick were in the Ram pickup lead car and Villar and Reynolds were in the third car, a Range Rover.

As money was no object, he had managed to convince Weber and Warner to bring together the very best men in his multinational intelligence security firm.

Addison, sitting behind him watching their six, was especially good. A former marine sergeant from Memphis, Tennessee, he had flown up from Culiacán, Mexico, where he was the lead military advisor to the Beltrán Leyva Mexican drug cartel.

"What's up, boss? What do you want me to do?" asked Coleal over the radio from the Ram pickup.

Westergaard consulted the phone map.

"We have an overpass coming up in a mile and a half. Just as you approach it, I want you to pit them, send them into a sidespin."

"Under the underpass?" Coleal radioed.

"Yes," Westergaard said.

"Done," Coleal said.

"Sounds dangerous," Stackhouse said. "You sure, Boss? That Novak guy is useless if he's dead or even brain dead. I want that bonus."

"The only ones who are brain dead are our bosses," Westergaard said. "We're in a box here. We don't have a choice. We have to grab him now."

"If you say so," Stackhouse said.

"Addison!"

"Yes, Boss?"

"Once Novak is culled," Westergaard said, "I want full fire on that Cadillac. Full fire."

"We're dealing with some pros here, huh?" said Addison.

"If this is who I think it is," Westergaard said, staring at the back of the speeding Cadillac, "once it's on, you put it to full auto and keep the trigger down until further notice."

107

The rev of the Cadillac's engine continued to rise as John Barber floored the accelerator.

Then Gannon turned as he heard another roar.

A dark truck was close on the left. It was a big jacked-up performance model Ram pickup truck.

Behind this truck was another vehicle, red in color. It looked like some kind of Jeep except it was easily keeping pace at nearly a hundred miles an hour. A third car followed it, a dark Range Rover.

Not good, Gannon thought as he glanced back around and saw the number 97 on the Escalade's digital dash.

"I count three following," Barber shouted. "You got three?"

"Yep. Three," Gannon shouted back.

"Sensational," John Barber said as their speedometer hit triple digits.

The only good thing about any of it, Gannon thought, was that Barber was the best driver he had ever seen. In Iraq they always had to drive at about a hundred miles an hour to not get shot and he'd seen Barber squeeze an accelerator-pinned Hummer through spaces you wouldn't think a moped could fit.

"Intersection, red light ahead," John Barber said as he put the SUV into the shoulder with a rumble.

Gannon held his breath as they flew through it safely, then looked back as the three speeding vehicles quickly followed suit, zipping neatly into the shoulder behind them.

Terrific, Gannon thought. The people chasing them seemed like some pretty good drivers, too.

"They're still coming," Gannon said.

They were approaching an overpass doing a hundred and ten when the Ram truck drove up on their left and sideswiped them.

"Shit!" Gannon yelled as the back end went skittering.

Rubber shrieked and smoked as the Escalade went in under the overpass sideways. They were perpendicular to the road when the front driver's side bumper clipped one of the concrete columns.

They whipped around even more violently and were in a full 180 when they went backwards off the road to the right.

The rear windshield smashed in a split second later as they bounced off another column. Then, still traveling backwards, they hit a chain-link fence with a jingling sound of tearing metal.

As Gannon's head whipsawed back into the headrest, he looked out, dazed, over the deployed airbag through the cracked windshield where the vehicles were shrieking to a stop.

"Shit," he said again as he turned and looked back through the glassless rear window and saw the tangle of ripped steel fencing.

When Gannon turned to the right, he saw the Ram truck that had pitted them was somehow on the other side of them now. It was parallel and almost touching them, only facing the other way.

Gannon turned back to see Kit gaping at him and then looked over at Novak as he started coughing and then looked forward at John Barber, who was pushing at the airbag that was in his face.

Past John Barber, he could see through the windshield as the doors of the Jeep and the Range Rover popped and men spilled out.

There were four of them. Each one was wearing a balaclava and bulletproof vest and was strapping a long gun. Some kind of lid flipped up on the red Jeep's roof and then a fifth armed man in a balaclava appeared, standing in the turret.

Gannon almost had to hand it to Novak at what he did next. Before any of them could so much as catch their startled breath, the spiky-haired dude was out of his seat belt and working the door latch with his cuffed hands.

Then he was out and running toward the balaclava men as fast as his feet could carry him.

Still dazed and confused as he breathed in the burnt chemical smell of the airbag, Gannon was frozen, watching Novak run, when he heard the sound.

From somewhere behind him through the shattered back window came a dull metallic quivering sound that was followed quickly by a dinging bell.

"No, no, no," Gannon said as he turned and undid his seat belt and scrambled past Kit over the seat toward the back.

Gannon didn't think his eyes could go wider as he poked his head out of the glassless rear window and saw the train track and train trestles almost directly underneath their SUV's jutting rear end.

His mouth worked wordlessly as he turned to his right and saw the approaching light of an oncoming train.

"John, move the car! We're out over the damn tracks!" Gannon finally screamed out as the train's horn suddenly sounded.

Which was the precise moment when the automatic gunfire started.

108

Gannon scrambled back to the third seat as every window of the Escalade seemed to shatter simultaneously.

Kit was already down in the footwell and he dove down on top of her. Through the rain of exploding glass, Gannon watched Barber bend low himself. He lay down flat on the front seat, almost under the steering wheel, as he rammed the transmission up into Reverse.

When Barber stomped on the accelerator, they shot backwards through the rip in the fence and bumped up onto the tracks.

Had they just kept going, they would have easily made it clear of the approaching train with time to spare.

But then the front right-side bumper of the Cadillac suddenly caught on something, and they stopped as their wheels began to spin.

"Why did we stop?" Kit cried. "C'mon!"

Gannon thought they were maybe held up on one of the trackside fence poles until he shot a look to his right and saw the side panel of the Ram truck beside them was slowly moving. As they reversed, it slid with them and then crushed up against the passenger side rear door.

Shit! Gannon thought. *No!*

The bumpers had locked!

More bullets whined and flew through the car. Then the burnt rubber reek of tire smoke started pouring in as Barber held down on the gas, trying to rip free of the pickup they were stuck to.

The Ram truck's tires started smoking a second later as the driver suddenly noticed it was being pulled onto the train tracks and tried to pull back in the opposite direction.

The train horn erupted again much closer now as the two truck bumpers' tug-of-war over the middle of a railroad track continued.

The bellowing train was maybe twenty feet away, its headlamp and rising roar and clank filling the entirety of the inside of the SUV, when the Cadillac's front bumper finally gave way with a wishbone-like pop.

Then the Cadillac lurched backwards in a bumping jolt and just cleared out of the way of the arriving train.

Gannon gaped as he sat up and turned back just in time to see the speeding commuter train T-bone the cab of the Ram truck dead center. In a fantastic howl of bleating horns and blue-white smoke and shooting sparks, he watched as the train plowed the pickup truck away to the south.

As this happened, Barber did the world's bumpiest reverse K-turn over a second train track and then squealed the shot-up Escalade through some weeds at the base of the overpass's embankment.

"Man, is the rental guy gonna love us!" Gannon cried as they arrived at the top of the overpass.

Barber squealed out onto the overpass into the left lane going the wrong way. Halfway across the center of the upper roadway, he brought the Caddy to a shrieking stop directly above where the truck had sideswiped them.

Gannon flipped over into the front seat with their long rifle gun bag. Tearing at the Velcro and grabbing up two cut-down M4 carbines, he and Barber leaped from the vehicle out into the street.

Reaching the overpass's rail, they could see the Range Rover below them already on the move a hundred yards to the north.

"Shit! You know Novak is in there. He's getting away!" John Barber said.

Gannon had just put one in the chamber of his carbine with a click of the charging handle when they heard the roar below them.

Gannon and John Barber looked straight down as the red Jeep broke cover out from beneath the overpass.

The armed balaclava man was still in the turret, standing backwards now.

He looked up straight at them as he began to raise the rifle at his side.

109

"Straight to the airport! Get Novak to the airport! Gun it!" Westergaard radioed to Villar in car three as he heard the burst of gunfire at his back.

The damned overpass, he realized as the Jeep's rear window exploded inward.

"They're up on the overpass!" he yelled at Stackhouse. "Turn in somewhere. We need cover. Cover! Turn in!"

Just as he said this, the automatic gunfire became one long thunderous staccato. Westergaard threw up his hands in front of his face as a decimating fusillade of bullets knifed through the center of the roof, blowing apart the console and the radio and the dashboard.

"Return fire! Covering fire!" he yelled at Addison, standing in the back.

But Addison wasn't standing in the turret anymore, Westergaard saw as he turned. He was kneeling now in the rear footwell, spitting blood.

"Addison!" he said just as the ex-marine turned cartel advisor caught one in the head.

The spray of his blood in Westergaard's face from the head-shot was horror-movie-level. The sudden sprinkler jet of blood got in his eyes, in his mouth. Blinded and spitting, he wiped at it, yelling. It was warm and sticky on his fingers.

As the withering barrage of firing continued, something caught him in the shoulder from the back. He felt the bullet slice down inside of him. It was a weird sensation. Like swallowing something hot.

Then something touched the back of his neck below the base of his skull. A moment later, wetness began trickling down the back of his throat like a nasal drip. The liquid thick and salty and metallic.

When he looked up, he saw they were still rolling rapidly even though Stackhouse was now slumped over dead against the driver's door.

He didn't even have a chance to look forward to see the telephone pole that suddenly sailed in through the shattered windshield.

He blacked out briefly and when he came to, everything was black-and-white.

Like the old TV his father kept on his workbench in the barn, he thought.

After a moment, he noticed that the horn was stuck in the On position. He pushed at Stackhouse over the shattered plastic and glass until he slumped back over off the horn. Over the deployed airbag, white fumes rose from the folded-back edges of crumpled hood like smoke from the nostrils of a dragon.

He tried the door. No go. It was wedged tight.

He heard car brakes nearby.

"Freeze, asshole!" said a man a moment later.

Westergaard turned out the shattered window to see a blocky man arrive beside him.

It was him.

The American.

The stumbling block had arrived.

110

Sirens started in the distance, and then John Barber turned and drew down on a car that slowed behind them.

It was a shiny black Mercedes-Benz, a small elderly couple in it, staring over at them with wide eyes.

Just a couple of curious onlookers, Gannon thought, waving and smiling as he lowered his own rifle. The old guy wisely peeled out.

"It's you," the bloody blond-haired guy in the passenger seat of the wrecked Jeep said with a funny accent.

"Dude, didn't I tell you?" Gannon said.

"This him?" John Barber said. "The sniper?"

"This is him," Gannon said as he reached in over the assassin and picked up the dropped phone between his feet.

"Look, John. There's a map and a blip on it moving near the highway. It's tracking Novak. Has to be. This ain't over. Let's go."

"One second," John Barber said as he stepped up to the window. "I want to say goodbye to our friend."

Barber leaned in until his face was an inch from Westergaard's bullet-nicked ear.

"How's it feel, fella?" John Barber whispered to the killer. "Hell's gates are gaping wide-open for you. Excited? How's it feel to bathe in your own blood?"

He watched as the assassin reached for a water bottle in the drink holder.

"This what you're looking for? Thirsty, are you?" John Barber said as he reached in and took it out.

He uncapped it and offered it to him, but just as Westergaard was about to take it, he dumped it out onto the street before chucking it into the weeds.

"I'm sure my brother was thirsty, too," he said. "You give him a drink?"

"C'mon, John. Let's go," Gannon said.

"Help me," Westergaard said.

"Help who?" Barber said.

"I have money," the killer said.

"I'm sure you do," Barber said. "You'd pay it now, too, wouldn't you? But there ain't nothing gonna stop what you got coming, fella. Not all the money in the world."

The sirens were getting closer now.

"We need to move, John. For real," Gannon said.

"But he's got money, Mike. What do you think? They got a cash machine in hell?"

"Of course. There's plenty of them. All you'd ever want," Gannon said as he pulled John Barber away.

"But what sucks," Gannon said as he patted the

dying killer on the cheek goodbye, "is that the stores are always closed."

They found a late 2000s Mercury Sable parked on a suburban street two blocks in from where they'd left the crashed Jeep and shot-up Cadillac.

"Do we have to?" Kit said, glancing over at a nice little house on the corner as Gannon removed a hammer from his kit bag.

"Desperate times," Gannon said as he smashed in the window and opened its door and sat down. He took out a big screwdriver and used it to chisel off the ignition lock. Then he slid the screwdriver into the steering column and turned the car over with a roar.

"Desperate measures," he said.

Gannon let John Barber in behind the wheel, and they all piled in, and John peeled out onto the road. They headed west, running red lights following the Novak blip on the phone screen. It showed that the Range Rover already had a nice head start up the 101 Bayshore Parkway.

When they finally made it to the four-lane highway's on-ramp off North Shoreline Boulevard, they saw that Novak was already far to the north past Redwood City, moving quick.

"They seem to be heading into San Francisco," Kit said.

They were still about five minutes behind around San Mateo when Kit saw the blip exit the highway.

"Exit 422," Kit said, checking her other phone. "Shit, that's the airport exit. Oh, no. They really are going to try to get him out. They're heading to San Fran International."

111

With its patterned fabric walls and sleek butter-soft cream-colored leather club seats and highest-end detailing possible everywhere you looked, the Bombardier Global 7500 jet was like a luxury penthouse that could do Mach 1.

Past the galley where you walked in, there was a dining space, and past that was a semi-portioned-off entertainment area and then the sleeping stateroom with a lavish spa-level lavatory at the aft end.

On the bed of the aircraft's stateroom, right beside the door of the closed lavatory, Dawn Warner sat with her hands clasped before her face as if in prayer. Ethan Weber sat just outside the open door beside her in the entertainment area, staring at the carpet, while the Chinese retinue sat forward cabin in the dining area, having drinks.

MICHAEL LEDWIDGE

Dawn looked up as Harris poked his head out of the bathroom door.

"How are we looking?" she said in a frantic whisper.

When Westergaard's two thugs had brought Novak into the Range Rover, the genius wasn't looking so hot. He was barely coherent and there was blood on his shirt. They'd cleaned him up some for the Customs inspectors, but once they were on the plane, she'd ordered Harris and Fitzgerald to take him in the back for a more thorough assessment.

Because if Novak had been shot or had a heart attack or something it was over. Even the Chinese Communists couldn't do anything with a dead artificial intelligence expert.

"He's fine," Harris said. "A little roughed up is all. The blood was from a scratch on his hand. He's in the shower now."

"You sure?" Warner said.

"Boss, honestly," Harris said.

"Honestly, my ass," Warner said hotly. "How close are they saying the pilot is now?"

"Ten minutes out," Harris said glancing at his phone.

Ten damn minutes, she thought.

They were waiting on another pilot.

The delay was a result of Weber's sudden change in flight plan. Originally, the plane was supposed to fly only Ethan back to his vacation place in Washington state. But now with all the excitement at the restaurant, the new plan was to fly Novak and all of them on the new plane straight to China along with their partners.

But by union laws, they now needed another pilot

because of the long-haul time of the flight. There was no budging on the issue, they'd been told. They would just have to wait.

This last-minute delay couldn't have come at a worse time since legally they were on extremely shaky ground. Novak as well as Sonexum were under Pentagon contract. Technically, Novak was not allowed to leave the country without authorized written permission from the Secretary of Defense.

Damn you, Hagen, Dawn Warner thought, glancing out at the tarmac.

And double damn that stupid screwup, Westergaard, for not putting her down on Grand Teton the way she had ordered him to.

She hadn't even told her husband yet about heading to China. How would that convo go?

Hi, Neil. I'm in China.

She would worry about Neil later. All that mattered was the pilot showing up so they could get in the air and get Novak to mainland China and get all of her side deal contracts signed.

"Why the hell are you still standing there like a congenital idiot?" she said to Harris. "Get back in there and put some clean clothes on that junkie prima donna. And wake him the hell up. I want him real nice and chipper and polite to join our Asian guests for the takeoff, okay? Either you do it or I will. If he thinks he's messing this up even more, I'll personally drag him out of that shower by the——"

"Dawn?" Ethan Weber said, suddenly standing by the bedroom door.

"Ethan. Hi," Warner said, instantly smiling at the billionaire as Harris closed the bathroom door again.

"How is everything? How's Alex?"

"Alex is fine. Clean bill of health. He was just shaken up a little. My guys are helping him to finish freshening up."

"Phew," Weber said making a mock swipe at his brow. "That's good news, Dawn. Very good. You know, I never did get a chance to thank you. About all of this, I mean. After we found out what had happened on Grand Teton, I must say with all of our, um, balls in the air as it were, I thought Sonexum was going to take its place in the annals of Silicon Valley next to Pets.com.

"If we didn't have you on speed dial to get Alex the help he needed as well as expertly guide us through every step of this utter catastrophe, there's no way this crucial Pacific Rim deal would have finally gotten solidified. That unfortunate call you had to make to eliminate the arriving FBI personnel especially. That was incredibly…"

"Necessary?" she tried.

"Critical," Ethan finished, nodding. "You committed yourself fully there, Dawn. That was incredibly loyal. It also bought us the precious time we needed to close this. I know this is a little premature—and you don't have to tell me now—but when the dust settles, it would please me greatly to personally nominate you as a Sonexum board member at the next meeting."

For one of the few times in her life, Dawn Warner was struck silent with joy.

"Thank you, Ethan. I…" she said, flummoxed. "Really, I'm so flattered. It was the least I could do."

"Happy to hear it," he said with a smile. "Any word on the pilot?"

The bathroom door opened again and Harris stuck his head out again, grinning.

"He's here. The pilot. He's in the parking lot," he yelled happily.

112

When they got to the airport exit, the blip tracking Novak's location had come to a stop not at the regular terminals but beyond them on an access road at the opposite side of the huge airport's northern edge near the bay.

"It's the private aviation terminal," Kit said. "C'mon, gun it, John. Dammit. Can't this thing go any faster?"

The access road they sped along went around the outer edge of the airport, and they passed cargo bays and the tanks for the fuel depot and the FedEx facility.

"How far out are Ferguson's buddies in the San Fran office?" Gannon said to Kit.

"Twenty minutes," she said.

As they drove, Kit had called everyone she could think of to tell them about Warner and Weber and how Novak and his AI secrets were about to get into the hands of the Communist Chinese forever.

"They're in there," Kit cried when they finally saw the line of corporate jets beyond the tarmac fence on their right.

The square steel-and-glass structure of the private aviation facility had the look of a high-end car dealership, Gannon thought as they screeched up before it.

They left the Mercury out in front behind a chartered party bus and dodged several empty luggage carts as they ran inside.

Two feet past the foyer, a young, extremely snotty-looking strawberry blond–haired woman was standing behind a curving silver metal desk.

"This man!" Kit yelled, showing the woman Novak's picture on her phone along with her FBI badge. "Have you seen this man? Where is he? We know he's here."

Gannon was already past the desk by the closed-off glass door of a lounge area that led through to the tarmac. He looked down at the killer's phone, then across the lounge through the tarmac-side glass on the other side.

There was a large, sleek white-and-gold corporate jet idling there with its lights on. 7500, it said on its tail fin.

"He's there! It's that white plane. The 7500. He's right there," Gannon yelled as he stared at the huge blip on the phone.

As Gannon watched, a white-shirted pilot crossed the tarmac and hopped up the plane's airstairs.

"They're closing the door!" Gannon cried as he

watched the airstairs shut and the plane was suddenly slowly on the move.

"It's leaving! Stop that fricking plane!" he cried.

"Open this damn door!" John Barber said, rattling it.

Two blue-uniformed Customs cops suddenly came in from a door behind the snotty receptionist.

"Whoa there. What is it? Slow the hell down," said the shorter and older of the pair.

"FBI!" Kit yelled. "We have a fugitive on that plane. This is a national security issue. Radio it now. It must be stopped!"

"Calm down now," the cop said. "That's not how this is going to work. Stop with the screaming and yelling."

"Not how this works?" Kit yelled. "Officer, I'm ordering you to stop that plane!"

113

Gannon turned and bolted down the corridor and out the front door back outside.

He could see the taxiing 7500 through the thick tarmac-side fencing as he hopped in the Mercury and reversed it at speed down the terminal's driveway and into its parking lot.

Back through the lot on its opposite side, there was a side wall of a hangar that fronted onto the tarmac.

Gannon bumped the Mercury up onto the sidewalk and turned the car in alongside it, almost touching its side.

He leaped out and lifted the M4 from the back seat. It was strapped to his back as he climbed up on the Mercury's hood and then onto its roof.

There was a knot of electric and phone cables that came out of the ground up the side of the hangar to its roof and he quickly tugged at them, testing their weight.

Then he began hauling himself hand-over-hand up the side of the building as fast as he could.

The hangar's roof was made of corrugated steel that rang hollowly under his heel when he swung his leg over on top of it.

Crouching low, he ran up the slope and at the top of the roof's pitch, he dropped to one knee and looked through the carbine's scope into the airport.

The 7500 was about two football fields away now, sideways to him, moving slowly as it turned off the taxiway right before one of the main runways.

Gannon lay down on his belly with a clatter. He laid the rifle between the corrugations, then thumbed the selector switch to single fire.

As he pressed in against the cheekpiece, he noticed the plane had come to a stop.

Gannon settled his right eye socket in comfortably against the gummy rubber edge of the scope.

Then he slipped his finger in above the flat trigger as he took a long, calming deep breath.

114

Warner had convinced the air hostess to let her sit in the pilot's jump seat right beside the cockpit for takeoff.

This close to the end zone, she was on her last nerve now. She wanted to be in position to instantly squelch any and all last-minute bullshit that came up.

She was in the leather-seated alcove leaning into the open doorway of the cockpit and listening to the sweet voice in the tower telling them it was safe to take off when an alarm sounded out.

She stuck her head out into the aisle to see better as one of the pilot's black computer displays began flashing stop sign red.

"What is that, James?" the second pilot said to the captain as the electronic alarm trilling continued.

"One of the front tires," the captain said, examining the screen. "That's funny. The pressure gauge is suddenly reading zero."

Another electronic bleep of an alarm sounded on top of the first one. The electronic trilling came in stereo.

"What on earth? Now the left rear tire is zero, too," the copilot said. "How can they both be flat? Did we run over something?"

"What the hell is going on?" Warner said, unclipping herself and standing.

"Sorry, Ms. Warner, but it looks like we have a problem," said the captain. "Looks like we ran over something. We've got two tires down. We're grounded."

"Grounded?" Warner said. "No, no, no. We're on the damned runway. Screw the tires. This is a plane, right? Not a car. You don't need tires. Just take off. Take off on the rims!"

The pilot peered at her curiously.

"That's not how it works, ma'am," he said. "No tires, no takeoff. Our fuel tanks are loaded to full capacity for the flight. You do realize we're all sitting on twenty-five tons of highly flammable and explosive jet fuel."

"He's right," the copilot said. "The tires are extremely essential to safety. Back in 2000, a tire problem caused the Concorde to crash on takeoff in Paris. One of the spinning treads came loose and ripped into the aeronautics and fuel tanks. All one hundred fifteen on board were instantly killed."

Warner began to seethe. She took a deep breath.

"I'm sorry, gentlemen. I'm really, really sorry here. But we have no choice," Warner said. "We must risk it. By the power of the United States federal government, I'm ordering you to take off."

"Well, well. Is that right?" the captain said brightly as he turned in his captain's chair and stood.

Captain James was a tall individual of around sixty with short white hair and a robust, clean-shaven tan face. He looked like he might have had some military in his background.

"Why in that case, I'll tell you what," he said as he put out his large muscular hands palms up.

"Anytime you want, you start pouring some of that federal government power in this hand here," he said with a grin, "and then you start pissing in this other one right here, ma'am. The fed power fills up first, scout's honor, I'll follow orders without another thought."

"This isn't amusing, Captain. This is a matter of national security."

"I don't care what it's a matter of, ma'am," the pilot said pleasantly. "We're powering down now. We'll have a car come out to take us back. We're heading back to the lounge whether you like it or not. Now take your seat."

115

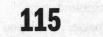

"What is the problem?" said a voice.

Dawn Warner turned.

It was one of the Chinese negotiators.

It wasn't Bob. It was the other one. The young one. Frank, she remembered. Frank didn't look happy.

"What is the problem?" Frank said again.

"The tires," she said. "There's something wrong with the tires. It's going to be fine. It's just a minor inconvenience. We just need to get another plane."

Dawn Warner's eyes were drawn toward the port-hole window. Outside past the tarmac fence on the access road, several vehicles were now approaching. They were driving very quickly and they all had spinning blue and red lights.

When she turned, she saw Frank watching with her over her shoulder.

"What's going on?" Ethan said, stepping up.

"We are at odds now, I'm afraid," Frank said as he passed him.

They both watched as Frank stopped before Bob and the two Chinese women. He said something they couldn't quite catch, but the three seated Chinese suddenly looked very frightened.

Then Frank pointed toward the rear of the aircraft, and the three Chinese stood and started walking back with him. They passed Novak, who was seated on the floor of the entertainment area, playing Xbox with Fitzgerald and Harris. They passed through the state room and entered the lavatory.

"Frank," Ethan Weber called as the door slammed closed. "Bob. I'm sure we can work this out."

"What's going on?" Novak said, standing.

"I don't know," said Weber.

"I'm sure it's fine," Dawn Warner said just as one of the Chinese women started screaming from behind the closed door.

"What the hell is going on back there?" said Captain James, coming up behind them.

Back in the rear cabin of the luxury aircraft, the door to the lavatory suddenly opened.

Then Dawn Warner started screaming herself as she saw what was coming out of the doorway.

116

Coming on an hour later, Barber and Gannon sat in a McDonald's on the strip just north of the airport.

"How's your joe there, Mike?" John Barber said. "You look like you're really enjoying it."

"This coffee here? Let's see," Gannon said, lifting the golden-arched paper cup from the other side of the plastic booth they were sitting in.

He made a moaning sound and rolled his eyes as he took a sip.

"Nice mouth coat. I'm getting notes of Hamburglar, a hint of clown sweat. Why, I think happy Ronald must have handpicked the beans himself."

Gannon smiled as his buddy burst out laughing. With all the traveling and shooting and racing around and no sleep, they were both running on nothing but pure adrenaline and were punch-drunk out of their minds.

Gannon jumped up as his phone rang.

"Hey, Kit," he said.

"You can come back now."

"Are you sure? We passed one hell of a lot of cops on the way out of Dodge. Maybe it might be better if we just got lost."

"No, it's okay. You're good. I smoothed things over. In fact, you have to come. This is something you really have to see."

They left the stolen Mercury in the parking lot of the McDonald's and took an Uber back to the private aviation lounge. Kit met them at the front door.

"What's going on?" Gannon said as he looked through the lounge window and saw the 7500 private jet still stuck way out on the tarmac. It looked like personnel in white Tyvek suits were climbing out of it.

"You'll see," Kit said, leading them in past the receptionist's desk into the back.

In the hall were the two Customs agents they had argued with. Beyond them in a small conference room, there were a half dozen FBI agents. They were watching a wide screen on the wall that was showing a plane cockpit.

"Now pan back," one of the agents said into his phone.

Gannon watched as the camera showed the luxury jet's cabin.

On the floor lay people. Motionless people with their eyes open.

Gannon looked at the Chinese men and women. At Alex Novak. Dawn Warner was there, too. As was Ethan Weber. All side by side.

"No!" Gannon said. "Dead?"

Kit nodded.

"All dead except one of the pilots. He managed to open the door but he's still messed up. He probably won't make it. They took him away in an ambulance."

"What happened?" Gannon said.

"Fentanyl," Kit said.

"Fentanyl?" John Barber said.

"Uh-huh. Courtesy of the Chicoms. Must have had some in a carry-on. Airborne high-concentration fentanyl is deadlier than a nerve gas. See the Chinese guy with the gas mask beside him there? He pulled the plug on them. On all of them. Then he took off the mask to do himself."

"But why?" John Barber said.

"Because of Alex Novak," she said. "This artificial intelligence thing is very much like the nuke buildup during the Cold War. Once they panicked and saw they were about to get busted, they must have figured if they couldn't have him, then neither could we."

Gannon shook his head.

"Look at them," he said. "So clever, right? MIT and computer science and even private jet planes. Oh, my!"

"Yeah, exactly," John Barber said. "Guess not, you stupid suckers. All your deep-thinking moves led you right into a pine box. Woops!"

"Exactly," Gannon said, laughing. "Your computer models indicated a zig when you should have zagged. So close though. Oh, well. Maybe next time we'll plug in pi at a further decimal point. Oh, that's right. They're won't be a next time."

"Hey, what's this?" John Barber said, going across the hall into what looked like a little kitchen.

He opened the door of a fridge. Inside there were bottles and bottles of champagne for the well-heeled jet-setters.

Before they knew what was happening, he had the foil off one and its wire twisted off and the cork out.

"To Owen," he said and took a swig and passed it to Kit.

"To Dennis," she said as she followed suit.

"And to large, highly visible luxury jet tires," Gannon said as the cold green bottle was placed in his hand.

Then he tipped the champagne up to his lips and closed his eyes and drank.

* * * * *

Read on for an excerpt of Michael Ledwidge's next novel, Beach Wedding, *coming in February 2022.*

PROLOGUE

DREAM HOUSE

1

A gull circling in the sea breeze banked into a clumsy slide, then settled gently on the tallest of the beach mansion's brick chimneys like it wanted to be the weather vane.

At the far end of the back lawn where the sod became beach grass, I stood with my brother Tom, looking up at the massive castle-like structure, taking it all in.

At least trying to.

Tom, playing tour guide, had just explained that the Southampton summer dream house he'd just rented was a proper traditional two-wing manor, built in the French Renaissance Revival style after a famous house of landed gentry outside of London. Past the sun terrace we'd just walked across, you could see the pool peeking out around the side of the thirty-thousand-square-foot house like a giant block of sapphire wrapped in travertine.

To say that Tom was a tour guide wasn't even an exaggeration, as the place was literally about the size of a museum.

"So?" Tom said. "What do you think?"

I turned away from the white elephant of a house and took a sip of my drink, studying the private staircase of weathered teak that dropped down the windy bluff at our back. I looked south to where the wood slat fence wound along the dunes, and beyond it, the Atlantic's infinite slate blue waves rose and curled and broke and crashed with a soft hiss as they washed up onto the private beach thirty steps below us.

Being from the poor man's Hamptons, Hampton Bays across the Shinnecock Inlet, Tom and I had been more of the to-the-split-level-born class. The only exclusive club we'd ever been members of was that of the hustling townie contingent. Up until now, the only times I'd ever gotten within spitting distance of these Southampton eight-figure beach castles was by working events as a busboy or a bartender or a valet. I'd never even dreamed of actually staying in one.

"What do I think of this beer?" I finally said, holding up my bottle. "Exceptional, Tom, really. What is it? Craft stuff? Head and shoulders above the cans of Miller Genuine Draft in my beer drawer back in Philly."

"Ha-ha, dummy," Tom said, elbowing me. "C'mon, really. What do you think?"

I turned, studying my brother. Tom usually looked pretty pale and stressed from his 24/7 Wall Street pressure-cooker managerial duties at Emerald Crown Capital Partners, the hedge fund that he had started. But he'd already been out here for a couple of days, and it had done him a ton of good, I saw. My dark-haired brother looked actually sort of relaxed for once, tan and handsome and happy in his preppy red shorts and half-unbuttoned cream-colored linen shirt.

"What do I think?" I finally said. "What do you think I think? It's impossible, Tom. That's not a house. It looks like a Park Avenue apartment building. I mean, where is Zeus staying now that you rented his house? Summering in the South of France? No, wait. Visiting Poseidon?"

Tom slowly put an arm around my shoulders.

"Zeus is right here, Terry," he said, winking at me with a wide grin. "I am Zeus, come down to stand here with you stupid mortals. Right here before your very eyes."

"Yeah, right," I said, shouldering him away. "I remember all those times Zeus clipped his divine toenails into my Captain Crunch at the kitchen table like it was yesterday. And all the birthday punches. With one for good luck, too. Every time. The gods are so benevolent."

As my brother cracked up, I smiled and took another sip of my beer.

Because I felt happy too then. Or maybe suddenly at ease was a better way to describe it. Truth be told, I'd been a little reluctant to make the trip up from Philly and all the way back home after all these years.

Actually, more than a little.

Even with the fact that my oldest brother was finally tying the knot.

There are reasons why some people leave the place they were born and raised and never come back. Usually, they're very good reasons.

But maybe, I thought as I took in Tom and the billion-dollar scenery some more.

Maybe this wasn't such a big deal after all. Time had passed. Quite a bit of it. And didn't they say that time heals all wounds?

At least it wasn't a big deal as far as Tom was concerned, I realized.

Despite his new ginormous pockets, Tom was still just Tom. Tom, who used to let me ride back home on the handlebars of his ten-speed from Little League practice when I was a kid. Tom, who let me read his comic books as long as I kept them neatly in the plastic covers. Tom, who hit a kid who was bullying me in the head with a basketball from half-court in the schoolyard that time.

Just Tom, I thought, looking at him as the summer wind scattered some more expensive sand across the back of my pale neck and knees.

Only with a couple of specks of white in his black Irish hair now and more than a couple extra zeros in his bank account.

"Okay, I'll bite," I said then. "Only because I know you're dying for me to ask. How much is it running you?"

"What? You mean with the staff and everything?" Tom said, comically wrinkling his brow.

Tom had already mentioned the chefs and the maids and the gardeners, and even the chauffeur and limo that the rental came with to heighten the full modern money-be-damned *Great Gatsby* experience.

"Yes, the whole kit and caboodle. Out with it, moneybags. How much?"

"Five," Tom said, staring at me calmly.

"Five? What do you mean? Five what?"

He looked at me again silently for a beat before I got it. If I hadn't already just swallowed my beer, I probably would have spit it all over him.

"That's impossible! Five hundred grand? Half a million dollars for the season?" I said in shock.

"Oh, no," my brother said, chuckling softly as he shook his head.

He gave me another wink as he brought his own beer to his lips.

"That's just for July, Terry," he said. "Just July."